The Body in the Gallery

ALSO BY KATHERINE HALL PAGE

FICTION

The Body in the Ivy

The Body in the Snowdrift

The Body in the Attic

The Body in the Lighthouse

The Body in the Bonfire

The Body in the Moonlight

The Body in the Big Apple

The Body in the Bookcase

The Body in the Fjord

The Body in the Bog

The Body in the Basement

The Body in the Cast

The Body in the Vestibule

The Body in the Bouillon

The Body in the Kelp

The Body in the Belfry

The Body in the Gallery

A Faith Fairchild Mystery

Katherine Hall Page

HARPER LUXE

ollins*Publishers*

THE BODY IN THE GALLERY. Copyright © 2008 by Katherine Hall Page. All rights reserved. Printed in the United States of America. No part of this book may be used or reproduced in any manner whatsoever without written permission except in the case of brief quotations embodied in critical articles and reviews. For information address HarperCollins Publishers, 10 East 53rd Street, New York, NY 10022.

HarperCollins books may be purchased for educational, business, or sales promotional use. For information please write: Special Markets Department, HarperCollins Publishers, 10 East 53rd Street, New York, NY 10022.

FIRST HARPERLUXE EDITION

HarperLuxe™ is a trademark of HarperCollins Publishers.

Library of Congress Cataloging-in-Publication Data is available upon request.

ISBN: 978-0-06-156194-8

08 09 10 11 12   OV/RRD   10 9 8 7 6 5 4 3

FOR MY DEAR FRIEND JEAN FOGELBERG

Acknowledgments

Special thanks to curator Nick Capasso, and others at the DeCordova Museum and Sculpture Park in Lincoln, Massachusetts. Also my thanks to Dr. Robert DeMartino; Carol Bischoff; Luise Kleinberg; Jeannie Rogers at Il Capriccio restaurant in Waltham, Massachusetts; my editor, Sarah Durand; and my agent, Faith Hamlin.

There will be time to murder and create.

—T. S. ELIOT, "THE LOVE SONG OF
J. ALFRED PRUFROCK"

Chapter 1

"Wait, let me get this straight. Isn't what you're suggesting called 'breaking and entering'?"

Faith Fairchild's fingers had been hovering over the plate of sticky buns her friend Patsy Avery had put out to go with the coffee they were drinking as they sat in Patsy's large kitchen on Maple Street—two blocks from Faith's house, the First Parish parsonage. Now she pulled her hand away as if the buns themselves might be larcenous.

"*Entering*, no breaking involved. All very legit. As president of the board of trustees I have the museum's alarm code. *Trustee*. Trust. We're not removing anything from the property, merely taking a look at something that's already there."

"Then why do we have to do it at night when the Ganley is closed? And why does it have to be 'we,' by the way?"

"Have a bun. You know you want one. I haven't been explaining this very well. To reiterate."

"You're sounding very lawyerly." Faith took a bun and started picking the pecans from the top. Patsy's mother sent the toothsome pastries up from Louisiana periodically, and even though Faith was a caterer, she had never been able to duplicate them. The recipe was a family secret—like the ones for jambalaya and cornbread.

"I *am* a lawyer."

"Just a reminder."

"Okay. When we were first married, Will and I bought a Romare Bearden. You saw it in the show that's up at the museum now."

Faith remembered it well. It was a Bearden collage from the 1960s, often considered the period when he was doing his best work. This piece was deceptively simple—a bass player in blue set against a background of more shades of blue. The rich brown of the musician's hands and face were in sharp contrast to the soft yellows and reds of the instrument itself, which merged to become part of his body. Looking at it, you could hear the notes—mellow, vibrant, pure jazz. Feel the intensity of the player, floating through the space the artist had created—Bearden, the figure, the viewer, all one with the music.

She nodded. "It's wonderful."

"When I was asked to join the board, Will and I decided to offer it to the museum as a permanent loan. We didn't plan to take it back, but we wanted to see what kind of commitment the museum would make, and continue to make, toward broadening its horizons before we gave it outright. *Loan* is the operative word here, my nervous friend. It's still *my* Bearden."

Faith nodded again. She was with her friend so far, recalling that African-American artists were severely underrepresented at the Ganley before the Averys' gift started the ball rolling. The Ganley, to its credit, was making up for lost time. A new acquisition, an Elizabeth Catlett mother and child bronze, that was also in the show was stunning. Faith had almost wept it was so beautiful. Catlett often portrayed mothers and children, which reminded Faith why she thought Patsy had asked her to drop by.

When Patsy had called Faith to come over for coffee, that she had something important to tell her, Faith happily jumped to the conclusion that the Averys were expecting their first child. They had been trying for a long time. A good-sized house and yard for the family they were planning to start was the reason they had moved from Boston's South End to Aleford, a western suburb. Patsy and Will had both grown up in large New Orleans families, and Faith had sympathized with Patsy at the announcement of each sister's, sister-in-law's, and cousin's new arrivals, while the Averys' cradle remained empty. "The way they're poppin' them out, must be something in that Louisiana air. We need to move home," Patsy had said at one point. But Will had made partner in a prestigious firm, and Patsy loved her exhausting job as a juvenile public defender. "These babies have no problem having babies, and that's the problem," she'd mentioned to Faith often. The Averys had seen specialists and engaged in all kinds of treatments without success so far.

Yet, it wasn't news of a blessed event, but of an unexpected one. Faith had no sooner sat down than Patsy had excitedly started talking about getting into the Ganley tomorrow night to look at the Bearden collage—one she strongly suspected was not the one the Averys had loaned the museum. Now she had calmed down and was patiently explaining it all to Faith, who had quickly gotten over her initial surprise and in one part of her mind was even starting to agree with Patsy's rationalizations. The woman *was* the president of the board of trustees, after all.

"It was all right at the opening, although it's hard to see what's on the walls with so many people milling around. That's why I went in today to take a last look by myself. I wanted to say good-bye for a while before it goes into storage. It could be a few years before it's in another exhibition. There I was, almost alone—there are never many people first thing in the morning—and right away I knew it wasn't our Bearden."

"How could you tell?" Faith asked.

"It was a vibe. I'm not one of those people who can spot a fake—I don't have 'the Eye'—but I've lived with this piece of art. I know it. The colors were right, the composition, everything, but something was off. Bearden's signatures were very distinctive. This one was vertical in black script so fine it looked like it was written with an etching tool—four lines, *Rom, are, Bear,* and *den.* As much of a work of art as the rest."

Faith had an art dealer friend from the years before her marriage when she had been living in her native Manhattan. Andy always said the way an artist signed a piece of art could make or break it.

Patsy continued. "The signature was very good, but not good enough. I'm sure it's a fake. And the signature is key. It's not a crime to copy a work of art—think of all those students on campstools at the MFA—but it *is* a crime to forge a signature. The show comes down tomorrow when the museum is closed, so we have to act fast. Early Wednesday morning it will all be transported to the storage facility in South Boston. I'll never be able to get at it! Before this happens I have to take some photos, and there's a tiny mark on the back that the forger may have overlooked. The frame looks the same, but whoever did this would have been smart enough to put the fake in the original one."

"But why don't you just go in and look at it during the day tomorrow? Surely Maddy wouldn't object to your taking it down from the wall."

Madelyn, "Maddy," Harper was the current museum director.

"Faith." Patsy sounded a bit impatient. "If there's something funny going on at the museum, the last person I want to alert at the moment is the director."

"Of course. I wasn't thinking. It's just that the whole thing is so implausible. This is Aleford, not London or New York. The Ganley is a small, New England museum, not the Tate or the Met. The idea that someone has switched an original for a fake here is hard to believe."

"Believe it. Romare Bearden died in 1988 and his work, especially his collages, has appreciated enormously. London and New York don't have a monopoly on greed. In fact, a fake at a museum like ours would be less likely to be spotted. Not only don't we have a large number of specialists on staff, but we also don't have the kind of traffic those museums have—traffic that includes connoisseurs from all over the world who might raise questions. And whoever's responsible knows the piece will be in storage for a long time—and in an off-site location. Maddy is hoping to launch a campaign for an on-site facility in the not too distant future, but it's a hard thing to get people to donate to—can't put your name on it or exhibit it. Too utilitarian."

"Which means whoever's responsible has to be on the staff or somewhat intimately connected with the museum to know the schedule of exhibitions," Faith said. "We're not dealing with Banksy here. You know that British artist who sneaks into museums and glues a piece of his own work onto the walls? He hit the Met, MoMA, Brooklyn Museum, and the Museum of Natural History all at once. Nobody noticed that what he calls his 'subverted art' wasn't supposed to be there for several days. I mean, the man disguises himself as Inspector Clouseau, although I guess in New York people wouldn't bat an eye."

"They would in Aleford, but although our crook is leaving something, it's not with the same intent. So here's the plan. We go in tomorrow night. Better wear dark clothes, and we can park at Have Faith and walk from there."

Faith had started her catering firm, Have Faith, in New York before moving to New England as a new bride, and after brief hiatuses when Ben, now twelve, and Amy, nine, arrived on the scene, had continued the business in Aleford. Faith only lied to her minister husband, Tom, when it was absolutely necessary and even then crossed her fingers behind her back. Patsy's plan would make both unnecessary. Faith could tell him she was going to work. Which she was. Kind of.

Lying to members of the clergy in some form was inevitable when one was the daughter and granddaughter of men of the cloth. Faith Sibley Fairchild and her sister, Hope, one year younger, had grown up on New York's Upper East Side. Their mother, Jane Sibley, a real estate lawyer, was descended from the canny Dutch who had made such a profitable—for them—deal with the original New Yorkers. The long-ago indigenous people who were unfortunately swayed as much by fashion—those blankets and beads were to die for—as present-day New Yorkers—got to have that Prada bag and Jimmy Choos.

Jane had no problem assuming the tasks a ministerial spouse inevitably inherits—Ladies' Aid, calls on the infirm in mind and body—but she firmly refused to leave her island, or her neighborhood. The Sibley parsonage was a very roomy duplex just off Central Park.

Early on, Faith and Hope had sworn never to enter even as well-appointed a fishbowl as the one in which they had grown up. Hope married Quentin Lewis, her counterpart on Wall Street. They synchronized their PDAs and produced Quentin Lewis III in due time.

Faith, however, had fallen. Fallen very much in love, virtually at first sight. The Reverend Thomas Preston Fairchild was in town performing the wedding ceremony for his college roommate, and Faith was catering the reception. Tom had shed his robes and collar. By the time she found out what he did for a living, it was too late. While she never regretted her choice, there were moments when she regretted *his*—members of the parish offering her "friendly" child-rearing advice or entering the parsonage living room and declaring in aggrieved tones, "You've rearranged the furniture." And then there was the omnipresent fact that with rare exception, Tom was on call twenty-four hours a day, 365 days a year.

"I don't want to park in the museum lot, and your place isn't far." Patsy was revved up. She was speaking fast again. Ms. Avery liked having a plan; she liked following up on one even better.

Faith had finished one sticky bun and was seriously contemplating another. This was what was so devastating about them—the first merely whetted your appetite for the second, and so on . . .

"You haven't explained why you need my company for your escapade. Certainly not to park at the kitchen. That's no problem. And it's not a large work of art. You can get it off the wall by yourself."

"Honey, I can get into the museum, but I can't shimmy under the laser beam into the gallery where everything will be wrapped and waiting to go. There's where you come in. And now that you mention it, it would be nice to have some company."

"Take Will. He can do the limbo number as well as, if not better than, I can."

Will Avery was thin. His wife was more ample, much more ample. She liked to point out that when they met, Will told her he didn't like to see bone on a woman, and thank goodness still didn't.

"Are you crazy, Faith! Can you imagine what he would say about all this? He's a *lawyer*, remember?"

Since she had brought it up before, Faith didn't feel it was necessary to remind Patsy of her own esquire status. The sugar rush or Patsy's enthusiasm was making Faith's skin tingle. It had been a slow fall so far at Have Faith with the downturn in the economy. She suspected many of her previous customers were transferring Costco's shrimp platters and other offerings to their own silver salvers instead of hiring outside help. Investigating possible art fraud would be a pleasant diversion, and as for entering the museum, Patsy had the code—no break-in involved—and the only things they would be taking were a few photos.

One more thought occurred to her.

"What about surveillance cameras? I've seen them on the outside of the building when we've catered events."

"Major secret, but they're there for show. I don't think the film has been changed since they were installed. Thomas, the security guard, told me that one was removed recently when he found mice had not only left little calling cards on the path below, but had had the further audacity to line their nest with the wires they'd chewed through."

Patsy paused for a moment.

"In or out?" she asked.

"In." Faith sighed. "Basic black and we meet when?"

As she walked home, rustling through the fallen oak leaves on the sidewalk, Faith wondered what had happened to September. Or the summer, for that matter. Time seemed to be speeding up. Is that what happened as you got older? She remembered longing to be more grown-up when she wasn't. Always waiting to be a certain age—old enough to wear makeup, old enough to drive, old enough, well, for all sorts of things. She was old enough now, but the funny part was that she didn't feel all that grown-up. Even with two very much wanting-to-be-grown-up children. Especially Ben. As she looked at the shadows that were growing longer each day, a shadow crossed her mind. Middle school.

Ben couldn't wait for the first day. All summer he and his best friend, Josh, had agonized over what to wear, what school supplies to buy. And then there was the mighty cell phone debate. Ben had started early—last spring—wisely avoiding the ineffective "Everybody else has one" for the canny "You'd know where I was all the time. You'd never have to worry." And "They have number blockers and limited-minutes programs, not that you couldn't trust me, but I'm just telling you." Faith and Tom had gotten to the point in life where they couldn't imagine how they functioned before cell phones, using them, on occasion absurdly enough, to speak to each other when they were both in the house—Tom in his study, Faith in the kitchen. Cell phones weren't permitted in elementary school, but the middle and high schools had given in to parental—not student—pressure two years ago. If little Jack missed the bus, he could call right away. If little Jill's soccer practice was canceled, she could let a parent know.

Latchkey children needed all the connections they could get. And in the post-9/11 world, the option many parents wanted above all was 911.

Although he didn't come home to an empty house, Ben got his phone.

Faith cut across her next-door neighbors', the Millers, backyard. The house was dark. In the past at dusk, there would have been lights on in the kitchen as Pix, Faith's closest friend, supervised her younger son Dan's homework and chose from an array of boxes with the word HELPER on them for something to put together for supper. Pix worked part-time for Faith, balancing the books and doing some of the ordering, a job she had taken with the proviso that she would not prepare any actual food. Dan was in his first year of college now; his older brother and sister already out. The nest was empty, and it looked as if Pix had flown off, too. Probably meeting her husband, Sam, in town for dinner. It was a good thing those boxes in the cupboard had a shelf life measurable by carbon dating.

The lights were on in the Fairchilds' kitchen and up in Ben's bedroom, one of the ones in the back of the house. Faith had left Amy doing math homework at the big round table in the kitchen. She was also supposed to keep an eye on the chicken dish simmering on the stove that they'd have once Tom got home from whatever parish meeting would delay him tonight. Ben had been at his desk writing a book report on a book of his own choosing. He'd picked *Eldest,* the sequel to Christopher Paolini's *Eragon.*

She opened the back door and was happy to see Tom home early.

"This is a nice surprise," she said, walking over to where he was sitting at the table with Amy. She put her arms around him as she planted a kiss on the top of his head. His rusty brown hair was as thick as it had been when they met and so far no silver threads.

"Where have you been?"

This was not the greeting she expected. The tone was accusatory, not friendly curiosity.

"Just over to Patsy's for a half hour or so. Why?"

"Aimster," he said, using his own special nickname for his daughter, "I'll be right back. You're doing a great job. Try the next problem on your own." He motioned Faith toward the living room. As she followed him she noticed that the flame under the chicken had been turned off. She paused to uncover it. It definitely needed to simmer longer. She replaced the lid and turned the burner on. It was an easy dish and a family favorite. She'd browned the skinless breasts in olive oil, then topped them with layers of thinly sliced onions, red and yellow peppers, plus two cups of fresh chopped basil—the last from the garden. She'd harvested the crop earlier in the afternoon, making and freezing pesto, saving one large bunch for this dish. Salt, pepper, and half a bottle of red wine—she'd had some leftover pinot noir in the fridge—completed the dish, which needed to simmer for at least an hour so the chicken could absorb the flavors. They'd have it with whole-wheat couscous, which has a lovely nutty taste, and a salad.

"When I came home, Amy was almost in tears over her homework, and there was no one to help her. She'd asked Ben, but he said he was too busy. When I went upstairs to check, he was busy all right. Busily instant-messaging a friend. He's lost his computer privileges except for schoolwork for the rest of the week. And I don't think Amy is old enough to be left in charge of dinner."

"Is this a talking-to?" Faith felt her cheeks flush. "If so, Amy was fine when I left and we'd gone over what she had to do. I told her if she got stuck to start reading her English assignment and wait for me to come back. I'm surprised she asked Ben, as he's never been known to help her out. Not sure what siblings would. Maybe in the Walton family. *And* she was not preparing dinner, although she's capable of it. Merely checking to make sure the chicken didn't start to cook too fast."

Tom, to his credit, looked somewhat chagrined. "It's just that I don't like coming home and finding the kids alone."

"I know. Your mom was in the kitchen whipping up cookies for you to have with your milk the moment any of you crossed the threshold. Those days are over, Tom. Not that I want the kids here on their own, either, and you know it's a rare event, but briefly stepping two blocks away—and they both knew where I was and have the number memorized—does not constitute abandonment. Or bad mothering."

They'd been standing in front of the bay window that overlooked the backyard. The swamp maples were turning red, and the last rays of the sun were setting the leaves ablaze. Tom sat down in the big wing chair and pulled Faith down onto his lap.

"Sorry, sweetheart. It's been a rocky fall, and I overreacted. What with starting this new capital campaign and the damn Harvest Festival, not to mention Ben." He looked so glum Faith didn't have the heart to be annoyed any longer, although she'd been about to move from peeved to mad.

"The vestry will handle the campaign. You just have to show up at the meetings, more's the pity, and deliver a few subtle sermons about stewardship on several Sundays. The Harvest Festival is another matter, and if it weren't such a moneymaker, I'd say ditch it. But since I'm on the committee, not you, try to stay away as much as you can. No, you don't have to thank me. It's my cross to bear and it's how I justify not getting involved in the Sunday school Christmas pageant. Maybe this year I can steer the group away from asking your opinion on where the cornstalk/hay bale display should go and how many pumpkins they should order to sell. What's really bothering you, and me, is Ben and you know it, not that we're mentioning him."

The shadow that had fallen across Faith's mind as she walked back from Maple Street thinking about her son and his entry into middle school returned. It loomed even larger now that Tom was beside her, sharing her anxiety. The greatly anticipated event had proved to be a major disappointment. His clothes were wrong. Even his pencils weren't the right kind. After hearing he never had time to go to his locker between classes, Faith had bought him one of those knapsacks on wheels, like luggage, to save his back. He'd thrown it across the room, shouted, "Are you crazy, Mom! Only losers have these!" and stormed to the sanity of his own room, strictly off-limits to his mother, father, and sister.

Ben had had his moments, but was essentially an even-tempered child, happy at school where he'd always done well, happy at play with lots of friends.

Now he never seemed happy, and his temper was on a hair trigger. Faith kept telling herself that it was the age. Hormones. Puberty. All those dreaded events such as when one's little boy stopped smelling like Johnson's baby shampoo and started reeking of Right Guard and hair gel. Pix, who was Faith's Brazelton, Spock, and Leach rolled up into one, had agreed, pointing out that Ben's choirboy soprano would soon be a bluesy bass and they'd have to start buying milk by the case. But, she cautioned, all else paled before the particular kind of hell, unknown anywhere else on the planet, that middle school brought. Once he emerged from eighth grade all would be well again. Faith hoped she could last that long, and more to the point, would Ben's bedroom door? The last slam had produced a hairline crack. She knew this was going through Tom's mind, too. They'd talked it to death.

"I should have called you to tell you I was going over to Patsy's."

"No, that would have been ridiculous." Tom had burrowed his face in his wife's thick blond hair and was nuzzling her neck. His words were muffled, but she could hear him. "You don't have to let me know where you are every minute of the day."

Which was a good thing, Faith thought, given her plans for the following evening. They'd decided to meet at a quarter to 10:00. Aleford shut down early. Most people would be in bed reading their library books or even asleep. It had taken Faith a long time to absorb the fact that the town ate dinner at 6:00 P.M. or earlier, possibly watched something on PBS, then settled down for their eight hours to be up with the birds. She'd tell Tom she was going over to the kitchen. Recently she'd been toying with the idea of offering carryout cuisine—main dishes, desserts, baked goods—in one section of the building that she occupied. Her assistant and only full-time employee, Niki Constantine, liked the idea, especially since desserts were her specialty. It needed much more fleshing out, though. The danger was ending up with too much leftover food. But if they did advance orders only, they'd lose all those harried customers running in for something for supper that night. Tom would assume she was going over to work on the plans, and she wouldn't disabuse him of the notion. Her other project was a cookbook, *Have Faith in Your Kitchen.* He might also assume she was working on that. Either way she wouldn't have to be too specific.

Reluctantly she got up. They didn't get too many moments together like this. "You go check on Ben. I'll see how Amy's doing, and we should be ready to eat in half an hour."

"Movie Wednesday night? We could catch something at Kendall Square and eat down in Chinatown at King Fung afterward."

"It's the first Harvest Festival committee meeting. Seven o'clock and you know I won't get out of there before nine at the earliest. Thursday night?"

"I promised to go see Joel Bishop. He's not doing too well."

"Maybe next year," Faith said ruefully.

Since so much of Faith's wardrobe was black, Tom didn't comment on her attire—black jeans and a black turtleneck sweater—as she left for work the following evening. It was 9:30 and Tom was on the phone with a parishioner whose wife's cancer had recently spread to her brain. Faith kissed his cheek, registering the pain in his glance, a look that told her how helpless he felt.

Today she'd made sure to be home well before the kids and their homework was all done before dinner. Ben's book report on *Eldest* was due tomorrow, and Faith had offered to proofread it, but he'd explained—to the Luddite unaccountably related to him—that he had a spell and grammar check on his computer. Said Luddite pointed out that you still had to go over what you wrote, since the programs wouldn't necessarily tell you if you'd used *it's* when you meant *its,* as both were spelled correctly, but this logic fell on deaf ears. Literally, since he'd plugged into his iPod as soon as she'd opened her mouth. She hadn't had the energy to pursue the matter further. Pix kept stressing the importance of choosing battlegrounds, and this one had *Waterloo* written all over it. The iPod had been a birthday gift from Tom's youngest brother, Craig, divorced, childless, and in this case, clueless.

Pix had warned her that two of the problems Faith would face as her children got older were that she'd have to wear increasingly opaque nightwear and that they'd eventually stay up later than she did. Ben was pushing this last item hard, complaining that no other sixth grader had to be in bed at 9:30 on school nights. Since he invariably fell asleep over his book once there, his parents knew they were right and stuck to it. At Back to School night, they felt further justified when the school nurse told parents the biggest health problem among the students was not enough sleep. "Send a note explaining why the homework isn't done. When your children were infants, you made sure they slept on their backs to avoid the tragedy of SIDS. Now you have to be equally vigilant, so they aren't overtired and pick up the colds, viruses, and flus that go around, among other things. Plus they'll have more energy for schoolwork, sports, and be more pleasant to have around the house without those drooping eyelids!" Ben wasn't all that pleasant to have around the house these days, but his eyes *were* wide open.

As Faith drove through Aleford, mindful of the rest of her outfit—a black denim jacket, watch cap, and flashlight—on the seat beside her, she thought about her day. As soon as the kids had left for school and Tom for his office—a hop, skip, and a jump among the tombstones in the cemetery that separated the parsonage from the church—Faith had headed out to Have Faith's kitchen. She'd spent the morning and early afternoon drawing up plans for the carryout counter with Niki, whose irrepressible and often outrageous conversation made most of their work fun.

Niki Constantine had married the man of her mother's dreams the previous December, resisting the fact that he was also the man of her own almost to the altar—"Harvard M.B.A., more than gainfully employed, tall, dark, handsome, wants a family, and is *Greek.* What could be worse?" she'd wailed to Faith, her matron of honor. The parade of bikers, communists, punk rockers, and men older than her father that she'd very deliberately brought home over the years hadn't fooled her mother for an instant, although Mr. Constantine seemed to sprout a new patch of gray hair after each introduction.

Mrs. Constantine even got her way with Niki's wedding dress—"Sort of like those dolls with the ruffly crocheted skirts my aunt Olympia makes to cover toilet paper rolls, except white tulle." Niki's choice, a Vera Wang strapless sheath, never made it from the magazine page to the dressing room. Niki had kept her name to use professionally, but was proudly introduced by her mother as "Mrs. Theodopoulos, my daughter. The one whose husband is an executive at Fidelity."

The idea for expanding the business was starting to become a reality, and it had been a productive day. Niki, normally so tuned into Faith's moods that she would have known something was up the moment she walked through the door, was preoccupied by her mother's ongoing campaign for a grandchild.

"If I hear her mention my 'organic clock'—she's started shopping at Whole Foods and has gotten a little mixed up on 'biological' and 'organic'—I'm moving to the West Coast."

"You know she'll follow you," Faith had said.

"I know, believe me, I know."

By the time Niki had described the various fertility advice being offered by the fiftysomething and up female Greek-American population of Watertown, Massachusetts, all her mother's best friends, Faith was helpless with laughter and had almost, but not quite, forgotten the night's escapade.

"Lying down afterward with your legs in the air would make too much sense. No, it's got to be a full moon and an empty stomach—nothing but hot water and lemon during the day. Oh, and a sprig of rosemary under the pillow. I tuned out when she got to the part involving a potato. Possibly you get to be naked, but we didn't go into that. However, on no account whatsoever are you to enjoy yourself. You should have seen my mother. She was so stern, looked me straight in the eye when she said it. I pretended not to know what she was talking about and she left the room in a huff. 'When you're an old lady and you don't have anyone to take care of you, you'll remember this.' I'm remembering it now and I'm not even thirty!"

There was some logic in Mrs. Constantine's thinking, the taking-care-of part, and Faith hoped Amy would prove to be the kind of daughter who would cut her mother's ugly toenails in old age. Or there would be a suitable daughter-in-law. Ben's taste in women at present ran to the waiflike girls with the big eyes in his Japanese manga books. They looked sweet, though.

Now Faith was sitting in her car waiting for Patsy. It was just ten o'clock. Aleford's Yankee thrift extended to streetlights, and aside from the outside light on her building, Faith was in the dark. Where was Patsy? A car slowed up. At last! Then it sped off. Faith suddenly felt very vulnerable. This wasn't a residential part of town, and at this time of night, no one was around. Another car, but this time it pulled up next to Faith's.

It wasn't Patsy's.

For a moment, Faith felt a strong surge of fear. Then the car door opened and her friend got out. Faith joined her.

"Sorry," Patsy said. "You must have been startled. I should have told you I'd be driving this. It's a loaner. Mine is in the shop. Let's go."

Patsy was wearing what looked like a dark monk's robe, but upon closer inspection it proved to be a long black cape, a black skirt, and cowl-neck sweater. The whole situation was beginning to seem like a scene from a movie Faith thought she might have seen or a book she might have read. Vaguely familiar and definitely bizarre.

"Love the cape, but Halloween isn't for a couple of weeks."

"I'll have you know this is vintage Oscar de la Renta and I wear it to Symphony."

They walked up a side street that dead-ended in the woods behind Aleford's Industrial Park—Faith's business, a small press, and a clipping service. The latter two were housed in one building. It wasn't exactly Silicon Valley. The woods were the start of the Ganley estate, now the museum and its sculpture park.

"There's a path, actually a former service road, left over from Theodore Ganley's day. It leads straight to the employee parking lot and the back entrance to the museum."

The path was easy to find. The dirt road was overgrown with alders and other invasive flora, but enough Aleford dog walkers and birders had kept the way open. The moon had risen, and Faith could see the glistening orange bittersweet berries looped like necklaces in the surrounding brush.

They weren't talking much, which was why the noise Faith heard behind them was audible. The sound of branches being pushed aside, leaves rustling. She put her finger to her lips and motioned for Patsy to stop.

"What's up?" Patsy whispered.

The noise behind them had stopped. Faith stood still for a moment. The whole escapade, including Patsy's cape, was spooking her out. The woods were filled with nocturnal creatures. Best not to think about them.

"Let's go. It's nothing."

She didn't hear the sound again, and it wasn't long before they reached the museum. Patsy led the way up the hill straight to the large double door—wide

enough and tall enough for all but the most gargan-
tuan artwork—at the rear of the building. There was
a loading dock next to the entrance and beyond that
an overflowing Dumpster. Unlike the rest of Aleford,
which trekked to the Transfer Station, better known as
the dump, each week, the Ganley had a trash collection
service. This convenience meant that they missed out
on the latest news, impromptu dinner invitations, and
most important of all—the swap table, which could
yield anything from a dog-eared copy of *Valley of the
Dolls* to an only slightly nicked set of Spode dinner
plates. Tom was addicted to the dump, and Faith often
had to surreptitiously return some of his "finds," a
frayed leather belt, "still good for working outdoors"
and clay flower pots, "do you know what these cost at
the garden center!"

The moon was waxing and had risen, sending its
bright rays across the parking lot and the pond below.
It would be full on Saturday. Mrs. Constantine must
have the date circled in red. Faith wondered what
stratagem Niki's mother would use to get her daughter
to fast—and all the rest. Watching the battle of wills
between these two equally stubborn women was end-
lessly fascinating. Now one was ahead; now the other.
She looked over at her friend, another stubborn lady.
Patsy was carrying a large pocketbook, one she'd had

before the luggage-size monsters had come into fashion last spring, bigger than ever this fall. Patsy's wasn't a Gucci or Fendi, but it would pass muster.

"Ready?" Patsy said softly, although their only company was a chorus of bullfrogs in the pond.

Faith nodded. She was as ready as she would ever be, and as doubtful. She took some comfort in the backup plan, the one they'd put in place in case the alarm went off or they heard someone coming. Patsy would stand her ground and Faith would run like hell into the woods and go home, thus avoiding the inevitable "Local Minister's Wife B and E Suspect" headlines. Patsy wasn't sure what she would say, but as a trustee she figured she'd be able to bluff her way out of it.

Patsy punched in the code, opened the door, and they slipped inside. They turned on their flashlights, and Faith noted that they were in the long, wide sloping corridor with shelving on one side that she knew from catering events there. They soon emerged through another set of double doors into the museum proper. The gallery that had housed the recent exhibition was to their left. Patsy stopped at the entrance, set her bag on the floor, and began to rummage through it. From the light filtering down through the high windows, Faith could see the artwork in brown cardboard boxes—some smaller pieces wrapped in brown paper—leaning against the walls, all ready to go into storage. Patsy had told her that the pieces were first wrapped in layers of bubble wrap before the final protective covering was added. Each work had a large label on the outside stating the artist's name, title of the work, and destination—Ganley's storage, back to the artist, owner, or another institution if a loan. Before any of it left the museum, the registrar would check it against the list that had been made upon arrival. A foolproof system—supposedly.

Patsy straightened up, leaving her bag open. "Take your jacket off," she instructed. Faith shrugged it off and put it on the floor next to Patsy's flashlight, a powerful lantern that any Scout would be proud to own. Patsy slid a roll of packing tape on Faith's wrist like a bracelet and handed her a box cutter.

"All you have to do is cut the tape on the top flap, remove the Bearden, and when we're finished, put it back, then tape it up, covering the place where you made the cut," she instructed as she bent down to get something else from her Mary Poppins–like bag.

Piece of cake so far as Patsy was concerned, Faith thought, hoping her friend's assessment would prove correct. Cakes had a way of falling.

Patsy stood up again. She was also holding a can of hairspray—extra hold. Her dark hair was straight, a legacy from a Native-American ancestor—"We *all* want to be part Indian you know, no nappy hair," she'd told Faith. "But not Condi Rice straight, no breeze would think of messing with that helmet." Patsy's hair swayed. Faith doubted she used any but the lightest spritz of spray. In any case, this did not seem an appropriate time for grooming.

"Watch carefully. You have to know how low the laser beam is."

"Wait a minute! It's invisible?"

"Don't worry. I saw this in a movie."

Before Faith could say anything more, Patsy sprayed the entrance, and sure enough, a thin red line of light was revealed. About two feet off the floor.

"Get down, quick, and slither under it. I don't know how long this lasts."

Faith crawled under, flattening herself as close to the ground as she could, although the knots in her stomach were raising her up several inches.

"You can stand up," Patsy said.

"But aren't there others?" Faith asked.

"Good point." Patsy rolled the canister along the floor, and Faith picked it up, trying hard to remember she was in Aleford and not Istanbul.

"How are we going to know where the Bearden is?"

"I'm assuming they took them from the wall, wrapped them, and left them more or less in place, so start with the ones on the wall nearest you. That's where it was hung. The package third from the left looks about the right size."

Spraying the air in front of her, Faith cautiously made her way over to the artwork. Burdened with hairspray, tape, and box cutter, she'd left her flashlight behind, but Patsy was training her lantern's beam on the wall. The Bearden, clearly marked, *was* the third from the left, and it only took a moment to slice through the tape and ease the collage out. She carefully unwrapped the protective bubble-wrap layers. "Bingo," she said.

"Slide it over to me and I'll be right back," Patsy said.

"Where are you going?"

"To the restroom. I can turn on the light there. Don't worry. It won't take long."

Faith wished she could go with Patsy, but it would be foolish to take the chance of setting off the alarm. She wanted to see what Patsy was talking about, the signature and the special mark. Even more, she had to pee. She shouldn't have had that second cup of coffee after dinner. She sat down on the floor. It *had* been a piece of cake so far, and if it was for them, why not someone else? She looked around at all the tidy packages. Since it was a small museum, the Ganley didn't have a full-time crew to hang and pack up shows, but Patsy had told Faith the museum had been using the same people from a company specializing in installations for many years. In addition, the curator and assistant curator were with them at all times. But, thought Faith looking around, during the hustle and bustle of packing up it would be easy enough to slip a small piece under a jacket on the floor to carry out later, filling the empty container with bubble wrap and something slightly heavy. The label was on the outside. No one would find out for years if the artwork was on its way to the storage facility. Or the switch could be made in the truck. Or the truck robbed. Last year thieves had broken into a delivery truck parked overnight in a lot outside a Pennsylvania Howard Johnson Inn and scored a Goya on its way from Ohio's Toledo Museum of Art to the Guggenheim in New York City. The Goya was apparently not what the thieves had had in mind—flat-screen HDTV more likely—and deciding it was too hot to handle even for them, they'd had a lawyer contact the FBI and arrange a pickup in New Jersey, no questions asked. The painting was unharmed, and what happened in Jersey stayed in Jersey.

Then there was Boston's own, still unsolved, 1990 heist at the Gardner Museum. The treasures—

a Vermeer, three Rembrandts, and eight other paintings—were still missing. The thieves had posed as police and gained entry at night where it was the work of a few minutes to grab what they wanted. Faith knew there were twisted collectors, whose pleasure would be increased, not lessened, by knowing they could never display a masterpiece. That it was for their eyes only.

Patsy was taking forever, but when she looked at her watch, Faith was surprised to see it was less than five minutes before her friend's return.

"I got some good pictures of the signature. I'm going to slide it back to you, then let's get out of here."

Faith quickly rewrapped the collage, put it back in the box, taped it shut, and placed it in what she thought was exactly the same spot, then made the return trip as fast as she could. Pulling on her coat, she followed Patsy out of the museum and waited until they were in the woods to speak.

"Well?"

"Without doubt a fake. Will didn't want to destroy the value of the piece by writing an inscription. It was an anniversary gift, but he wrote the date in pencil on the back. The numerals were so tiny they looked like dust spots. It was our secret." She paused. "They're not there."

"What now?"

"I'll send the photos to a couple of places I know that can tell me about the signature. Two very discreet dealers in contemporary African-American art. Once I hear from them, we'll go to plan B."

"Plan B?"

"This being plan A."

"I got that, but what's plan B?"

"Plan B is you, sweetie."

Chapter 2

The Ganley Museum of Art is a well-established Aleford institution. The cognoscenti affectionately call it the "Teddy," a reference to its founder, wealthy industrialist Theodore Ganley. Theodore and his wife, Julia, were omnivorous art collectors with passions that spanned many centuries, as well as cultures. With no offspring to bless their union, they regarded their collection as progeny—and legacy. In the early part of the twentieth century, they purchased forty acres in Aleford and built an estate overlooking a scenic body of water that supplies some of the town's drinking water. Its name—Otter Pond—struck a pedestrian, rather unaesthetic note, and since "Walden" was already taken, the Ganleys renamed it "Gododdin Pond" after the early Welsh poem that first mentions the noble King Arthur.

Both Theodore and Julia were devout followers of the Round Table. This penchant for the Arthurian also influenced the design of the main house, a castlelike stone edifice with crenellations, turrets, finials, parapets, a moat and drawbridge complete with portcullis. When it was done, they traveled the world over, scouting bazaars, auction houses, upscale as well as lowly emporia, and shipped their finds to Aleford. The stables were soon crammed with packing cases. When their contents were removed, the rooms in the mansion overflowed with objets d'art, much to the couple's great delight. Without a Berenson or Duveen—they saw no need to have their keen eyes instructed—the Ganley purchases ranged from the rare to the ridiculous with a great deal in between. While they eschewed antimacassars and left the piano legs undraped, there was more than a whiff of Victoriana in the four-foot-high Chinese porcelain vases stuffed with peacock feathers and a phalanx of Benares brass bowls filled with potpourri.

As might have been expected, the Ganleys were an easy mark for anything fit for a king. They created a timbered Great Hall where the wall's tapestries vied with the carpets on the floor, and both fought to hold their own against the brilliant stained-glass windows and heavy, intricately carved Gothic furniture. Glass-fronted cabinets revealed a mix of archeological "finds" and art glass, Julia's obsession. They purchased as many Pre-Raphaelites as they could, some quite wonderful, others merely illustrative. Suspicious of the Impressionists at first, they eventually took to Degas, covering one wall in the library with drawings and several pastels of his dancers. Other surfaces reflected their fondness for landscapes, especially the Barbizon School, as well as a few choice pieces by American Hudson River painters, including Asher Durand. These gems, however, were outnumbered by rhinestones, especially sentimental renderings of dogs, horses, sheep, milkmaids, and damsels in or out of distress. Chaste alabaster cupids and putti gazed down upon the collection from their own special niches. A large marble Saint George stood guard at the entrance. There were many suits of armor. Not a wall, ceiling, floor, staircase, banister, or newel post remained unadorned.

Apart from a few select gatherings for their friends, the Ganleys preferred to dwell amid their treasures alone. As lord and lady of the manor, they did lower the bridge twice a year for two townwide gatherings—a merrie olde Yuletide open house complete with wassail and strolling minstrels and a garden party in July marking Julia's birthday, the day they had chosen to move into Aleford, making it the estate's natal day, as well. After Julia's untimely death at age fifty-five—she had a heart, as they used to say—Theodore continued to live in the house by himself with his longtime retainers. There were fewer dinner parties, but the Aleford events were sacrosanct, particularly the birthday party. A small, dapper man who did not bow to fashion, having made a deep obeisance in his youth, Theodore Ganley cut an unvarying figure in a swallowtail coat and silk cravat.

When he turned seventy-five, his lawyer came before the board of selectmen with a proposal. Mr. Ganley was concerned about what might happen to his estate after his death. He was without issue, and his nearest relative was a distant cousin with no ascertainable artistic sensibilities. Therefore Mr. Ganley had decided to leave his entire property—the house, its contents, outer buildings, and acreage—to the town of Aleford. The institution would be known as the Ganley Museum of Art upon his death and belong in totality to the town. Unlike Boston's Isabella Stewart Gardner, Theodore would make no restrictions regarding the collection or the buildings. If at some later date, a curator wanted to move the furniture around and rehang a painting, that was fine with him. None of the acreage could be sold, however. The paths he had created in his park, which had never been public, would be made available to Alefordians immediately. If his offer were accepted, he would set up an endowment that would be administered by a board of trustees upon his demise to maintain the buildings and purchase art "contemporary to the period." The endowment would throw off enough interest to see the museum well into the next century, by which time it was his fervent hope that the museum would have attained such renown as to be self-supporting. In return, he asked only for life tenancy and tax-free status.

The board could barely control its glee. For years the town had speculated about the fate of the property. Millicent Revere McKinley, one of Aleford's self-described leading citizens, and oldest, this last vociferously denied, had tracked Ganley's cousin down at one point. Since she was a descendent of that famously resourceful silversmith through a cousin of his twice removed, and since genealogy was not simply a hobby but a calling, finding the man was child's play. After speaking with him by phone, she'd enjoyed dropping heavily veiled hints in line at the post office and Shop 'n Save. Some eavesdroppers had the impression Theodore Ganley was leaving everything to his cousin, a dentist living in Milwaukee; others that the cousins had quarreled as children and the estate was being left to the ASPCA. These listeners were under the impression that the relative was a shoe salesman in Akron. After a week of fun, Millicent had told all. The cousin was a plumber in Spokane with only a vague idea of what his distant kin had been up to all these years. When she'd asked him what was hanging on his walls, he'd replied, "Wallpaper." As for sculpture, he'd volunteered that "the wife was partial to garden gnomes and birdbaths." The obvious heir had been eliminated, but Aleford was still no closer to knowing the disposition of the Ganley loot. Not until the lawyer made his presentation.

It took all of ten minutes in executive session for the board to accept the offer. There had been a modest attempt to wish Theodore a long and healthy life, but facts were facts, and New Englanders never shy away from the unvarnished truth. Ganley was an old man and from the look of things—it wouldn't take a nor'easter to blow *him* over—his maker would be calling soon. The papers were drawn up and signed, the town moseyed along the paths that traversed the property, enjoying each season—vales of rhododendrons and drifts of daffodils in the spring, cool shade trees and lush green flora in summer, fields of wild aster and milkweed against a backdrop of vibrant color in fall, and a wonderland for snowshoers and cross-country skiers in the winter. It was a sweetheart of a deal, and the board was reelected with no opposition. And then the years went by. Exactly twenty-two tax-free years.

Theodore Ganley lived to be ninety-seven. It was indeed a sweetheart of a deal. For him.

As Theodore joined his beloved Julia in the mausoleum he had erected on the grounds, modeling it on the one they'd seen in England at Castle Howard, the selectmen hastened to call a meeting of the Ganley Trust Committee, which had been set up at the time of the initial arrangement. Only one of the original members remained, Harriett Spencer Potter, a young bride at the onset, who was interested in art.

After years of waiting in the wings, *always* the understudies, the Ganley committee got right to work. They opened the main house up to the town for the first time in many years (as Theodore aged, he'd dropped the Christmas revels, then the birthday fete) and then they convened a special Town Meeting.

"Tear the monstrosity down and start over," "I love the way the towers look silhouetted against the sunset," and "Who could possibly dust all that!"—a wide range of opinions were expressed, but everyone wanted to keep the access to the park as open as possible and use the bequest in an educational capacity, perhaps have the museum run some courses.

In short order, the committee thanked people for coming—especially on such a fine day when normally they would be engaged in vigorous outdoor Aleford pursuits—appointed themselves the new board of trustees and hired Alexander Harvey as the Ganley Museum's first director. He was a local boy who had gone on to Yale and was working as a curator in its art museum. The fact that he had never served as a museum director bothered them not at all. Sandy would know what to do and do it well. He always had.

They were right.

Sandy immediately advised serious winnowing and made a list—not a long one—of artworks that would form the basis of the permanent collection. He also asked that the trustees take Theodore's words literally and start acquiring art "contemporary to the period" as soon as possible. His goal was to start the sixties with a bang—the Ganley as it had never been seen before. The trustees were infected by his enthusiasm and gave him free rein. An auction was held, the tapestries came down, the moat was filled in, the drawbridge and portcullis were sold to a theme park in New Jersey, and the first new sculptures—kinetic ones—a Calder and another by George Rickey, were set in place in the park. Sandy wanted movement, inside and out.

The castle retained its turrets and finials, but the inside was mostly gutted to create exhibition space. The architect retained some of the Romanesque archways and set some of the capitals in gallery corners. Theodore's immense oak-paneled library at the top of the house was divided into the offices and a meeting room/art book library. When the Ganley Museum of Art officially opened its doors in September 1961, all Aleford flocked through them, as well as a large number of artistically inclined visitors from the Boston area. It was easy to identify the two groups. Local residents wore what they wore every day around town—the women in corduroy wraparound skirts and Liberty round-collared blouses from Johnny Appleseed's; the men in khakis from Bean's and oxford-cloth button-downs from Brooks. The Cantabrigians and Bostonians favored brightly colored shirts and dresses—Marimekkos from Finland sold at Design Research. The women wore jewelry that, like the new sculptures outdoors, moved when they moved. The novelty of these birds of paradise intrigued Aleford, and since it was a onetime thing—the Ganley was *their* museum, after all, and it was unlikely these people would be around again, at least not in the near future—they nodded amiably and tried to understand what was hanging on the walls. They knew it was art, but they weren't sure *why* it was.

Besides Sandy, no one was more conspicuous on the opening day than Harriett Spencer Potter. Her husband, Channing, had died on Omaha Beach, leaving her a widow with a posthumous child. Their son, Channing

Jr., had been at his late father's old boarding school throughout his adolescence and was now starting at the pater's alma mater, Harvard. That project completed, she'd been at loose ends when the Ganley call had come. She considered herself Sandy's right hand, and he was not averse to her help—unpaid time *and* a hefty annual pledge. Harriett supplied the funds for the purchase of the Nevelson that greeted museum visitors in the large foyer. She'd given it in memory of her husband and felt its massive, dark presence was an apt representation of her grief. They'd married the Saturday following her graduation from Mount Holyoke and they hadn't had much time together before he went to war. Of course, he'd never known his son.

And so the Ganley blended gracefully into the Aleford landscape. As the years passed, Sandy proved adept at fund-raising, both through grants and individual donors. Admission was free for Aleford residents, but many adopted it, along with the Audubon Society, WGBH, various institutions of higher learning, the church, and Emerson Hospital Auxiliary, as an appropriate recipient come the end of the tax year. Twenty years later, a tasteful wing doubled the exhibition space and the greatly enlarged sculpture park was a destination in itself by the nineties. The school became a reality early on and offered courses for children and

adults in ceramics, drawing and painting, silversmith-
ing, woodcarving, basketry, and more. Sandy revived
the picnic celebrating Julia's and the Ganley's birth-
days. He had held on to most of her glass collection
and was validated by the enormous rise in prices for
Tiffany, Gallé, Lalique, and some Roman, Greek, and
Egyptian finds. He bought contemporary glass, much
of it Scandinavian, discovered Dale Chihuly at the start
of his career, and organized a very successful show—
Through a Glass Brightly—that successfully mixed all
these fragile works together.

Boyish in appearance, Sandy never seemed to change.
He'd been twenty-seven when he took on the job. Forty-
three years later when Harriett found him slumped over
his desk, dead of what appeared to be a massive coro-
nary, her first thought was that he was much too young
for that sort of thing. Ironically, they were meeting to
discuss the purchase of an Andy Goldsworthy piece for
the park, yet another memorial. Channing Jr. had not
been the son she had hoped for—and thought she had
molded so well. He'd finished Harvard with barely a
gentleman's C and proceeded, with diligent abandon,
to go through the trust fund set up for him at birth.
At thirty-five he'd eloped with a nineteen-year-old au
pair he met while visiting his college roommate down
on the Cape. She was not Swedish—a North Dakotan

who *looked* Swedish, and that was good enough for Channing. After a very brief visit home, which netted him several valuable, highly portable, and pawnable objects, the couple did not return to Aleford for some years. This time they didn't take much, but did leave something behind—a six-month-old boy whom Channing Jr. had had the foresight to name Channing III, pleasing Harriett enormously, as was intended. III's grandmother, however, was surprised to discover an hour after she'd waved good-bye that the baby was still in the Potter ancestral cradle she'd dragged down from the attic upon their arrival. What she had taken to be her grandson in the infant seat in the back of the car was actually a lovely small Afghanistani Buddha she'd acquired many years ago swaddled in blankets. Never one to shirk her duty, Harriett resolved to raise the latest twig on the ancestral tree to the best of her abilities—and get new glasses.

Postcards arrived sporadically, then when Channing was a senior in high school, his mother—still quite the babe—herself arrived, attractively clad in black jersey and clutching an urn, much the size and shape of both that Buddha and Channing III years earlier.

Channing Jr. had met death in Venice. His widow stayed in Aleford for the funeral, made sure the allowance the departed had been receiving would continue, and took the next plane back to Italy where they had been living when too many Bellinis resulted in Channing's lethal stumble into an unforeseen canal. If Harriett was bereft, she did not show it. In fact, her son had meant little to her for most of his life, although she did express regret that she had given in to his complaints about early morning practices and allowed him to leave his prep school swim team. There were only two things that mattered to Harriett Spencer Potter—her darling grandson and the Ganley.

Faith was watching Tom eat a late supper. She'd started him on a sandwich she'd thrown together—sourdough bread, smoked turkey, a little cranberry conserve with a slice of farmhouse cheddar and lettuce—while she made her emergency "Pantry/Fridge Soup" (see recipe, p. 385). She'd thought the good ladies of the parish were providing sustenance for tonight's vestry meeting, scheduled as it was during the dinner hour—six o'clock, this was Aleford. Sustenance, that is, in the form of hideous casseroles—tuna, bacon, tomato, creamed corn, Velveeta, and mushroom soup topped with cornflakes had been a recent offering—but there had just been coffee and crumb cake. Faith's soup was a delicious concoction that started with a sautéed mixture of what she happened to have in the pantry and fridge—leeks, onions, scallions, and/or shallots—simmered with chicken or beef stock with more of what was on hand. Tonight's featured chickpeas, tomatoes, rosemary, garlic, mushrooms, and slices of applewood-smoked chicken sausage.

The vestry meeting had been unusually contentious—and long. Now that First Parish had decided on a capital campaign to raise enough money to repair the steeple, everyone had a favorite candidate for the job.

"Thank goodness for some sane voices," Tom said. "Who knew there were so many steeplejacks in the area? Prescott Wainwright finally interrupted and told them their 'steeplechase' was a bit premature and once we had some pledges and money in hand, we could solicit bids, which would be considered in due course."

Reflecting on the name—none of the movers and shakers at First Parish were simply "John Smith" or the like—Faith made a few sympathetic comments while she bided her time. She'd had a particularly irksome scene with Ben earlier and she needed to give Tom an abbreviated version—enough information to keep him up to speed on this ever increasingly stranger in their midst, but not enough to upset him more than his parishioners had, especially as Faith had won with Ben, more or less.

The argument had been about going to Maine for the long Columbus Day weekend on Friday, a family tradition. Sanpere Island in Penobscot Bay was the place that was most home to the Fairchilds. A parsonage never belongs to its occupants. They are merely passing through. The cottage, which they would be closing up for the winter, was another story—a long one. It was theirs forever, and Ben had previously talked about how great it would be to show his kids how to sail someday just the way he'd learned from his dad. Faith, whose own childhood voyages had been limited to Manhattan's Circle Line and the Staten Island ferry, loved that her offspring were growing up knowing that lines were never called ropes and port was not only a fortified wine from the Douro Valley in Portugal.

She'd brought a pile of clean laundry into his room, remembering to knock, and had reminded him about the trip. Ben didn't say anything. Faith was finding these one-sided conversations one of the most annoying in her son's new repertoire of behaviors. He simply didn't respond. No back talk, mouthiness, just nada.

"Ben, I'm talking to you!" Ah, exactly the right thing to say, and so original, she'd said to herself. I'm sure I must be the first parent to think up this effective line.

"I'm not going," he'd said over his shoulder, then turned his head back to the computer screen.

"What could possibly be more important than going to Maine? I know there aren't any soccer games scheduled. And this is something we have always done as a family, Benjamin," she'd said. "I don't know what's getting into you these days, but I do know that I don't like it!"

Ben had swiveled his desk chair around to face his mother. He'd regarded her calmly and explained the new facts of Benjamin Sibley Fairchild's life in a voice that sounded as if he were explaining a rudimentary concept to a two-year-old, like why eating crayons is bad for you. "I like Maine all right. But things change. Kids my age don't always want to do everything with their families the way they did when they were younger. Parents need to understand this and give them some space." He resumed his prior position.

Faith had had a sudden flash-forward to a much older Ben giving the old "I need some space" line while kissing off a girlfriend, or maybe a wife. It was not a pretty picture. Immediate corrective measures were in order.

She sat down on his bed, still hugging his laundry. The smell of Tide—that at least was immutable—was reassuring.

"Your dad and I realize you're growing and changing, which means becoming more independent. If you only wanted to do things with us, we'd be in trouble.

But there are some parts of our family life that we do expect you to participate in. Closing the cottage is a little like a rite, like a ceremony. You know we always have a special dinner Sunday. When you and Amy were very little, we'd go down to the shore and wave good-bye to the ocean."

She'd thought she heard a gagging noise, but Ben's back was to her, and the computer did tend to emit odd, weird sounds. She'd pushed on.

"That's not to say we can't alter what we do. How about inviting a friend to come along? Josh always has a good time in Sanpere."

Ben had whirled the chair around and scowled. "Not Josh."

Before Faith could ask what was going on—Josh was Ben's best friend—he'd forestalled her question; "I don't want to talk about any of this anymore. I'll go to the damn cottage."

Faith had left the clothes on his bed and walked quietly out of the room. It was a victory, but a Pyrrhic one.

Tom was spooning up the last drops of his second bowl of soup and did not appear to be unduly upset at his son's behavior.

"I probably should have said something about the 'damn,'" Faith said, "but things would have escalated, and I didn't have the energy. Besides, it was clearly a test to see whether I *would* react. I'm glad he's coming, though, even under duress. Once he's on the island, he'll be his old self."

"A long weekend outdoors away from his computer is just what he needs. We have to haul the mooring and put the kayaks away. If the weather's decent, we can get one more trip in." Tom's face shone. No steeples, Harvest Festivals. Hopefully no phone calls. The sea, a whole lot of pine trees, and his nearest and dearest. "Ben will be fine."

The weekend had come and gone. While it hadn't been quite so idyllic as previous years, it had been a good break. Ben had veered toward meltdown when he'd discovered his cell wouldn't work on the island, but was diverted by Tom's suggestion that he walk along the shore since Swan's Island to the north had a cell tower. This activity, eventually resulting in two bars of service, had kept him happy for hours.

There was a message on the machine from Patsy when the Fairchilds returned late Monday night. "Hi, Faith, give me a call when you get a chance." Nothing in her tone of voice to indicate anything other than "Let's have coffee."

With Tuesday taken up with settling back in—Faith often felt the packing and unpacking part of any trip made the whole thing almost not worth it—she didn't get around to calling Patsy until Wednesday morning.

"I was right," Patsy said.

The previous week's nocturnal escapade had been eclipsed by the Fairchild family ups and downs to the point where Faith was beginning to regard her time at the Ganley as a figment of her imagination. Patsy's words changed all that.

"You're absolutely sure?"

"I was always absolutely sure, but now I have proof. I consulted two different experts and each confirmed that the signature was a forgery. I didn't show them a photo of the piece, just a blowup of the name; no need to reveal which Bearden it is, even though as I said they're very discreet. And I didn't tell them why I wanted to know, although I'm sure they could figure that out."

Faith wasn't listening. Instead she was remembering Patsy's words, "Plan B is you, sweetie."

A heavy silence hung on the line.

"So?" Faith said.

"So we have to talk. What are you doing for lunch?"

Someone was stealing artwork from the Ganley. Patsy and Will's artwork to be precise. Something had to be done about it. Faith felt more cheerful than she had all fall.

"I'm not doing anything for lunch."

Patsy's office was in downtown Boston, so they met halfway at Za on Massachusetts Avenue in Arlington. Patsy was a big fan of their macaroni and cheese pizza with caramelized onions. Until Faith had tasted it herself, she'd viewed it with the same suspicion as the Handmaidens of the Lord casseroles. The ten-inch pizza did have something in common with the spirit of the aforementioned—first bite to last was in name heavenly, but the resemblance stopped there. Za used four cheeses, none of them Velveeta or Cheez Whiz. Besides the mac and cheese pizza, they'd ordered one of the day's specials—gorgonzola, mission figs, and prosciutto—and the beet salad with red onions, toasted hazelnuts, orange sections, chèvre, and pea greens, those delicious tendrils that would soon disappear until next year.

While they waited for the food, Faith suddenly experienced déjà vu. She was sitting at another restaurant—the old Upstairs at the Pudding—again with Patsy and again with a problem.

"This plan B of yours. It doesn't happen to have me going 'undercover' at the Ganley by any chance?" she said.

Patsy smiled broadly. "I knew Mrs. Sibley didn't raise any stupid children. Or maybe I just knew it worked once, so why shouldn't it work again?"

"But that was teaching a cooking course. I don't know anything about art. Yes, yes, I know what I like, but . . ."

"Who said you have to know anything about art?"

The large salad arrived, and they dug in. One of the things Faith liked best about Patsy was her willingness to share food.

"I figured you want me to pose as a docent or something similar."

Patsy finished chewing.

"No posing. You can do what you do best while you're figuring out what's going on. You'll be doing something for the museum, something for me, *and* something for yourself. Win, win, win."

Faith was skeptical. Things that sounded too good to be true usually were. She raised an eyebrow. Her mouth was full.

"You've been talking about opening up a carryout section at Have Faith," Patsy continued. "What about taking over the restaurant at the museum instead? Right now the food is so bad, only the staff eat there and only when they're desperate. Maddy has been searching for an outfit to take over and doesn't want to close down in the meantime since it's advertised that we have a place to eat. The company that currently provides the food service has been put on notice, which could be why the coffee has become even more execrable, now that I think of it."

Faith started to say something, and Patsy put up her hand. The rest of their food was arriving.

"Eat some pizza and hear me out. You'd transform the place. We're open from ten to three, closed two days a week, so the hours should be all right. Soups, salads, wraps, some baked goods. Maybe a special daily dessert—nothing complicated. Once the word gets out, it will become a destination for the town apart from the museum. Other than the Minuteman Café, there's no place to eat. You know the layout of the Ganley's food prep facilities from the times you've catered events. Oh, you also have to provide an easy-to-eat dinner—currently it's leftovers from lunch—for trustee meetings, about eight a year. When you and Niki do open up your new venture, your reputation will be even more established."

Faith had to admit she was intrigued. Investing in the refrigerated cases and other equipment for the carryout was going to be expensive. Running the operation at the Ganley would be a test run, and if successful might remain the only run. There was a compact but well-equipped prep kitchen on the top floor where the small restaurant was located. The dining area had been added in the most recent remodeling project and

THE BODY IN THE GALLERY • 57

overlooked the pond, a terrific site that should have food to match. In addition, a large outdoor sculpture terrace with a few tables and chairs was used during the warmer parts of the year.

"I'd have to discuss it with Niki—and Tom." She was yielding. "And I'd need at least one more person at the Ganley. I can't be there all day, nor can Niki. Pix might fill in, operating the cash register, but she's busy enjoying her empty nest."

The pizzas had disappeared. Patsy looked down at the table. They were in a booth away from the street. Faith thought her friend was looking for crumbs on the platters, and the look of slight dismay on Patsy's face when she did raise it would have confirmed the notion, excepting the words she blurted out.

"Actually, you already have an assistant. I mean, there's someone who has, so to speak, life tenure, even though he's only in his twenties. It's Channing Potter. Harriett Potter's grandson. She's a trustee—has been since Noah—and also some relation of Maddy's, since Harriett's nephew, Spence, is Maddy's husband. Besides that, he and Harriett are some kind of relations of the Ganleys."

"Nepotism, incest, or both?" Faith laughed. Aleford was just like any other place when it came to handing out jobs, although perhaps the family trees were a bit more root-bound. She vaguely remembered Harriett from a discussion at Town Meeting about sodium vapor streetlights for Main Street. Harriett was firmly opposed. Too orange.

"Channing dropped out of Dartmouth several years ago to find himself, and he's still looking. Meanwhile he's firmly ensconced at the café."

"How bad can he be? He can ladle out soup and put a sandwich on a plate, I assume? Ring up a bill?" The restaurant did not have table service. Patrons picked up trays and placed their orders at the counter.

Patsy pursed her lips. "Well, yes, he can do those things."

Faith was getting excited and decided to ignore the dubious tone in Patsy's voice. Niki and she could do much of the preparation at the catering kitchen in the morning. The job would provide a steady income that could be invested in the new venture later on if they decided to go that route. For a brief moment she'd forgotten about the reason behind it all.

"But how is this going to help unmask the thief?"

"I'm convinced it has to be an inside job. You couldn't walk in and then out with the collage without being spotted. Once they know the food is good, the staff will eat at the café again, and no doubt you'll have other opportunities to do what you do so well—snoop."

Faith wasn't sure whether to take this as a compliment or not. Before she could ask for clarification, Patsy said, "I already have the name, Have Faith at the Ganley. We'll do a lot of promotion. Have a grand opening. What do you say?"

Faith said yes.

Not for the first time, Faith reflected on the status the position of servant, or in her case, server, conferred. It was as if she were clothed in Harry Potter's cloak of invisibility. The Ganley trustees were tucking into the roasted butternut squash soup garnished with diced Macoun apples and the trays of assorted sandwiches—wraps that had been cut so they were easy to eat. They were also pretty to look at; the various fillings resembled pinwheels. Standing off to the side, she had only to replenish the sandwiches and remove the soup bowls. Niki had made a medley of dessert bars—blondies, Toll House, apricot walnut, and raspberry shortbread—which would come later with coffee or tea. As the group feasted, they talked. And Faith was listening intently.

Have Faith at the Ganley had been open a week, and it was a rousing success. Patsy's prediction had been correct. If you cook it, they will come. Faith's interview with Madelyn Harper had been pro forma. The director could barely contain her joy, and relief. The specter of spoiled tuna fish salad—and a major suit—would no longer stalk her. Maddy had other things on her list to worry about.

After Sandy Harvey's sudden death, the trustees, with Harriett at the helm, once more turned to their own backyard. Yes, they followed the correct procedure, appointed a search committee, and advertised the position, but there was really no need. Spencer Harper, the son of Harriett's own sister Eleanor Spencer Harper, had married a girl with advanced degrees in museum and curatorial studies who had been working at the ICA in Boston and before that in New York City after graduating from Williams. Granted, she was from Ohio or one of those places, but Spence was homegrown. His mother had died of cancer when he was in college and his father had remarried, moving to Weston, much to Harriett's displeasure. She had been widowed a great deal longer, and you didn't see her rushing off for a replacement. Or worse, moving out of Aleford. Spence was an artist, which was fine since his mother had left him well provided for and since, as Harriett liked to point out, "Art is in our blood." She was eager to get her nephew back to Aleford—the Ganley directorship came with housing, the gatehouse that Sandy had made so comfortable.

Maddy had been at the museum for four years, and they had become increasingly rocky. Aleford was shocked when she filled two vacancies on the board of trustees with non-Alefordians. She defended her decision by explaining that she felt it would help broaden the museum's base of support, i.e., annual giving, to go beyond the town. And it did. Patsy told Faith the amount donated by the board and their contacts doubled. The Aleford residents on the board had tended to take the museum and its financial needs for granted. It was stuck in a rut. Maddy shook things up. She appointed Patsy when another vacancy occurred and got her to volunteer to serve as president. The director also replaced the retiring assistant curator with a young woman, Elizabeth Canning, who mounted a controversial photography show that was more Robert Mapplethorpe than Ansel Adams. But what really upset the town was Maddy's leash law. All dogs had to be leashed when on Ganley grounds.

Forget war and pestilence, gas and tax hikes, what brought Aleford residents into the streets was anything dog related. The issue of leashing or unleashing dogs on Conservation Land had been debated for six hours on the floor of Town Meeting, preceded by weeks of letters in the *Aleford Clarion*, mostly from the Let Them Run Free group, before it was finally resolved that dogs must be within call at all times and disobedient dogs should be reported to the town clerk. Presumably that meant disobedient owners, as well. Residents were incensed that Maddy did not follow the precedent set forth, even when she wrote a column for the *Clarion* explaining the reasons behind the restriction—unleashed dogs were causing damage to the sculptures in the park, specifically one that resembled a hydrant, and dogs were finding ways under the fencing that protected Gododdin Pond, a source of the town's drinking water. The trustees were divided on the matter, but it was within the scope of Maddy's powers to make the rule. She had also removed the trash barrels in the park upon her arrival, pointing out that the sight of overflowing refuse was unaesthetic and that people would be embarrassed to be seen littering, taking out any juice boxes or what-have-you when they left. She was right. Patsy had supported the leash law and received some angry letters, but nothing like Maddy's, one of which described in detail what the writer would do to Maddy with a leash—it was anonymous, of course.

The agenda for tonight's trustee meeting was brief. The main portion was a discussion of the show opening in early November. The opening, intended as a major fund-raiser, was a ticketed black-tie event with several of the artists speaking. Have Faith had been engaged months ago to provide an elegant autumn buffet dinner. Much of the talk was about how to get the word out. Ticket sales had been good but not great, and the publicity director, Ben Conklin, an amiable-looking young man who bore a remarkable resemblance to Robin Williams as Mork, was urging the trustees to call their friends, relatives, neighbors, everyone.

"You are our best ambassadors," he said.

Faith had been briefed sotto voce by Patsy as to names and functions upon each person's entry into the room. They were in the director's large conference room on the top floor, which was lined with art books and also served as the museum's library. The head curator, Marvin Handler, who had been appointed by Sandy, was describing the upcoming show in detail.

"Elizabeth and I wanted to start the season with some pizzazz. At the last meeting we showed you some of the artwork, and we can do that again for those of you who might have missed it. In essence, we're paying tribute to the New England contemporary art scene. We've limited the artists to those living and working here. Of course that's no hardship. It's such a vibrant and creative group. The biggest problem was selection. I think the title is a good one: New England Rocks! As you know from your invitations, its subtitle is Twenty-first Century Contemporary New England Art."

Appearances could be so deceiving, Faith thought. It was what made life so interesting, and occasionally dangerous. The curator was a rotund man in his sixties with a fringe of white hair. He wore a tweed jacket, frayed at the elbows without patches, and was sweating profusely. However, as if to assert his claim to his hip position, he was wearing a tie printed with broad, neon-colored stripes.

The trustees were a mixed bunch. They ran the gamut from Harriett in a proper white silk blouse and navy blue St. John suit with a bijou from Firestone and Parson on the lapel, a family piece—people like Harriett didn't buy diamond brooches for themselves, they inherited them—to a young man in jeans and a T-shirt that proclaimed Thoreau's maxim BEWARE OF ALL ENTERPRISES THAT REQUIRE NEW CLOTHES. Patsy had whispered that he was a hedge fund manager from a wealthy Boston family, one of Maddy's appointees, who enjoyed both art and playing against type. His name was Jack Winston.

Faith cleared the table, and when she was finished, placed platters filled with the dessert bars at each end with carafes of coffee, hot water, and a selection of teas. While everyone was busy getting more to eat and drink, Faith noticed Harriett in heated conversation with the director.

"I told you!" Harriett said, raising her voice.

Maddy flushed, but did not reply.

When everyone was seated again, Harriett turned to Marvin. "I think you *should* show those who were absent some of the highlights from the show."

Was the venom in her voice—it positively dripped—aimed at the absentees, Marvin, or the show? Faith wondered. It wasn't long before she found out.

The lights in the room were darkened, and Elizabeth Canning flashed the first piece of art on the wall. One of Henry Horenstein's Aquatic Life photographs—a jellyfish transformed by his eye into an ethereal creature. This was followed by several other pieces by Sarah Walker, Walter Crump, Jon Petro, Reese Inman, and Stephen DiRado. Faith glanced at the slides, but kept her eye on the watchers, particularly Harriett, who seemed about to explode. Her thin cheeks were puffed out and her eyes were narrowed into mere slits.

The final work consisted of a large Plexiglas rectangular box filled almost to the brim with Caribbean turquoise-blue water. It contained one small, solitary bright orange goldfish.

Mount Harriett erupted.

"I told Maddy last time that this was *not* art and that it was an affront to the Ganley to even consider it for a show, let alone display it! Poor cousin Theodore must be spinning in his grave."

Maddy flicked the lights on in an angry gesture.

"We've been over this and over this, Harriett. Aside from the fact that at the Ganley we do not censor our curators' choices, this is *not* an objectionable piece of art. It's not even a Damien Hirst shark in formaldehyde— we should only be so lucky, although I hear the poor things are disintegrating and having to be replaced—or Andres Serrano's crucifix in urine. Both of those are most definitely works of art, but perhaps too out there for the Ganley. This, entitled *Looking at You Looking at Me,* is an eloquent postmodern statement about the world as a fishbowl—spectators looking in and being looked at in turn by an iconic American symbol, a goldfish. The artist plans to sprinkle Goldfish crackers around the base for consumption, so that by eating some we become part of the work."

There was an uncomfortable silence broken by one of the younger trustees, a slim woman in bright green from top to toe, who tried to lighten the mood by saying she hoped the crackers would be the cheddar variety, her favorite. No one laughed. A hirsute man in his fifties who, Faith had noticed, was wearing Birkenstocks without socks, raised the question of the goldfish's well-being. He was, he declared, a proud member of PETA, and goldfish were among the most abused pets in the country.

"How many have all of you flushed away?" he thundered.

Maddy quickly explained that the artist was a fellow member and had made provisions for the safety of little Swimmy. At the close of each day, the fish would be transferred to a state-of-the-art aquarium kept in one of the upstairs offices, and at the slightest sign of malaise—lackluster scales, off its feed—would be replaced by a plastic replica.

Once more there was silence. Faith saw Maddy nod to her assistant, Kelly Burton, who apparently knew what the director wanted and left the room.

Throughout the discussion, Harriett had been seated with her arms folded across her chest. She stood up, walked to the end of the table, and faced the room.

"I don't care what it's supposed to mean or how much loving care the fish gets. If it remains in the show, I'll resign from the board—and change my will."

The heavy oak door, one of the period touches from the Ganley house the architect had retained, slammed shut. Harriett was gone. A hairline crack in the ceiling appeared. Faith thought of Ben's bedroom door. There was a lot of this going around lately.

Chapter 3

"It isn't worth having an extra hour to sleep in on a Sunday when it's going to be getting dark so early. I hate it when we go off daylight savings time," Faith complained to Tom, who was enjoying Nature's snooze alarm. He opened his eyes and rolled over toward his wife.

"Then let's not sleep," he said.

Despite or because of the extra hour, the Fairchilds were almost late for church and Sunday school. Tom made a mad dash across the cemetery, fastening his robe on the way. It streamed out behind him, fluttering in the breeze, making him look like an extremely large raven. Faith left the kids with their teachers and slid into the pew just as the organ started to play the first hymn, "When on My Day of Life the Night Is Falling," appropriately enough. She had not suspected that Will Werner, the organist and choirmaster, had such a keen sense of humor.

At coffee hour after the service—Tom had acquitted himself well, managing to tie thoughts on the tapestry of life to the eye of the needle, a subtle reference to the capital campaign—Faith pulled her friend Pix into a corner. Pix had been happy to fill some of her free time working at the Ganley, and Faith was eager to talk to her about what was fast becoming a flourishing enterprise.

"I'm thinking of adding a kids' menu—pb&j, tuna fish without anything except mayo, cookies and milk, hot chocolate and marshmallows when it gets colder. What do you think?"

"It's a great idea, especially if you decide to keep the café open on Sundays. Even so it would work. I watched a group of moms with toddlers in strollers having lunch there this week, and they were constantly taking out Baggies with carrot sticks, crackers, and raisins. I'm sure they'd love to have something all done for them. The café has become *the* place to meet. Ursula told me she hasn't been to the museum in years, but had two dates, one for coffee, one for lunch, next week," Pix said.

"Anything would be an improvement on the old café. I ate there incognito before I took all this on, and it was truly horrible. My salad had black slime on the lettuce and two prehistoric tomato slices. The split pea soup was inedible—too salty and tasted like liquid smoke, not real ham hocks. My chicken salad sandwich smelled so high, I didn't dare explore it any further. I skipped dessert—questionable brownies."

"How can a brownie be questionable?" Pix asked.

"Questionable as to the use of a packaged mix or the real thing—no offense intended."

Pix's reliance on packaged mixes was a sore point for Faith. Her often repeated comment "It's just as simple to make some of my recipes from scratch" had fallen and continued to fall on deaf ears.

"It's time to change the subject," Pix said firmly. "What are the kids going to be for Halloween?"

"Amy's finally outgrown the unicorn costume Tom's mother made, much to both their sorrows, but last Saturday Marian drove up from Norwell with her trusty Singer and whipped together a princess number with a generous hem. It should last until Amy moves into the horse phase. So far she's been a pretty predictable girly girl."

"Write that down someplace, so we can laugh or cry in a few years. There's no such thing as predictable when it comes to kids. Kind of like your questionable brownies—an oxymoron if I ever heard one. I've never met a brownie I didn't like, no questions asked. Now, what about Ben?"

"Oh, Ben's not trick-or-treating this year. Too old. Twelve is the new sixteen, by the way. And I don't need to write it down. I'm living with it."

"My kids were all so greedy, they'd still be ringing doorbells if I hadn't put my foot down when they were juniors in high school," Pix said. "Aside from scaring people—Mark had hit the six-foot mark the last time he went out, donned in a King Kong mask and a black cape that I used to wear to Symphony—it got to be embarrassing. Rather than have all Aleford know what candy freaks they are, I bought extra each year."

What was with Symphony and capes? Faith asked herself. First Patsy and now Pix. The Fairchilds did not have season tickets, but went often. Next time she'd have to be more observant. In the past what she had noticed most about the fashions was the smell of mothballs.

"Ben's got a sweet tooth, too. I mentioned that he might miss the treat part, but all I got was one of the world-weary looks he's recently perfected. Tom will take Amy around; Ben will probably hole up in his room with his computer and some kind of cyber Snickers."

Pix patted her friend on the shoulder. "It will all be over eventually and you won't miss these days at all. Not like when they were babies."

Babies had meant a lot of spit up and not much sleep, Faith recalled. The golden age was from walking and talking through elementary school.

"I've got to go," she said. "I have to feed everyone, then get back here for a Harvest Festival meeting. Too bad it just happens to fall on the weekend that you're going with Sam to that lawyers' meeting in Vegas."

Pix had the grace to blush. "I'll probably hate the whole thing. I'm not a gambler."

"Hmmm." Faith continued to tease her friend. "And you'll really dislike all those fantastic restaurants." She gave her a quick hug. "I'm glad you could get out of the fair. You've more than put in your time. Try some slots. Go nuts."

"How about I donate any winnings to the capital campaign?"

"How about you buy yourself the equivalent of a new cape."

Halloween came and went with its own melodrama. Ben had foresworn trick-or-treating, but not going out. He'd announced at their early dinner that he was spending the evening at a friend's house watching horror movies. The boy's name wasn't familiar to Tom and Faith. They'd wanted to know who was going to be home and if Josh was going, too. Ben had exploded and knocked over his milk, which spilled on Amy's dress on its way to the tile floor where the glass shattered. Before Faith could say not to worry, it was an accident, and let's talk about this, he'd left the room. His bedroom door slammed as Amy burst into tears. Tom had waited, helping Faith clean up the shards and calming Amy down before confronting his son. He'd also been counting to ten, Faith had sensed. Order—and the princess costume—was restored, but Tom had not made much headway with his son, coming downstairs in much too short a time.

The first Saturday in November had marked the date of First Parish's Harvest Festival for as long as anyone could remember. Faith always imagined it rooted in some pre-Thanksgiving get-together with Squanto and his tribe. A kind of dress rehearsal with the Native Americans playing Rachael Ray: "This is maize. You'll like it. Steamed for exactly eight minutes—you don't want it to get mushy. Mushy is for when it's ground into cornmeal. Very yum-o. And this feathered creature is a turkey. After it's plucked, which only takes a few minutes, we like to slip slivers of garlic under the skin. . . ."

The food at the Harvest Festival took the form of baked goods and preserves. First Parish—all Aleford—

was big on baked goods and preserves. Faith was presiding over a table that groaned under the weight of things like cranberry nut breads, sour cream coffee cakes, lemon squares, real brownies, blueberry muffins, plus sparkling jars of bread-and-butter pickles, dilly beans, jams, jellies, chutneys, apple butter, and lemon curd. Pretty packages of fudge—divinity, peanut butter, dark chocolate, maple walnut, penuche—spiced nuts, peanut brittle, and peppermint bark stood stacked and waiting for customers. This was the kind of food at which the ladies of the parish, those Handmaidens of the Lord, dubbed Tom's Groupies by Niki, excelled. Tried-and-true New England basics that had never heard of a casserole dish.

Across the parish hall Faith could see Amy, who was helping at the plant table, and Ben, who was quite human today, giving a hand to the volunteers frantically unpacking the last of the boxes for the book table, always popular. Tom was roaming about, eyeing the white elephant table the way he looked at the swap table at the dump. Who knew what Antiques Roadshow find might be lurking beneath the slightly yellowed pile of embroidered hand towels or behind the set of five-cut glass sherry glasses, with only a few nicks?

The doors opened and people swarmed in like biblical locusts, stripping the tables of their goods faster than

the real insects cleared a field of wheat. It was the signal
for First Parish's answer to the New Christy Minstrels
to strike up a tune. Despite being poorly miked from
the small parish hall stage, site of the Sunday school
Christmas pageant, they belted out a lively version of
"This Land Is Your Land" that had Faith humming
along. In between pushing the breads—"they freeze
so well"—she watched the group. She was particularly
interested in Joseph Sargeant, who was on the Ganley
Board of Trustees. Joseph was strumming his banjo
and dressed in a blue striped shirt with red suspend-
ers holding his chinos up. And they were not just for
show, Faith surmised. Joseph was as thin as a whippet.
A runner. She often saw him on Aleford's back roads,
never failing to think of the title of the Sillitoe novel
and subsequent movie—*The Loneliness of the Long
Distance Runner*—when she did. Joseph, never Joe,
was in his late fifties. He'd come from money and made
a whole lot more, retiring in his forties to take care
of his wife, who died soon after and much too young.
Faith never heard what the cause was. Probably some
kind of cancer, she thought. Although he was smiling now, she imagined she could see a trace of sadness
around his eyes. They were bright blue. His hair was
Andy Warhol white. She'd never seen it any other color.
The effect was startling—and attractive. Although he

needed a little more meat on his bones; some of Patsy's mother's sticky buns would do the trick. Faith finished her inventory of his appearance and began thinking about the man himself. Alone. Lonely. He had never remarried. A poet, some of his work good enough to be published in various literary magazines, he was a quiet man. The natural world was his subject. Trees, not people, or perhaps trees as people. He'd made one comment the night of the trustees' meeting she'd worked at. It had to do with the treasurer's report. Something about the interest thrown off by the endowment. She hadn't paid much attention, nor it seemed had anyone else. There had been no response except from Patsy as president who said it would be noted in the minutes. Now the group had moved on to "Tom Dooley" and when the singers wailed out "poor man you're going to die," the room grew quiet for a moment before the chatter resumed. It was startling to hear such a line amid the lively guitar and banjo strumming

Joseph Sargeant. He'd have no need to steal artwork. He could buy almost anything he wanted. Still, he could be doing it for the thrill. A kind of Thomas Crown stunt. She decided to put him on the list.

"Faith, I've been standing here for hours. Are you going to sell me these watermelon pickles or not? Mine are all gone."

It was Millicent Revere McKinley, and of course she hadn't been standing in front of Faith for hours, but that was the story she was telling at the moment and would forever after.

"Sorry, Millicent, I was listening to the music," Faith apologized.

"Never liked that folk stuff myself. Who was the girl with the long hair? Joan Bias, something like that. Voice like chalk on a blackboard. Give me Dinah Shore any day. Always a smile on her face. That Joan always looked as if she'd had to drown some kittens."

"Baez. Her name is Joan Baez and she has short hair now." Faith was tempted to go on about the way Baez could reach a note, so pure it seemed unearthly, hanging suspended for an instant before she reached for another and another, but you could never win with Millicent, so Faith simply took her money and put the jar of pickles in a small bag. And as for smiling, Millicent wasn't one to turn the corners of her mouth up much. In fact, when you saw her smile, it usually meant trouble.

"Don't forget our Christmas fair is the first Saturday in December. I think you'll find some delicious goodies there." She gave First Parish's offerings a withering glance, the cakes, cookies, breads, et cetera, so many Little Debbie snack cakes or Hostess Twinkies. Millicent was not a member of Tom's congregation, for which Faith was profoundly grateful. The Almighty did come through. Millicent was a lifelong Congregationalist, as were her ancestors before her, world without end, amen, and she only darkened First Parish's doorway for events like today's or funerals.

"Be sure and tell Pix, too. I understand that she and Sam are in Las Vegas." From the inflection in her voice, there could be no doubt that Sin City *was* Sodom and Gomorrah.

It occurred to Faith that Millicent, who had had her finger on Aleford's pulse ever since she herself had one, might be a source of information about the Ganley, particularly its board of trustees and staff. The question was how to go about asking for the information without seeming to be asking. It wasn't that Millicent didn't pride herself on her broad knowledge of everything happening in town; it was that she enjoyed keeping said knowledge to herself, dropping tantalizing hints, but never coming across with the real goods. Faith decided to let it lie for the moment and drop in on Ms., sorry, Miss—Millicent thought feminists were no better than fallen women—McKinley after church.

"I meant to put up watermelon pickles myself this summer, but didn't get to it. I have a superabundance of green tomato chutney, though. I'd be happy to drop some off. Maybe tomorrow afternoon?"

"Very thoughtful, Faith dear. I'd like that. It makes a nice change from mint jelly for lamb chops. And then we can have that chat you want."

It was very difficult to put anything over on Millicent Revere McKinley.

The festival was a huge success. Faith's table was almost bare—only a few jars of calves' foot jelly that everyone avoided each year because of the free-spirited maker's reputation for unusual additions. This batch seemed to have olives floating in the aspic. Tom was very happy with a box of old flatirons that he said would make perfect doorstops as soon as he cleaned the rust off them. Ben was also cheerful, lugging an ancient Mac LC that had gone unsold at the white elephant table and that he had been able to get for "Only three dollars, Mom! Boy, are they stupid. This is a rare collectible. I bet I could sell it on eBay for a whole lot more."

Amy hadn't bought anything, but had scored a treasure herself—a slightly limp cyclamen that needed water and TLC. Her reward for helping out.

After "Good Night, Irene," the singers and musicians had departed. Joseph had asked if they needed help cleaning up and was lugging a box down to one of the storage closets in the crypt. The white elephants remaining would make their appearance as "attic treasures" at the Maypole Festival. Faith tried not to think about it. Spring was many months off. Instead she reflected on the way the same stuff kept circulating. Much of what was purchased from today's table would come back as donations for the next event once the owners realized they had more than enough vases, trays, candlesticks, and of course, doorstops. Not that she was optimistic about getting Tom to part with *his* finds. The Fairchilds as a clan were notorious pack rats. She'd been married to Tom for several years before she realized the reason his parents' cars were out in all weather was because there wasn't an inch of space in the garage. She'd been in their basement once, and it was enough to convince her never to attempt the attic. Her mother and father-in-law made the Collyer brothers seem anal-retentive.

Joseph Sargeant appeared to say good-bye. As she thanked him, Faith decided to ask him to dinner soon. Aside from the Ganley connection and her investigation, he was an eminently eligible male. An inveterate matchmaker, Faith mulled over her list of eminently eligible females. It was longer.

She was tired, but she'd enjoyed herself. Complaining about the festival beforehand had become a habit. Like the town of Aleford itself after so many years, the event was growing on her, much like the mosses on the Old Manse. The festival had been appealing to various senses all day—the music, the happy squeals of kids and steady drone of neighborly talk; her food table, the chicken and dumplings served for lunch, and the harder-to-define odor of plants and the parish hall's own slightly oaken smell. The hall looked festive decked out in bright autumn hues, and if there wasn't a smile on someone's face before entering, there was as soon as the threshold was crossed.

"One down, one to go," Tom said, bringing Faith her coat. For a moment she was startled. The mystery of the missing Bearden had been lurking in the corners of her mind even as she endeavored to get rid of every last banana nut bread.

"Oh, the steeple!"

"Yes, what did you think?"

"Nothing," said Faith. "Absolutely nothing"—and crossed her fingers in her pocket.

Millicent Revere McKinley lived in a small, eighteenth-century white clapboard house that sat facing Aleford's green, as did the First Parish parsonage. Millicent had a better view, though, if your idea of a better view was a clear shot down Main Street. Generations of McKinleys had used the front garden behind its white picket fence as an excuse to get an even closer look. Birders virtually in utero, they'd usually had binoculars around their necks. Millicent was no exception. In the winter and during inclement weather, there was the bow window in the front parlor to occupy. Even the males of the family had knitted—idle hands were the eighth deadly sin—as they sat in one of the wing chairs gazing out at Aleford and its citizenry.

Faith had barely lifted the heavy brass knocker when Millicent opened the door. Besides Main Street, the McKinley perch had a clear view of the green and all the houses bordering it.

"Come in, dear. No little ones?"

Faith tried not to grind her teeth. Millicent, having watched her leave the parsonage, knew very well that she was alone. Her remark was meant to imply that Faith had once again abandoned her children, irresponsible mother that she was.

"They're busy with schoolwork. Tom's home."

It paid to keep responses to this kind of remark short, although Millicent usually came back with a knockout punch. Today was no exception.

"Poor Tom. He must be tired after the service. Plus he's so busy all week. I don't know how our men of the cloth do it. And then to have to watch the children when no doubt he'd like a little time to himself or a nap. He looked terribly tired at the Harvest Festival . . ."

Bad mother *and* bad wife.

"Here's the chutney." Faith had lined a little basket with a checkered cloth napkin and put two jars of chutney inside. Carrying it to Millicent's, she thought of all the capes she'd been hearing about lately and thought she should be wearing a red hooded one. She was certainly going to see a wolf in grandmother's clothing—not that Millicent had any grandchildren, or children, preferring instead the life of a vestal. She carried her torch high, all the better to illuminate the past—those glorious founding fathers and mothers were her household gods. This was expressed in the décor of her house. Dark portraits of gloomy ancestors with ill-fitting teeth stared down from the walls. Ornately framed certificates for service to the Commonwealth and the nation were tucked in between, and to fill things out, Millicent went in for funerary art. Mourning wreaths woven of mostly raven tresses looked slightly moldy under the flyspecked glass. It was all so familiar Faith barely noticed any of it, intent instead on wending her way through Millicent's forest of tables—tilt tops, piecrusts, candlestands—without knocking one over. With customary relief, she made it to the horsehair sofa that was reserved for Millicent's company and wished she had thought to change from the skirt and pantyhose she'd worn to church into pants. The coarse surface was excruciatingly uncomfortable and snagged at the hose behind her knees.

Over the years, Faith had tried many approaches when she wanted to get information from Millicent, and none had worked, so now she simply asked her questions and hoped that crumbs of information might fall in her path.

"You may have heard that Have Faith has taken over the operation of the Ganley restaurant."

Millicent was knitting mittens—no doubt for her church's fair. They were an impossibly intricate Scandinavian design. She never looked down.

"Yes, and I understand the food has gotten much better."

Encouraged by the equivalent of a four-star review from Frank Bruni in the *New York Times,* Faith pushed on.

"I don't really know much about the museum. We've been there, of course. They have wonderful programs for families. I keep meaning to take a course, too, but never seem to have the time. I thought you might be able to fill me in a bit. About the museum's history, the trustees, staff . . ." Faith's voice trailed off. Damn, why did Millicent always have this effect on her!

"It was very generous of Theodore to give his estate to the town, although it was also a good thing for him in the end. I don't think the selectmen thought Theo would live *quite* as long as he did." Millicent chuckled. She loved it when someone pulled the wool over someone else's eyes, no matter what the circumstances, Faith had observed.

"I know all of the trustees, of course. I was asked to be on the board originally and several times since, but I have my work. It doesn't pay to spread oneself too thin, you know." Like having what amounted to two businesses and a family, Faith read between the lines.

"I'm hoping to finish my research soon and start writing," Millicent continued. For years, she had been delving into what she called the "French Connection"—never, apparently, having seen or heard of the movie. Her illustrious ancestors, the Reveres, were originally from France and Millicent had been giving little talks at various historical societies on Apollos Rivoire and his descendent, Paul Revere, using what she called her "catchy" title. If some of the audience had been expecting a different sort of discussion, she had never picked up on it, and Faith wasn't about to enlighten her.

Hoping to get her back on track, Faith said, "I supplied dinner for one of the Ganley's board meetings recently."

"How nice for you. Well, it's a good board from what I can tell. A working board, not like some where two or three people do everything. But then they would be, they're all so interested in art, although I imagine both Ganleys would look askance at some of the things that have been hung on the walls of their old house."

"It's my impression that the Ganleys wanted the museum to be a contemporary art museum, not just one that preserved their collection intact."

"Gracious! Collection! More like a flea market, although they had some nice landscapes. I went to dinner there several times. Not a single ancestral portrait—and they were both well connected." Millicent shook her head. "A question of values. But you were asking about the trustees—for some reason." Her gimlet eye speared Faith just above the bridge of her nose. She almost winced.

"Joseph Sargeant is in your church, so you know him. And Patsy Avery is a friend of yours. I don't know the ones who live out of town." Faith could almost hear, "poor souls." "There's Harriett Potter, of course, the heart and soul of the place. She was a Spencer. Her younger sister, Eleanor, married a Harper. Your current director is married to her son, Spence. Poor Eleanor died some time ago and her husband remarried. The two sisters were always very close. Eleanor was the pretty one, and terribly sweet. You know how it is when there are two sisters. One is always better liked than the other."

Faith fumed silently. Millicent knew she had a sister and it was obvious which one was the pretty, likable one.

"Not that Harriett didn't have her admirers. Very athletic and a keen horsewoman. I believe there was talk of the Olympic team. Still rides plus I hear she plays golf and tennis almost every day. Channing Potter was a sportsman, and that's what attracted him to Harriett. That and the fact that her sister was already taken—engaged and biding her time until she was eighteen. Her parents were insistent that she wait, and in any case, she couldn't get married before Harriett. People didn't do things like that then." Millicent pursed her mouth at what Faith could only imagine were the foibles of youth—and their irresponsible parents—nowadays. Girls getting married out of birth order! Scandalous. Better to be an old maid—no, spinster was a nicer term—than flaunt tradition.

"Poor Channing was killed in the war. He'd barely gotten a foot on foreign soil. Harriett had a baby afterward—quite a trick to get enough black material to make mourning maternity clothes. We needed it for the blackouts, but she managed. Harriett always manages. Anyway, she had a baby and it was Channing's all right."

Faith hadn't considered otherwise and opened up her mouth to say so, but Millicent, blessedly enough, was on a roll.

"That long Potter face, and tall. Not a bad-looking family, although of course the face is horsey. Still, being such outdoorsmen, they were never bothered by that. Channing's son, Channing Jr., inherited both. The Spencers were tall, too, so Channing got a double dose. Harriett's nephew Spence got the height, but no Potter blood, for which he should be grateful."

Faith was beginning to get muddled, what with all these gene pools and generations, but here was a fact to which she could cling. Spencer Harper, "Spence," *was* tall—and dark, and handsome. Faith thought back to the scene at the trustees' meeting, the last time she'd seen him. His aunt had just given his wife an ultimatum, and it looked as if things were going rapidly downhill regarding the upcoming New England Rocks! exhibition. Maddy had conveyed some sort of silent signal to her assistant and it wasn't long before Spence appeared, Maddy's secret weapon. He'd strode into the room with Harriett—who had just stormed out—beaming on his arm. He announced he'd come to walk his wife home and run into his aunt, who had agreed to join them for the stroll since she lived nearby.

"Sorry for barging in," he'd said, pulling out a chair for Harriett and sitting next to her. "Thought you'd be finished." He'd flashed a grin at everyone and immediately started a whispered conversation with Harriett, their heads close together. Harriett had actually giggled—that was the only word for it—at one point and given Spence a light, "oh, go on, you" flirtatious slap on the hand. It was quite a show. The crusty grande dame was obviously besotted by her nephew—and who could blame her? a small voice inside Faith's head had asked. The end result was Harriett's announcement that if Maddy didn't have the good sense God gave her to know what was and wasn't art, she, Harriett, couldn't do anything about it and the fish tank could stay. "But I'm not looking at it." Spence had said he'd drag her over to it, and the prospect clearly thrilled her. The meeting had then adjourned.

"Yes," Millicent was saying. "Spencer got the best of the Spencers and the Harpers in looks as well as other departments, but as to the next generation, Channing III—oh, gracious, you'll have to excuse me, I didn't realize the time! Do come 'round again. I so enjoy these little visits of ours." The audience was over just before the good part. *Conversatus interruptus.*

Faith made her way out, bumping into a whatnot, evoking the comment, "Do be careful. That's an extremely valuable piece! Great-great-grandmother got it to hold her wedding china. Every piece is still intact, not a single chip. It's only used for *very* special occasions."

That would do it, Faith thought, although her own wedding china—Royal Copenhagen's Gemina—had stood up almost as well despite frequent use.

She trudged home swinging her empty basket. What had Millicent been about to say regarding Harriett's grandson, Channing? Even without Millicent's remarks, the young man was providing much food for thought.

Faith prided herself on her open embrace of fashion, but Channing pushed the limits as far as work attire was concerned, contemporary art museum job not-withstanding. He was very tall—and now she could trace the trait back through the generations thanks to Millicent. Channing also habitually wore cowboy boots, which made him taller still. He dressed completely in black from the T-shirts to tight jeans that reminded Faith of the lengths she and her friends went to in ado-lescence to achieve this effect—sitting in a tub of boil-ing hot water to shrink the denim, lying on the floor to zip the pants up. Channing had long light brown hair pulled back in a ponytail. It wasn't the monochromatic outfit that set him apart, though. It was his penchant for metal—the shinier and spikier the better. His boots sported lethal spurs—which she requested he remove during working hours—and he wore several spiked leather bands that evoked the Ganley's medieval mace collection, cleared out when Sandy Harvey had taken over. Both ears were pierced wherever a hole could be made—studs, rings of various sizes adorned the lobes. If there was other body piercing, it wasn't public. The tough-guy look was at odds with a slightly round, soft, very young-looking face. If Faith hadn't known how old he was, she would have thought maybe he'd be shaving soon. His face didn't match the rest of his body, which besides being lean looked as if he spent quite a bit of time working out. He was not happy about wearing one of the new aprons Faith had had made for the staff and for sale—a silhouette of the museum and its name in white against bright green. At their first meeting, he'd listened to her, asked a question about his hours, balked at the apron, and that was it. Since then, she'd tried to draw him out on numerous occasions, but failed. He did his work, not well, but not poorly enough to warrant dismissal—Faith certainly didn't want to go there, not with grandmamma in the background—and most of the time she forgot he was there. She remembered he was going over to the catering kitchen on Tuesday so Niki could show him how to serve the new desserts they were adding to the menu: a mixed-berry crisp, chocolate brioche bread pudding, and a blood orange flan, plus walk him through making the specialty coffees yet again. Perhaps she'd have better luck conversationally than Faith had.

"He's kind of pathetic, but he doesn't know it," Niki said. "I mean he's still living in his grandmother's house, although from the sound of the setup even I might have been tempted at his age. The only separate entrance in my ancestral home is a storm-cellar door. Channing's leads upstairs to a third-floor apartment, complete with home gym and what sounds like a spa bath. The only whirlpool when I was growing up was my mother, who could pull you down in a maelstrom before you knew what was happening. Oh, and the blue one when you flushed in our only john, if you were lucky enough to have your number come up and get in."

When Faith finished laughing at all the mental images Niki's words conjured up, she returned to Channing. "I heard from Patsy that he started at Dartmouth, but dropped out to 'find himself.' " She was not surprised Niki had been able to draw Channing out. Aside from the fact that they were closer in age—Channing had a way of looking at her that made her feel more than over the hill—Niki was very, very good at getting information from people.

"He's still looking. At the moment he's taking courses at the MFA's Museum School. He's been doing some kind of art all his life and is sure that it's his passion—his word, not mine. His grandmother thinks he's very talented. See what I mean? Pathetic. What kind of guy tells you his grandmother thinks he's brilliant? All grandmothers think their grandchildren are geniuses, otherwise they get drummed out of the grandmother club. And not just pathetic. Passive. He's been at the Ganley doing various things—taking admission fees, working in the store, and now this—for a long time. He doesn't seem to like where he is, but hasn't tried to find anything else. He can't make much."

"I don't think money is a problem for young Channing—by the way, doesn't he have a nickname? He can't be called Channing by his friends. But back to the money—grandma's loaded."

"That would explain the BMW convertible. What would the nickname for Channing be? Chan? Channy? Maybe they call him Bud or something totally removed."

"Does he seem to have a lot of friends?" Faith asked. Trying to fill in the tantalizing blank left by Millicent wasn't easy.

"Hard to say. He did make a pretty bitter comment about being dumped recently. Something from the movies like 'I guess *I love you* doesn't always mean forever.' I made sympathetic noises. Asked if she was an artist, too. He started to open up—they did meet at the Museum School, but not in a class. She must work in one of the offices or something. Then he clammed up. Oh, one last thing—he said maybe we could hang out sometime. I said sure, that he'd like my husband and that was that, except he's bringing his portfolio to show me. My overall impression is that he gets up in time for work, goes home, maybe does some crunches, and heads into Boston for his classes, then 'hangs out' until it's time to head back to bustling Aleford and Granny. But I'll see what else I can find out since Mr. Potter seems to be such a burning issue with you, and I'd ask why, but I get the feeling you don't want to share this one."

"Oh, I'm just curious about him because in a way he's working for us at the museum."

"Sure, sure," Niki said, laughing. "And by the way, we just happened to get the Ganley gig out of the clear blue sky, right?"

"Let's do the menus for the week, then go over the food for the opening Friday night," Faith said firmly. It was time to change the subject.

Life was truly unfair, Faith thought as she looked out at the line in front of the buffet for New England Rocks! Put a homely man—no, make that ugly even—in a tux and suddenly he was Cary Grant, James Bond, Fred Astaire. And there was no decision to make. No "does the red make my hips look too wide?" No "everything in my closet is dated." Tuxedos, like diamonds, were forever. Shawl lapels, thin lapels, satin lapels, even no lapels—you could wear the outfit on into the sunset and never be out of style; a tux never was in or out of fashion. Grandpapa's was "vintage"; grandson's "hot."

Tonight she hadn't had to worry about dress herself—white chef's jacket and checked pants; well, she did have them made to order so they fit well. She was hovering behind the table, replenishing the food. There was nothing worse than waiting in line and finally arriving at the buffet to find the cupboard bare. Tonight there was beef tenderloin—the meat from Savenor's, that incomparable market in Boston and Cambridge beloved by Julia Child—with a choice of horseradish sauce or au jus; two kinds of ravioli: butternut squash with brown butter and sage and wild mushroom with a very light béchamel; roasted root vegetables—parsnips, golden beets, tiny carrots, and sweet potatoes—with halved brussels sprouts and purple cauliflower that had been blanched, all tossed in olive oil and minced garlic before being baked at high heat. The breadbasket at each table was filled with yeast rolls, olive rolls, slices of buckwheat walnut bread, focaccia, rosemary bread sticks, and zingy cornbread with a touch of jalapeño in the batter. Early in her career as a caterer, Faith had learned that platters of crudités, no matter how beautifully presented, went virtually untouched after the first guilt-induced foray, but breadbaskets were always emptied. Tonight, since Maddy would be speaking and introducing several of the exhibiting artists before the stampede to the buffet, Faith had made sure to have a superabundance of tempting carbs for people to munch while they listened. They were pouring two Italian whites—never reds in an art museum. Her friend Jeannie Rogers, the sommelier and co-owner of Il Capriccio in Waltham, had introduced her to a real find, a sleeper—a 2006 Coroncino Verdicchio Castelli di Jesi "Il Bacco," a dry white. Faith loved the taste and loved saying its name almost as much. They were also pouring a great Adami '05 Prosecco.

In addition to Niki, she'd called on Scott and Trisha Phelan, mainstays for years as waitstaff at Have Faith; and two sisters, Helen and Mabel Jenks, women of a certain age who'd worked at the much lamented, now defunct Willow Tree Kitchen, where their white uniforms and starched peacock-hued handkerchiefs had been as much a part of the place as the always reliable chili. The sisters were staffing the buffet. Scott and Trisha were seeing to the wine. Everyone had passed hors d'oeuvres earlier out in the center hallway. Faith was especially pleased that the new one she was trying, suggested by the pizza at Za—spears of pale green and lavender endive with chèvre and figs (see recipe, p. 384) had gone over well. She was tired of serving mini crab cakes and things on sticks, although she'd had those, too. People expected them. Channing was out of sight in the kitchen.

The response had been good, and there were very few empty places at the round tables set up in what had been the tapestry hall. It had been transformed during the initial remodeling. The vaulted ceiling and clerestory windows had remained untouched, but the dark walnut walls were removed—the wood was used as wainscoting elsewhere, replaced by plaster walls, painted a creamy white. At one end of the room the floor was raised to provide a platform for speakers, while not sacrificing exhibition space, which a stage would have meant. The wall behind it was covered in canvases, as were the walls to the sides. The works were from the permanent collection. New England Rocks! was in the main gallery.

Faith had made a lightning tour earlier; she had to see *Looking at You Looking at Me*, the fish tank. It was set apart from the rest of the show in an alcove, which may have been discretion on Maddy's part, or simply because it looked best there. Faith thought it was visually stunning and not at all gimmicky as she had thought it would be. The lighted Lucite platform upon which it rested illuminated the turquoise water. The tiny ripples made by the goldfish—little "Swimmy" Faith found herself calling it—were enough to send thin shadows streaking across the adjacent walls, extending the work outside the boundaries of the glass tank. Bright orange Pepperidge Farm Goldfish were artfully scattered around the perimeter of the work, interspersed with cards the artist had lettered in a variety of fonts saying "Eat me."

She resolved to see the rest of the show with Tom and had gotten to work on the reception.

As far as Faith could tell, all the trustees were in attendance, as well as much of the staff and also some of the instructors from the school. Patsy and her husband, Will, had made a point of telling Faith how good the food was, and Patsy had winked at her. Faith wished she had a solution to her friend's mystery, but so far, she hadn't turned up a thing relating to the forgery. Both Marvin Handler, the head curator, and Elizabeth

Canning, assistant curator, had started eating lunch at the café every day, telling her how much easier and happier their lives were now that they didn't have to drive to the Minuteman Café for takeout (Marvin) or eat a cup of yogurt at her desk (Elizabeth). They were, of course, both very much in attendance tonight. Faith wondered at their relationship. Elizabeth was Maddy's pick and Marvin was a carryover from the old days. According to Patsy, Maddy had been given carte beige, not carte blanche, when she was hired. The staff that wished to remain was to be allowed to do so. Marvin had stayed. The two curators were all smiles tonight, but Faith wondered if they always saw eye to eye. Elizabeth's photography show had raised a lot of eyebrows in town and Marvin would have been forced to defend it. How happy had that made him? It had been a very well attended show, Patsy had told Faith gleefully. All Aleford had to see what it was they objected to, of course.

Jack Winston, the young trustee, had traded his jeans and T-shirt for a tux—Armani—and was sitting at the same table as the woman in green, whom Faith had since learned was Lynne Hollister. She was in purple tonight with what appeared to be the stems of broken wineglasses dangling from a heavy silver chain around her neck. Thank goodness it was an air-kissing crowd, Faith thought. The necklace looked lethal. The Birkenstock trustee, Harold Prizer, was at another table. Faith couldn't see his feet, but he clearly hadn't been able to button his tux in many years, and from the way he'd attacked the bread basket, wouldn't be any time soon. Joseph Sargeant, looking most urbane in his penguin outfit, had been up and down from his seat all evening, peering out into the lobby and occasionally leaving the room. He seemed to be looking for someone and there was an empty place next to him. Stood up? Faith hadn't heard that he was seeing anyone, but she hoped he was.

Maddy's assistant, Kelly, wasn't sitting down, either, but darting about, the capable factotum she seemed to be. Maddy and Spence were sitting with Harriett, resplendent in sapphire-blue taffeta.

How was she going to discover who was responsible for the theft of the Bearden? Faith wondered. It had to be someone close to the Ganley—an inside job—but everyone close seemed such an unlikely candidate. She'd give it a bit more time, then advise Patsy to tell the director and let Maddy take over. Maddy had had a glass of wine, which had caused her face to flush in a rather unattractive manner. The woman wasn't bad looking, although sadly lacking acumen in the what-to-wear department—tonight's outfit appeared to consist of burlap gunny sacks, accessorized with a necklace and bracelet made from chunks of . . . could it be coal? In contrast, her husband was by far the best-looking person in the room. The low light seemed to bring out his finely modeled features, the dark brown velvet of his eyes, intensified by the dark black tux. The Reverend Thomas Fairchild still turned heads, and Faith never tired of looking into *his* velvet eyes, but she wondered what it would be like to be married to someone who was so off the charts. Every woman at his table was trying to talk to Spence or looking his way, and it had been like this whenever Faith had passed by.

Dessert was a light lemon mousse with plates of pastries and fruit dipped in chocolate. Scott and Trisha were pouring coffee. It would all be over soon, a successful event. Faith had done so many similar ones, here at the museum as well, that an inner voice told her not to worry. Yet, that same voice would remind her of past catastrophes—a portable stove that would not get up to temperature, a flu that decimated her waitstaff the very day of an event, the nondelivery of crucial supplies necessitating entire menu changes hours before. And then there was always the guest factor—someone imbibing too much (having arrived well lubricated), a scene between two exes that suggested Albee's *Who's Afraid of Virginia Woolf*, the odd fall resulting in a sprained ankle, once a broken wrist and the threat of a lawsuit, and always a gate-crasher or two or ten. Not much chance of that tonight, she thought. Besides being a ticketed event, the Ganley turnouts tended to be the same people, so a stranger would be spotted immediately and either encouraged to join the museum or firmly turned away.

Eventually everyone left to look at the show in the main gallery, which was impossible since everyone was going at once. But they could then say they had seen it. Word of Harriett's opinion regarding the fish tank—no one called the piece by name—had gotten out and Faith had picked up snatches of conversation about it. The artist, from western Massachusetts, was apparently thrilled to be in the show, his first major one. A number of the attendees were friends of his, but Faith hadn't been able to figure out which person was the artist himself. Keeping a low profile except with his near and dear, Faith thought, which was wise—unless he wanted his Goldfish crackers thrown in his face by Harriett. Earlier Faith had spied Spence leading his not unwilling aunt to see the piece, and now he was teasing her by pulling crackers from his pocket, tossing them into the air, and catching them in his mouth, much to her delight. But Spence was one thing, the artist quite another, and fortunately their paths did not cross.

Cleaning up was always faster than setting up. Niki departed in the van with the leftover food, tables, linens, dirty cookware, china, glasses, and cutlery—everything would be washed in their own industrial washers. Helen and Mabel left next, then Channing.

"Do you mind if Trisha goes now?" Scott asked Faith. "We don't like to keep the sitter out too late. So far she seems to like us. I mean we leave enough food for a month, pay her more than I make at the garage in a day, and get the kids all ready for bed before she comes. But there's always that chance that someone will come along with plasma TV and surround sound or God knows what else. 401(k) plan maybe."

"Of course she can leave. You, too. There isn't much more to be done."

Scott shook his head. "If anyone should go, it should be you. I want to do the vacuuming in here and in the hall and main gallery. Despite the sign asking people not to bring food or drink into the main gallery, I saw plenty of people walk right by with loaded plates and glasses in their hands."

She was grateful he was taking on the job. She *was* tired. "Thanks, I'll stay and keep you company, though."

"Yeah. We'll have a great conversation with the vacuum running. Go home. Go to bed. It won't take me long." This wasn't the first time Faith had left Scott on his own. She gave in.

"Okay," she said. The end of a big event like this always left her feeling like someone had let all the air out of her balloon.

Thomas, who'd been the security detail for the night as usual, had gone off duty, telling Faith to leave by the rear door. "Nobody's coming in, so the alarm's set," he'd told her. She reminded Scott and cautioned him to pull the door tight—it didn't close properly unless you did. Then she went out to her car, got in, and started for home.

It was a beautiful fall night, unusually warm for the time of year. Before it got too dark, people had been out on the museum's terrace. The fresh air was reviving her, and she once more turned her thoughts to Patsy's Bearden. The thief had to be an artist or know an artist. Which included everyone who was there tonight, all one hundred and fifty of them.

"I'm just going to stop by the museum and make sure we didn't leave any mess, then I'll meet you at the game," Faith told Tom at breakfast. Ben had tried out for the middle school soccer team, but didn't make it. The fact that sixth graders almost never did was of little consolation. He was still playing in the town's recreation league, however, as was Amy. Both had games today; Ben's started first.

It wasn't that Faith didn't trust Scott to do a thorough cleaning. She just wanted to set her mind at ease. She was the boss, and suppose he'd left one of the vacuum cleaner attachments in the gallery—he'd been tired, too. It wouldn't matter too terribly much, since visitors would assume it was a piece of sculpture, but Faith thought it was worth a few minutes' detour to check.

"No problem," Tom said. "Looks like it's going to be a beautiful day. I can't believe this weather. It's like spring. I hate to think it might be because of global warming."

Faith kissed her husband. "I hate to think so, too, but don't worry. We'll have a major blizzard before the year is out, and just think, you haven't had to turn the heat on yet."

Every year the Fairchilds faced one of the ongoing crises in their marriage—when to turn the furnace on. Tom, in accord with most of Aleford, opted for waiting until the temperature outside got almost, but not quite, cold enough to freeze the pipes. Faith, in layers of wool and polar fleece, believed that when you could see your breath in your own bedroom, it was more than time. This year all had been sweetness and light—and warmth—so far.

"See you later," she called to the kids upstairs and left.

As she drove into the lower parking lot, not the staff one, she could see that Thomas was already on duty, so she stopped and went in through the main entrance.

"Nice shindig," he said. "I liked that lemon thing you had for dessert."

"Thanks," Faith said. "Next time we make it, I'll bring you some to take home." Thomas lived alone in a small cottage on the estate. Judging from the amount he ate for lunch—and he'd been one of the only staff members to eat at the old café—she didn't think he cooked much for himself. "I'm going to take a quick look upstairs to make sure everything's okay."

He nodded. "I just got here myself and came straight down, but you folks always leave the place in better shape than it was before. Not like some of these out-fits." He looked disgusted.

Faith started in the kitchen, and it looked fine, as it had when she'd left. The same was true of the former tapestry hall where they'd eaten. She spot-ted a lone wineglass on the stone wall surrounding the terrace and went out to retrieve it, propping the door open with her shoe just in case Thomas hadn't unlocked it from the outside yet. She tucked the glass into her bag.

The main gallery appeared all right, too. She walked to the end and glanced into the alcove. Kelly Burton, whose job it seemed to be, had carefully removed the fish to its pied-à-terre in her office, so Faith was not surprised to see that Swimmy wasn't in the tank. What was a surprise was the human being who had replaced him, occupying almost the entire space.

It was a young woman, and she was dead.

Chapter 4

Faith dropped her bag and screamed. She felt her legs start to give way under her, and she leaned against the gallery wall only to stand up immediately, aware that she was contaminating the crime scene, had done so the moment she walked in.

Thomas wouldn't have heard her. No one would have. The gallery was as silent as the grave it had become. Fearful, she backed away, then stood still, unable to take her eyes from the horrific sight in front of her. From the look of the woman's wrinkled and swollen bare arms and feet, she had been in the tank for many hours, which meant the murderer was long gone. Faith wasn't in any immediate danger. Her rapid heartbeats slowed.

Murder. Suicide? Could the young woman have somehow gotten past the alarm system and drowned herself? A flamboyant gesture? Faith looked to see if there was anything on the floor that might indicate it. A note? There was nothing. Nothing except a few stray Goldfish crackers. No note—and no shoes, socks, purse, or jacket. It had been cold last night, too cold for just the T-shirt and jeans the corpse was wearing. Faith tried to remember whether there had been another car in the parking lot, a car with these missing items. Thomas would have parked up in the staff parking. She closed her eyes and thought. She was almost positive hers had been the only vehicle.

The alarm system! Had Scott remembered to pull the door completely shut? Thomas would have come in that way this morning before going downstairs. Surely he would have noticed if the door hadn't been closed properly. Otherwise, the archaic alarm system wouldn't have been set, and anyone could gain entry. But how would she—or her killer—have known that the door would be ajar, if, in fact, it was? And what about the laser beams in the gallery? There was no sign of hairspray. No need of hairspray. Faith felt her mind start to spiral out of control and almost laughed. No, this woman didn't need hairspray.

Faith took a deep breath. She knew she was in shock. 911. She had to call the police and she had to go tell Thomas to keep museum visitors away. That the Ganley was closed.

She reached for the cell phone in her bag, groping for it among all the vital and unnecessary things she carried around. When she dropped her bag, the wineglass must have broken, and one of the pieces sliced into her ring finger. Rings. No rings on the Nereid's hands. The sight of her own blood made Faith feel faint. She wrapped a tissue around the wound and watched as the bright red stain soaked through it. She reached for another and pulled it tighter, dropping the first as she did so. She flipped her phone open and saw that she wasn't getting any reception. Typical Aleford. The town had fought cell towers for years and only last spring, facing a suit from several phone companies, grudgingly allowed two installations at either end of town, which produced only spotty service. She raced out toward the terrace and opened the door. Three bars. It would be enough.

Deputy Dale Warren answered. He and the chief would be right there. Was she sure the victim was deceased? Faith was sure. She knew there would be emergency vehicles anyway. But it was too late. Much too late.

She went down the main staircase, a dramatic one that looked out over the pond through long plate-glass windows on one side and had glass vitrines set into the wall on the other with changing exhibits of small objects. A plethora of Theodore's snuffboxes filled one;

in another, gleaming contemporary ceramic and metal boxes fashioned to hold nothing. Her finger was still bleeding. Maybe Thomas had a Band-Aid. She reached the front desk.

"Now, now, what have we here? Let me get the first aid kit, Mrs. Fairchild," Thomas said, looking up from his newspaper.

"We have to close the museum. We need to put a sign on the door. The police will be here any moment. There's . . ." Faith's voice gave out for a moment. "There's a body in the gallery upstairs."

"What! Now you just sit down, put your head between your knees if it will help, and I'll get that kit. How did you cut yourself?"

Faith reached across the desk and grabbed his arm. "Thomas, listen. It's not the cut. That's nothing. There's a young woman in the tank where the goldfish was and she's dead."

Thomas was the one who looked faint now, and he sat back down in his chair—hard.

"Lock the door and only let the police in," Faith said. "It's early; there won't be many people yet, but make a sign. Say the museum is closed for the day due to unexpected . . ." Her mind searched for the best explanation. Unexpected death? "Due to an unexpected repair situation."

He nodded and got out a sheet of paper and a black marker from under the desk. Having a task was something he could get his mind around, something that would block out the unimaginable.

"Maddy. We'd better call Maddy," he said, reaching for the phone.

Faith shook her head. "Let the police do that." She knew from experience they didn't like it when those on the scene made decisions.

"I'm going back upstairs to make sure that any staff coming in don't enter the gallery. We'll need to put a sign on the back entrance, too."

Thomas reached for another sheet of paper.

Faith started to leave, then turned back and asked him, "Was the back door closed securely when you came in this morning?"

"Tight as a drum. I punched in the code, came in, and didn't see a thing that wasn't the way it always is. Here, wait, you need that Band-Aid."

Faith leaned back against the desk and looked toward the parking lot. Hers *was* the only car. What was taking the police so long? Not that it made any difference to the victim, but it did to Faith. She wanted to know what had happened here late last night, and she wanted to know now.

Thomas, still pale and disbelief written large on his face, gave her a fistful of Band-Aids. As she went back upstairs, she wound one tightly around the cut. She walked back into the gallery and toward the tank, noting that the tissue she had dropped had made a small bloodstain on the carpet. She left it, knowing she'd have to explain how the mark, so fresh, got there.

With the first shock of discovery passing, she stood in the doorway of the alcove and looked at the body again. As was the usual case with bodies in water, the victim was facedown, her head lower than the rest of her body, which was curled in a fetal position due to the size of the tank. Faith crouched and saw that her face was unlined—a young face, which had been Faith's first fleeting impression. There was a faint rosy glow on it, echoed on her arms, hands, and feet. A healthy glow, which gave the lie to death—except Faith knew that this lividity was what happened to drowning victims, along with the wrinkled swelling and small goose pimples that covered the skin. Skin that was unblemished in any other way. No age spots, no visible tattoos. The tight jeans and white T-shirt clinging to the corpse revealed well-formed breasts, firm arms—a taut body. She'd been in perfect shape. Faith forced herself to look at the young woman's head suspended in the turquoise water. It was this part of the body that had so disturbed Faith earlier. The woman's face was lovely, small, heart-shaped, and her eyes were closed. Rigor had not set in—the gallery had been at its low nighttime temperature, and the water was also cool. The young woman's mouth was curved in a slight smile. But what had upset Faith, and continued to cause her stomach to contract, was the fact that the woman's head had been shaved. No curling tendrils in the water, no tendrils at all. Just a gleaming, perfectly smooth skull. She was a piece of art, a statue submerged in a replica of the Aegean, a replica herself. Not real. For an instant Faith questioned her morbid conclusion. Perhaps it was a statue, a dummy? An art school prank? No, that had never been a possibility. This had been a living, breathing, human being only a short time ago.

A voice behind her startled her from her thoughts. How long had he been standing there? Staring as she stood staring.

"Come on along, Faith. You can tell me what this is all about while we wait for the boys to get here." It was Aleford's Chief of Police Charles MacIsaac, "Charley" after all the years Faith had known him. The "boys" he was referring to were the state's crime unit, male *and* female, that would swoop in with their high-tech equipment to photograph, measure, and collect—squeezing every drop of evidence possible from the scene.

"I dripped some blood on the carpet," Faith said.

"Did you now?" Charley was leading her away to the open foyer outside the gallery, where there were chairs near the glass doors. "Sit down and have a swig of this." He was carrying the thermos that went everywhere with him, its contents varying with the situation. She sipped strong, sweet milky tea and told him what had happened with her finger, then backtracked to her movements that morning and the night before.

"Oh, Tom! I have to call Tom. I'm supposed to be at Ben's soccer game."

"Why don't you just tell him you've been delayed? We don't want this to get out just yet."

Faith called and was happy to note that Tom barely listened to her. Ben had scored, and his team was ahead now.

Faith put the phone away. There was a tremendous noise on the concrete staircase. It sounded as if a brigade was marching up, and in a way, it was. The man at the front stopped at the top, his face registering disbelief and intense annoyance. He walked over.

"Chief MacIsaac." He nodded toward Charley. "And Mrs. Fairchild. Don't tell me. *You* found the body."

It was Massachusetts State Police Detective Lieutenant John Dunne. Faith hadn't seen him for several years, but there was no mistaking the face only a mother could love—scariest when Dunne grinned, fortunately a rare event. He was a mountain of a man, well over six feet, solid muscle. Faith noted that his salt-and-pepper hair, tight curls that resembled wood shavings, had more salt than pepper now. He was elegantly dressed, as usual. She had a theory that his sartorial splendor was a deliberate attempt to make up for what Nature had so unfairly denied him. She recognized the topcoat as Joseph Abboud, and was that an Ermenegildo Zegna tie?

Together they had been involved in several murder investigations. She liked to think of them as partners, especially at the denouements when he was forced to concede that her help had been essential. Yet his memory conveniently reset itself, and each time was just like the first when he had considered her a major nuisance in *his* investigation.

He sighed heavily. "Where's the body?" She and Charley stood up, and Dunne motioned to the troops behind him, busy putting paper booties over their shoes and pulling on latex gloves. They all followed Faith into the gallery. She waved them on toward the alcove, bringing up the rear. It was a tight squeeze. The sight invoked silence, and then Dunne said, "What the hell is this? Some Damien Hirst snuff piece?"

Dunne had grown up in the Bronx and had never lost, or wanted to lose, his accent. It reminded Faith of all the things she missed about home—the whoosh of traffic, the smell of roasting chestnuts, the sight of the Chrysler Building at night. Damien Hirst. Dunne never failed to surprise her with his knowledge about everything and everyone.

"The show opened last night. This piece is entitled *Looking at You Looking at Me*. A single goldfish swims in the tank during museum hours. It's kept in an aquarium at night."

"Who is she?" he asked.

Faith had been asking herself the same question ever since she'd first walked into the gallery many long minutes ago. She was positive she'd never seen her. Trying to imagine her with a variety of hairstyles only served to strengthen her conclusion. She wasn't at last night's event. Faith was sure of that.

"I've never seen her before."

Dunne gave her a cross look. Why *didn't* she know who the victim was? Life was never simple. He gave some orders to the force accompanying him, put Detective Ted Sullivan, "Sully," in charge, and asked Faith where they could talk.

"We can go to the library upstairs. But shouldn't we notify the museum director, Madelyn Harper? We've closed the museum and staff is being turned away. She'll be wondering what's going on."

Maddy *had* been wondering after getting calls from several of the staff. She was in the foyer, panting, having run up the stairs.

"Thomas says there's a dead woman in the gallery!"

"This is Detective Lieutenant John Dunne of the state police, Maddy. He's in charge. I came in this morning to make certain everything was cleaned up and found her. She's, well . . ."

"Excuse me, Mrs. Fairchild. I'll take it from here if you don't mind." Faith saw him glance at Maddy's left hand. "Mrs. Harper, would you mind coming with me? It's possible that you might be able to identify the victim. I can assure you that while it will be upsetting, there was no obvious violence involved."

Maddy blanched, but went with him. Faith followed, despite the look Dunne shot at her, a look that said, "Stay out of this."

"The tank? The tank! She's in the tank," Maddy said. In short order, she stared, stumbled away from the sight, and reached for Faith, who put her arm around the woman's trembling shoulders. "I have no idea who she is. How did she get here and why doesn't she have any hair? Oh! This is a nightmare. I have to call the trustees before they hear it on the news."

"All in good time, Mrs. Harper, but I'd like to get statements from you and Mrs. Fairchild for a start right now. At the moment, the media is ignorant of the event. Now, I understand this exhibit opened last night with a reception. We'll need a list of everyone who attended the event. Is that possible?"

Maddy nodded. "It was ticketed, and we checked names off at the door. My assistant will have the list."

"Until we get the medical examiner's report as to the cause and approximate time of death, we'll have to assume it occurred after the last person left the building and before the security guard came on duty this morning. We'll be looking at those hours."

Was it Faith's imagination or did Maddy suddenly look terrified? The director had seemed to be coming around, eager to provide the list, administrative things. Maddy was a good administrator. Then Dunne's statement sent her careening back into shock.

"I left at about ten. There was no need to stay. The caterers were seeing to everything. I left with my husband, and we went straight home and straight to bed." Her face was flushed and she was agitated, speaking rapidly. The redness that spread across her cheeks did nothing for Maddy's appearance, just as it hadn't the previous night after one glass of wine—or was it more?

"Could you supply the name of the caterers for me?" Dunne had his BlackBerry out.

"Yes, Mrs. Fairchild's company, Have Faith."

"Of course." Dunne turned glumly to Faith. "And what time did you finish?"

"We'd been able to do much of the cleanup while people viewed the exhibit after dinner, so it wasn't much past eleven."

Scott was the last to leave. She had to think about this—and think quickly. There was no way he could be involved, and it would just confuse things. In his youth, Scott had had several brushes with the law. Nothing serious—unregistered, uninsured vehicles, some speeding tickets, but he had cultivated a *Rebel Without a Cause* image. Husband, father, part owner of a body shop in Bedford, he was a very law-abiding citizen now, but if she told the police he was here alone, he'd instantly become a suspect and valuable time tracking down the real killer would be wasted. She decided her conscience could rest easy if Dunne didn't ask her specifically whether she was the last one out or whether it was someone else. He didn't, and she made a mental note to get in touch with Scott as soon as possible. Maybe he'd seen something, a car? She could report it.

"Please make out a list of your staff and how to reach them, Mrs. Fairchild. Now, Mrs. Harper, I presume I can talk with you now? There's a library upstairs?"

"Yes, or we can talk in my office."

"Good. I'll be along shortly. In the meantime, Deputy Warren will be with you." He waved Dale over.

What did Dunne think? Faith wondered. That she and Maddy had committed the crime together and if left alone would work on their alibis?

She followed Maddy upstairs with Dale Warren trailing along a few steps behind them looking uncomfortable. Maybe he was annoyed at being so far away from the action, relegated to babysitting duty, or maybe his briefs were too tight. In any case, his face was indicating some kind of problem.

The phone was ringing as they walked into Maddy's office—a spacious one carved out of Theodore Ganley's former library. A wall of leaded-glass windows overlooked the pond, and although the ceiling had been lowered and its beams plastered over, it was still higher than normal. The architect had used the wood from the tapestry hall to line the new walls. The contemporary office furniture and artwork were in marked contrast to the feel of the room, but then the entire museum was a study in contradictions like this.

"May I?" Maddy directed her question at the deputy.

He nodded, and she grabbed the receiver.

"Yes? Madelyn Harper here."

"Oh, thank God! I didn't know where—" She stopped abruptly to listen to whoever was on the other end of the line.

"Yes, the police are here. One of them is with me now, also Faith Fairchild."

"Well, she found the body. Yes. Yes. No. No." The *nos* were quite emphatic, Faith noted.

"I have to go. The policeman in charge, a Lieutenant John Dunne, is coming to talk to me in a few minutes. Yes, like the poet. Spence, this is no time to make jokes!

"All right. I'll be home as soon as I can. No, we're not supposed to tell anyone."

She hung up and sat down in the chair behind her desk—collapsed would have been a better description, Faith observed. Obviously Spencer Harper had made one of any number of "for whom the bell tolls" jokes after hearing Dunne's name. Faith was sure John had heard them all. She'd heard a lot of them herself.

Dale was looking out one of the windows.

"You know about these things. I've heard about you. What happens now?" Maddy asked.

Faith drew up a chair. It was one of those Philippe Starck Ghost chairs, molded clear plastic that played with the Louis XVI style. It was surprisingly comfortable.

"They'll collect evidence—pile from the rug, any hairs, threads." My bloody tissue, she thought, chagrined at having dropped it, not professional at all. "Take photographs. The medical examiner is probably there by now and will make preliminary observations, then they'll remove the body for an autopsy." She was about to go into more detail. About all the scut work that would start—interviews with everyone who was at the event last night, inquiries in the neighborhood about unfamiliar cars, anything out of the ordinary. And the biggest question of all—who was she? They'd run her prints, search databanks for missing persons. But Faith didn't get to continue.

"I think I can take it from here, Mrs. Fairchild. You're free to go after you make that list." He handed her a piece of paper. "Deputy Warren will give it to me when you're finished." Dunne loomed in the doorway and stepped into the room, sucking all the air from it. Faith could take a hint. She took the sheet and walked past him into Maddy's assistant's office.

"I'll be home this afternoon if you need to reach me. Charley has my cell, too. This wasn't a poor girl—at least she spent a lot on clothes."

"What are you talking about?" Dunne sounded annoyed. "No, don't tell me." He paused; had his mother's, wife's voice chided him?—where are your manners! "I'm sorry you had to experience this and you know we have counselors available to help you. Please let the department know if there is anything we can do. We are grateful for your help."

Faith doubted it.

An hour later she was at the soccer field. It had taken longer to write down the names and contact information for her employees than she thought it would. After she gave the list to Dale, she thought she'd better swing by the body shop to let Scott know what was going on. She didn't want a record of the call on her cell. She knew she shouldn't be telling him anything, but no one had specifically told her *not* to, and she didn't want him to be caught unawares. That would almost guarantee him as a suspect, since he always reverted to his earlier attitude when confronted by the guys in blue. Besides, she reasoned, in a matter of hours, it would be all over the news. There hadn't been any sign of the media when she left the museum and she'd been surprised. Wasn't anybody listening to the scanners these days? Maybe Millicent, but she was of the generation that believed one got in touch with newspapers only for a birth, a wedding, and a natural death. She'd never drop a dime for anything else.

Scott was working on a car he'd bought on eBay—a 1939 Jaguar SS100 Duke replica—that he already had a buyer for, otherwise Faith knew Tom would have been sorely tempted. Not exactly a family car, though. Quickly she told him what had happened and asked him whether he'd seen anything unusual.

He'd tipped his welder's hood back when she'd approached, and now it seemed to be covering his handsome face again—figuratively, not physically. As a younger man he'd looked like Dennis Quaid in his prime, very sexy smile included. If anything, the more mature Scott was even better looking and totally unaware of the effect he had on people—something his wife, Trisha, had corroborated, adding, "Thank goodness."

"Seen anything? Like somebody walking past me carrying a stiff and dumping it in the fish tank? No, I don't recall anything like that."

"Come off it. I know you didn't have anything to do with this. I just don't want you to be blindsided when the police question you."

"Of all the nights to be Sir Galahad—no pun intended." He smiled ruefully, and her Scott was back. "Seriously, Faith, you do what you have to do. Tell Dunne or MacIsaac or any of the other cops that I was the last one out. As for me, cooperation is one thing, putting my head in a noose is another. If they want to know what time it was when I left, I'll tell them that and no more. If they ask me point-blank if I was alone, I'll have to say yes, but I'm not volunteering anything."

"That's pretty much the conclusion I came to," Faith said.

Their parting was an uneasy one—on both sides.

Racing to get to the field before Amy's game started, Faith wished she had time to stop at Patsy's and see if she was home. She didn't dare call yet. Not until the murder at the Ganley was common knowledge.

From the moment she had seen the body in the gallery, Faith had been plagued by the thought that somehow the forged Bearden and the murder were connected. But how? Had the young woman learned about the forgery, the switch? Was it confined to the Ganley or more widespread, affecting other area museums? Faith recalled what she'd learned from Patsy about art storage. A phony work could be packed up with a legitimate label and put into storage for four or five years before anyone found out it wasn't what it said it was. How many years ago was it that the team of John Drewe and John Myatt had been exposed in Britain? Six, seven? Myatt had done the forgeries, and Drewe had faked the provenances, inserting false ones into inventories so skillfully that the authorities were not sure to this day that they had spotted them all. Myatt was out of prison now and was exhibiting what he was calling "Genuine Fakes." His most recent show had sold out.

She pulled into a parking space and tried to switch her mind from the endless number of possibilities and improbabilities crowding into it to the simple, bucolic scene in front of her. The unusually warm day had continued sunny and bright. The small bleachers were filled. Families had brought blankets to spread out on the grass, and there was a holiday feel to the afternoon. Monday was Veteran's Day, but it felt more like Memorial Day. Faith had noticed her forsythia was budding out. It was unsettling. November was supposed to be cold, even snowy.

Ben came charging over.

"It's about time," he said in an accusatory tone.

"And hello to you, too, sweetheart," Faith said, leaning toward him to give him a hug. "Congratulations on your goal. What was the final score?"

"If you'd been here, you would know," he said, sidestepping her embrace. She remembered she wasn't supposed to engage in any public displays of affection with him now—one of Pix's tips. Her arms fell to her sides.

"You're the one who made me play on this stupid little kids' team," Ben said. " 'It will be good practice. You don't want to lose your edge. I'll come to all the games.' " It was eerie to hear her words mimicked back at her so accurately, Faith thought. Eerie, humiliating—and infuriating.

Tom had been at Ben's heels. "I'm sure your mother has a very good reason for not being at your game," he said over his son's head. His look was almost as peeved as Ben's.

"I had to work," Faith said, flushing. What was up with Tom? He'd feel terrible when he heard why she was delayed. It gave her the only moment of satisfaction she'd had all morning, but it disappeared before it could be of any comfort.

"I'm going to be with my *friends*," Ben said and walked off.

"I need to talk to you—in private. Let's sit in my car," Faith said.

Tom nodded. "Yes, we need to talk. Amy's game doesn't start for another ten minutes. I left my jacket saving two seats in the bleachers."

"You don't need it today, that's for sure," Faith said, struggling for some semblance of normality, but as she said it, she was reminded of just how abnormal the weather was. Sixty-seven degrees in New England; snowing in Texas.

She reached for her husband's hand. The back was covered with a few fine red-gold hairs. His touch was warm, and she felt transfused, connected. It was such a powerful sensation after all that had happened that she felt herself start to cry. A young woman was dead. Murdered. Behind her the crowd was cheering. Someone had scored. Above her the sun was a yellow ball like something a child might draw in a cloudless Crayola-blue sky.

"What's wrong? What's happened?" Tom cried out in alarm.

She almost dragged him to the car. They got in and she managed to blurt out the important details before burrowing her head on his shoulder and sobbing—sobbing the way she had wanted to from the moment she encountered death in the gallery.

Tom was stunned.

"Who would do something like this? The police are dealing with a psychopath! Kill a woman, shave her head, and then put her in a tank of water!" He was shaking, thinking what she hadn't wanted to put into words. The first detail she hoped to get from Chief MacIsaac. How had the victim been assaulted?

"I know! It's insane." Faith sat up and wiped her eyes. It was almost time for the game. She needed to compose herself.

"It has to be someone who was at the opening last night—or knew that this work of art was part of it. I should remind Charley or Dunne that there's a catalog with a picture and description of the piece. Anyone with an advance copy or working at the printer's could have seen it."

"Faith!" Tom had been opening the car door to get out, and he slammed it shut. "You can't honestly be thinking of getting involved in this any more than you are! Aside from the fact that I would not be a happy widower, you have to consider the kids! It was a near thing last summer out on Bishop's Island when you were only supposed to be doing the cooking for those Pelham College alums' reunion."

"This isn't like that at all, and of course I'm not going to do anything that would threaten my life and family. Today I was in the wrong place at the wrong time. The police are going to be questioning me. That's it. If I can help by telling them anything, I will. Case closed."

"Okay." Tom sounded relieved, but skeptical. "Just make sure it stays that way."

They walked back to the field, the harsh afternoon sun stretched out in front of them, bringing everything into sharp focus. This was what she needed, Faith thought. Something that would illuminate the facts at hand; something that would bring them into focus. Something that would show no mercy to anything, or anyone, in the shadows.

Ben was with a group of middle-schoolers half out, half under the bleachers. She waved, but he didn't respond. She knew he'd seen her, and she was tempted to go over and say something, but she heard Pix's voice in her head and stopped. Choose your battlegrounds. Playing fields, particularly at Eton, were of course made for war, but Aleford's gentle, noncompetitive recreation soccer was not. She went to her seat, waved at her daughter, and was gratified by an enthusiastic response.

"You made it, Mom! Watch me! We're psyched!"

Faith allowed herself to be drawn into the game. Ben and his friends emerged to shout from the sidelines. She didn't recognize the boy immediately to one side of her son. Tom didn't know him, either.

"He must be new in town. Nice of Ben to take him under his wing," Tom said.

Faith wasn't so sure. She trained her gaze on Ben, not the action on the field, and she didn't like what she saw. The other boy was doing most of the talking and he had what she could only describe as a sneer on his face. Expert at snap judgments that she was, Faith decided this kid was trouble with a capital *T*, which rhymes with *P* that stands for—she was sure it wasn't anything as benign as *Pool. The Music Man* was dated in that respect, but as she hummed the song's refrain softly, the words boomed like a big bass drum inside her head, "Trouble, right here in River City."

He was larger than Ben—taller, broader. She wasn't sure, but there seemed to be a hint of a five o'clock shadow on his face, but maybe that was just a real shadow—the one cast by the Patriots cap he was wearing. Nothing wrong there. Nothing wrong that she could put her finger on. Just an inkling. Just something about Ben's body language, which was running the gamut from bantam strut to groveling Igor. She'd have to find out more about this new boy. If he was older, as he appeared to be, what was he doing hanging out with a lowly sixth grader? She knew the way the food chain worked at middle school.

Amy's team lost, and she was crestfallen. The two kids piled into her car. Ben surprised Faith by treating his sister like a human being, offering words of comfort and reassurance. "Hey, everybody loses some of the time, Ames. And you didn't screw up. It was the goalie."

Amy beamed, and the ride home was a pleasant one. Both kids were thrilled by the news that David Beckham was coming to their very own country to play for the L.A. Galaxy soccer team. This increased the possibility that they might someday see this august personage a hundredfold.

"They have these really cheap flights to California, Mom. I've been checking on the Internet. And maybe we could camp. They have national parks all over the West, right?" Ben said.

Faith didn't want to burst his bubble by telling him that the only kind of park they'd be likely to find in L.A. would be a parking lot. She turned into the parsonage driveway and wasn't surprised to see an unmarked police car at the curb. Tom wasn't home yet. He had a parish call to make; one that he assured her wouldn't take long, but that he couldn't put off in spite of how much he wanted to be with her. She'd assured him she was okay, and she had been, but now, seeing the car, she wished he were here. There had been no reason to tell the kids what had happened this morning and she hoped there still wasn't. She'd think of something to explain why the police were paying them a visit.

She parked outside the garage, and they got out.

"Look, somebody's getting out of that car that's in front of our house," Amy said. "Oh, it's that police guy you know, Mom, and Chief MacIsaac."

Faith started to say something to the children when she was stopped by the look of panic on Ben's face. He mumbled something about homework and dashed to the kitchen door. It was locked. Since the house had been burglarized several years ago, Faith set the alarm and locked up tight even if she was just going to get milk.

"Hurry up, Mom!" Ben called.

Before she could think about what his response could possibly mean, John and Charley were upon them—in

Dunne's case, monumentally upon them. Amy gave them both bright smiles and started in on the soccer game. Charley listened attentively, offering his condolences for her team's loss.

Maybe Ben had to go to the bathroom and was too embarrassed to say so in front of Dunne and the chief. He was certainly hopping up and down. The moment Faith opened the door he ran straight through the kitchen and upstairs.

"We tried calling both phones," Dunne said. "No one was home here and the cell didn't answer."

"Cell service is new and a little unreliable in Aleford," Faith said. "There are residents who are still getting used to the pushbuttons instead of a dial, so there hasn't been much pressure to improve things. Why don't you come on in to the living room and sit down. I'll make coffee."

Offering coffee wasn't simply a polite gesture in suburbia, but a rule.

Charley said fine as John Dunne said no, thanks. It wasn't a social call, as Faith well knew. Charley backtracked and said he'd had enough caffeine already today.

"Amy, why don't you get a head start on your homework, and that way you'll have two free days before school starts on Tuesday."

"Sure, Mom. Good-bye, Chief MacIsaac and Mr. Umm." Amy blushed.

"'Dunne.' You say it the same way you'd say, 'I done good,'" the detective said with what he perhaps thought was an amiable smile, but the show of teeth was as grim as a spooky jack-o'-lantern. Amy didn't blanch, however.

"Oh, you silly! You can't say 'I done good.' You have to say 'I did well,' right?"

"Right you are, but now you'll never forget my name."

This was a side Faith had never seen. A kindler, gentler Dunne. A Dunne good with children. She'd met his wife once—five feet nothing and a hundred pounds of a very tough lady—but he'd only referred to his two kids a few times in passing. They were out of college now, one in New York City; one in Minnesota, married. That had been the occasion for some information—the point being that only his son's wedding would drag him to Minneapolis in August: "hotter than hell, but then hell freezes over in the winter. Go figure."

Faith knew her mind was wandering over a wide terrain in an effort to escape.

"Tom out?" Charley asked.

"Yes," Faith answered, adding hastily, "He'll be home soon."

Dunne lowered himself into one of the big wing chairs by the fireplace, the only one that fit his frame. Charley, a big-boned Nova Scotian, grabbed the other, and Faith was forced to sit on the sofa facing them. She moved to the middle so they'd be in stereo.

Dunne took out a BlackBerry. He'd obviously abandoned his Filofax for a tech toy. Charley reached for a small, battered spiral notebook and a pencil. They looked like the same ones he'd been writing in and with since she met him, but that was impossible. When he came to Aleford as chief over thirty years ago, he must have bought reams of them.

"Okay," Dunne said. "To satisfy my curiosity. Why did you say the victim obviously spent a lot on clothes just as you were leaving?"

"Why are you asking now? Was there something special about what she was wearing? What *was* she wearing? All I could see was jeans and a T-shirt. No bra, by the way."

"We know that," snapped Dunne.

"No labels," Charley said. "Somebody cut the labels out of the pants and shirt. And that's all she had on."

Dunne glared at him.

"I thought so," Faith said. "Those jeans were pretty tight." Before Dunne could explode at her—or Charley—she went on. "She was wearing J Brand jeans. The kind Angelina Jolie favors. They cost about a thousand dollars, although since these looked like the faded ones, I'd add a few hundred dollars more onto that."

"Jesus, Mary, and Joseph! Are you trying to tell me that someone would pay over a thousand dollars for faded blue jeans? I thought they came from Goodwill," Charley said, his face totally shocked.

Dunne looked taken aback, as well.

"It's obscene, I agree, but apparently the fit is great. The T-shirt is from Agnès b. and I won't bother to tell you what that cost, but more than Hanes. The important thing here, besides the fact that she had the money to buy clothes like this, was that she was projecting a certain image. If you can't be Angelina Jolie, the next best thing is to dress like her."

Dunne nodded and made a note or two.

"She'd also had a good pedicure and manicure recently. A French manicure. White tips, pale polish. Classy. Not bright red talons. Maybe the lab could figure out what brand the polish is and ask around at the salons on Newbury Street. She has Newbury Street written all over her, unless she turns out to be from New York. We'd know more if we knew how her hair was styled. Wait! Find out whether anyone has had her head shaved recently at one of the hairdressers. She could have wanted it done herself, a sort of retro Sinead O'Connor thing. It would have to be very recently. There isn't a hint of stubble, which means we have no idea what color her hair was."

"She was a redhead," Charley said.

"A redhead? How could you . . . ?" Faith started to say *tell*, but the answer was obvious, and she had a hard time keeping a straight face. Both men looked so uncomfortable.

"Don't worry," she assured them. "You don't have to say anything more. I get it."

Chapter 5

If Faith thought she had the upper hand, she was sadly mistaken.

"We didn't come here to talk about hair color. I want to know what you're doing at the Ganley, Faith," Dunne said.

For a moment she was cheered by his use of her first name. It had been "Mrs. Fairchild" since their eyes locked at the top of the museum stairs. Then she sighed inwardly. This was no olive branch, no "let's solve this thing together," just an attempt to draw her out and tell all. Good cop.

"What do you mean what am I doing?" The police tended to answer a question with a question. She could play that game, too.

"Just what I said." He looked at Charley with an "I told you so" expression plainly written on his face.

"What are you doing there? Yeah, yeah. You catered the opening reception. You cater for them a lot. But why did you recently take over their restaurant? Don't you have enough on your plate?" He didn't smile at the pun, nor did she.

"I've been thinking of expanding Have Faith for a while now, offering carryout. I mentioned it to one of the Ganley trustees, a friend, and she urged me to take over the museum's restaurant instead. It's been steadily losing money. The food was a notch below vending-machine quality. I thought it would mean less of an initial investment on my part, and since I'd be offering the same kinds of things I would in carryout, it would be a dry run."

"Who was the trustee?"

"Not that it relates to any of this, but it was Patricia Avery."

Dunne nodded at Charley. For a moment no one said anything. Faith knew what they were thinking. That it was the same Patricia Avery who had had Faith go undercover at Mansfield Academy here in town just before a body was discovered there.

"Quite a coincidence. You two women get together again and another corpse appears on the scene," Dunne said.

"Completely isolated incidents. We get together all the time without bodies turning up." Faith was peeved at finding herself on the defensive. It was too stupid. "I had lunch with her recently in town and we often stop by each other's house for coffee. She was merely offering to help me—and the venture has been very successful from my point of view. Good financially plus a good schedule, since as you pointed out I have a lot on my plate, by which I presume you mean as a wife and mother. That reminds me, I have to start dinner and see how my children are doing."

"Now don't get all huffy," Charley said. "Nobody's accusing you of anything. We all want to find out the same thing—who committed this terrible crime and, to start with, who the victim is. You've helped already with the clothes, and maybe something else will occur to you. Here's the little we know so far."

He flipped open his notebook and ignored Dunne's irritated glance.

"We've shown a Polaroid of the body to the entire Ganley staff, a few of the trustees, and are starting on the museum schoolteachers. The only person who reacted at all is Thomas, the security guard. He thought her face looked quote 'kind of familiar,' but he couldn't say when or where he'd seen her. Almost everybody said if she had hair, it might help. A couple of computer portraits with different hairdos should be ready any minute, so we'll go back and show those. Plus get them out to the media."

"Any idea how she died? I can't imagine that she drowned, unless she was drugged before someone put her in the tank. There were no signs of struggle—no bruise marks on the body and very little water on the carpet, which would indicate someone held her down."

Dunne had had enough. He stood up. Charley did, too—a fraction of a second later.

"Thank you for your time, Mrs. Fairchild. We'll be in touch," Dunne said.

Faith took them to the door, happy to see them go. At the moment the secrets she was keeping threatened to fall off that full plate of hers. It wasn't like Dunne to make a joke in the middle of an investigation, or too often at any time. But what was it Freud said, there are no accidents? Charley hadn't answered her last question, but she was pretty sure she'd be able to worm that and more information as it became available from him. He was getting close to retirement and had loosened up a lot.

As soon as they left, she went upstairs. Amy was curled up in the window seat that overlooked the street. Jane Langton's *The Fledgling* lay open beside her. She was staring out at the departing figures.

"Is something wrong, Mom? Why were the police here?"

Faith put her arms around her daughter. "There was an accident at the museum. Let's get Ben and I'll tell you both about it."

It would be all over school when they returned on Tuesday, but Faith hoped without the gruesome details.

Faith started to open Ben's door when Amy said, "He likes us to knock, remember?"

Faith knocked and, after a while, was granted permission to enter. At least that was how she interpreted the grunt she heard.

She gave them the facts, leaving out the shaved head and saying the body had been found near one of the pieces of artwork, not in it. Amy's eyes were wide with fear. Faith hastened to assure her that they were all safe; that it had nothing to do with them or anyone else they knew.

"But you work at the museum!" Amy cried.

For the second time today, Ben surprised his mother. He reached across Faith and took his sister's hand, squeezing it tight.

"So do a lot of other people, and besides that there are tons of visitors. It doesn't mean that this, this thing, has anything to do with them—or us. Right, Mom?"

He needed reassurance, too. One foot in childhood, one in adolescence, it was the little boy who was sitting beside her now.

"Absolutely right. I'm sure the police will find out who did this soon. Now, how about waffles for supper tonight? And afterward we can watch one of your animes, Ben. I'm in the mood for *My Neighbor Totoro*. In fact, why don't we start it now?"

"The cat bus!" Amy jumped up and headed over to the shelf where Ben kept his treasured DVDs. He dashed over before she could get there.

"I have them in order. Don't touch them!"

Too good to last, Faith thought, but at least she knew her old Ben was still alive and well. The Body Snatchers hadn't gotten him—yet.

"What was her name? The lady at the museum," Amy asked as the two of them went downstairs. Ben said he had to close some files and would be right there.

"We don't know her name yet, honey."

Amy teared up. "You mean her parents could not even know she's dead? Or maybe never know? Didn't she have her name in her pocketbook or something?"

"They haven't found her pocketbook, but they'll find out who she is, don't worry. Chief MacIsaac and Detective Dunne and a whole lot of other police are working on it right now."

Amy giggled. "Dunne. He was funny."

Faith nodded. She wasn't thinking of Dunne's sense of humor or lack thereof. She was thinking about the victim's total lack of identification. Somebody had wanted Jane Doe to stay that way for as long as possible.

Faith had called Patsy as soon as she had left the museum and left messages to call her back immediately on the Averys' answering machine and Patsy's cell. The phone rang just as she was letting herself be pulled into Hayao Miyazaki's lush anime world, blotting out the image that had been haunting her all day, not simply an image of death, but death distorted.

"Faith!" Patsy said. "Maddy just reached me. I can't believe it. I'm coming over right now."

"Yes. Come now." Faith hung up the phone and slumped into one of the kitchen chairs, the energy that had been propelling her through this nightmare suddenly sapped. A friend was just what she needed.

By the time Patsy appeared at the back door, Faith had made a pot of steaming Darjeeling tea and set out a plate of spice cookies. Comfort food, even though she wasn't hungry.

The first thing Patsy did was envelop her friend in a long, tight hug.

"Will and I took off early this morning for a spur-of-the-moment getaway weekend to the Berkshires. Neither of us has to work on Monday, so we thought we'd go out to North Adams and Williamstown, hit MassMoCA and the Clark. Find some B and B. I'm rambling."

Faith shook her head. Rambling conversation was just what she needed. She poured the tea.

"Maddy reached me and we drove straight back. She didn't tell me you were the one who found the body until I called her when we got home." She covered Faith's hand with her own, warm from holding the steaming mug.

"The whole thing is surreal." Faith smiled at the apt word choice given the context. "It keeps running through my head like that horrible movie *Groundhog Day*."

She filled Patsy in on what had happened from that first moment of discovery to Dunne and Charley's recent visit. As she recounted their conversation, she thought briefly about Ben's reaction to their arrival. Like almost everything else lately, it had been the direct opposite of earlier behavior. She didn't mention it to Patsy.

"Maddy has asked me to call a meeting of the board for tomorrow afternoon once the police let us back into the museum. I want you there; see if you pick up on anything. In any case, we'll need coffee, lots of it, and something to eat."

What was appropriate for a postmortem like this? Faith wondered. No funeral yet, so no baked meats.

Patsy was continuing. "I can't imagine what this has to do with the forgery, but I don't believe in coincidences. We have two crimes at the Ganley now."

Faith was well aware of that.

The day was finally over. The kids asleep—or at least Ben was pretending. Knowing it would be all over the news and tomorrow's papers, Tom had called their families, sparing Faith that exhausting chore.

"No, the victim has not been identified. No, Faith has no idea who she is." Over and over and over.

At 9:05 the phone rang, late for Aleford. A call made after this hour was not merely considered rude, but taboo, acceptable only in the case of an extreme emergency. It was Pix and murder was an extreme emergency. Faith took the phone from Tom and filled her in. The Millers, too, had taken off for the weekend, leaving at the crack of dawn on this sunny Saturday. They'd headed north to visit friends in Cape Elizabeth, Maine, picnicking on the Two Lights Beach. Sounding as if she were in shock, Pix was describing their whole day finishing with Sam's hitting the button on the remote for the *Nine O'clock New England News.* Faith had not been identified by name, but somehow it had leaked out that it was the caterer from the event the night before who had found the body.

"Now, you must be about to go to bed," Pix said. "You need to go to sleep and try to forget about today, although I know there's fat chance of that."

Oddly enough Faith thought she might be able to do just that. She had never been so tired in her entire life. She said good-bye and was about to hang up when she had an idea.

"Pix, are you still there?"

"Yes? What do you need? Anything."

"Could you come with me tomorrow when the Ganley board meets? I'm to provide coffee and something to eat. It's Patsy's idea. You know a lot of these people and can tell if someone is behaving out of character more easily than I can."

"I'm happy to come, but won't it seem a little odd? Two people to pour coffee and serve whatever else?"

"Things have been so 'odd' at the Ganley, I seriously doubt anyone will notice we're there."

Patsy called the meeting to order after everyone had something to drink, and for those who also wished, something to eat. Faith had decided to treat the meeting as if it were a coffee break, filling platters with Danish pastries, crumb cake, and lemon pound cake, adding sliced fruit for those who didn't do sweets or carbs. Pix's job was to keep circulating with the coffee and teapots. Faith's was to pass the platters once plates were empty. At the moment, the two women had melted into the drapery at opposite ends of the room. Faith had been correct. Aside from a brief thank-you from Maddy, no one had taken any notice of them.

All the trustees were there—every chair around the large oval table was taken. The staff and a few unfamiliar individuals were sitting in chairs against one wall. Faith assumed those she didn't know were teachers at the museum school. Patsy thanked everyone for coming and turned the meeting over to Maddy.

At her arrival, Faith had been shocked at the director's appearance. She now knew what it meant when people said someone had aged overnight. Maddy's face was deeply etched with worry lines, and she had neglected to put on any makeup, even lipstick. Her hair was pulled back untidily into a scrunch and her clothes were wrinkled. Granted, Maddy was no slave to fashion, or rather any fashion Faith had been able to detect, but this was a new low—a ratty navy blue turtleneck and pilled black wool slacks. The director took a sip of coffee, cleared her throat, and said, "Thank you all for coming at such short notice. This has been—is—a tragedy, but we'll get through it together."

It sounded like "Win One for the Gipper"—Team Ganley.

"The police have said that we can open for business as usual . . ."—she stumbled over the words—"tomorrow. The artwork involved has been removed as evidence."

Where could they be keeping it? Faith wondered. And what about little Swimmy? Someone else had the same thought. Mr. Birkenstocks, Harold Prizer.

"Hope you're remembering to feed that fish." His face registered more disapproval than concern.

Maddy nodded. "Kelly is taking good care of it until we can return it to the artist."

"What about the artist?" Harriett demanded. "He's the logical suspect. Anyone perverted enough to create the piece in the first place would think nothing of doing something like this just for the publicity."

"Oh, really, Harriett," Jack Winston said. He was wearing a dark suit as befitted the occasion. "You can't seriously be suggesting that a man would commit murder just to get his work noticed."

"That's exactly what I mean." Harriett was just getting started.

"The artist has been cleared of any involvement," Maddy interrupted. She sounded very weary. "He was here at the opening all evening and with friends afterward celebrating down at someone's house on the Cape. He has been ruled out as a suspect."

"Could have had an accomplice," Harriett muttered.

Maddy ignored her. "I'd like to turn the meeting over to Chris to talk about how we should deal with the media. You've all seen the morning papers, and it's only going to get worse."

Chris, the publicity director, was the Mork/Robin Williams look-alike Faith had noted at the other board meeting. He'd tried to tame his curls with gel and was also dressed in a dark suit, but his somewhat manic energy refused to stay below the surface.

"It could have been much worse. We're lucky that this is the first Sunday following the elections, so most of the news is about our new governor, what Nancy Pelosi is wearing, and the outcomes of some of those close Senate and House races. The *Times* buried us in a paragraph under New England news and only the *Herald* ran the story on page one."

Faith looked at the faces around the table. They were studiously blank with the exception of Elizabeth Canning, the assistant curator, who looked frightened, and Lynne Hollister, the trustee, who looked frankly bored. She wasn't in green, nor was she wearing any sharp objects around her neck. In a vintage dark orchid dress, she'd been fiddling with her purse and drawing curlicues on the pad in front of her.

"However, I don't think this moratorium will last as more information leaks out—sorry, bad word choice. Anyway, we've prepared a little script in case any of you are contacted by the media, or anyone else for that matter—neighbors, friends, relatives. It basically says that the police are handling the investigation and you have no comment except to express your sorrow at the tragic loss of a young life."

"Do the police know who she is yet?" Marvin Handler asked.

"Not to my knowledge," Chris said. "Maddy?"

"No, or if they do know, no one has told *me* anything," she said bitterly.

Faith felt very sorry for her. What a thing to have happen on her watch. No matter where Maddy went, she'd always be "that director who had a body in her gallery."

Joseph Sargeant had been staring into his cup of tea as if looking for answers in the leaves. "I don't know how to say this any other way, but I sincerely hope we all keep our mouths shut."

Lynne stopped doodling, and all eyes were on Joseph.

"Most of us live in this town—have lived here for a long time—and you know how rumors get started. In the short run, we'll have an increase in attendance as all the ghouls in the Greater Boston area will want to come and see where 'it' happened. But then we run the very serious risk of losing visitors. Murder leaves an indelible mark, and even if people don't realize it, they'll shy away from our doors. If we all avoid talking about it and continue to mention the new show and our programs, the rumors will die down."

He was right, Faith thought, and watched to see what the reactions would be from his fellow trustees.

Harriett was the first to weigh in—of course. "I don't think we need to worry too much, although sealing our lips is certainly called for at this time." She pursed hers. "The untimely death of an unknown young woman won't keep people from our marvelous park and museum. And if it does, then we didn't want them in the first place."

The illogic of it all was mind-boggling, and Faith noted she wasn't the only one struck—Marvin Handler's mouth had actually dropped open.

Chris jumped in. "I appreciate all your comments and you'll find my contact information on the sheet. Please call me if you hear from a reporter or anyone else pressing you for information."

"Even our near and dear?" said a tall rake of a man with a neatly trimmed Vandyke beard who was sitting with the staff.

"I leave that to your discretion, Roland—and everyone else's," Chris answered and passed out his sheets.

"Any other questions, comments?" Patsy said preparatory to adjournment.

Lynne Hollister snapped her purse shut and tore off the sheet of paper, crumpling it into a ball. "Only the one we're all thinking about. The elephant in the room? Why was she murdered at the Ganley?" She graced everyone with a bright smile. "It can't be a coincidence, now can it?"

It was dark by the time Faith got home. Somewhat cheered by the fact that daylight savings time would start three weeks early next year, she put the plate of food she'd saved from the event on the kitchen table and went in search of her family. Tom was fast asleep on the couch, and Amy was curled up like a kitten at his feet reading. She put her finger to her lips and motioned her mother back toward the kitchen.

"Dad was reading to me, but he was so sleepy I told him I'd do it myself. Ben went to a friend's house. I can't remember his name."

"Not Josh?"

Amy paused a moment. "No," she said, hesitating still more. "Not Josh."

"Well, Dad knows, right?"

Again she hesitated. "Dad may have been asleep when he left."

"Amy Sibley Fairchild! Was Dad awake or not when Ben left?"

"Not awake."

Faith glanced out the window. It wasn't late, but it *was* dark. Ben knew he wasn't supposed to go out without permission unless it was next door to the Millers, an infrequent destination now that Dan, Ben's idol, was in college.

"You're sure he didn't go to Josh's?"

Josh lived only a few blocks away. If that was where Ben was, Faith wouldn't be upset.

Amy shrugged and reached for a slice of pound cake.

"Can I have some cake and a glass of milk?"

Faith nodded and went to the phone. She'd wiped the message board clean yesterday morning and there was still nothing on it. No word from her son. She quickly dialed Josh's number. His mother answered.

"Hi, Carolyn, it's Faith. By chance is Ben there?"

"No, he's not—and I'm surprised you would call."

Faith was stunned. She had never heard Carolyn use this particular tone of voice. Greenland was warmer.

"I'm sorry. Is there something going on that I don't know about? Has anything happened between Josh and Ben?"

"Josh and Ben haven't been friends all fall." The temperature rose a degree. "I don't know myself what it's all about. Josh won't talk about it, but whatever it is, it was Ben's doing, not my son's."

"But they've been friends since kindergarten!"

"Exactly," Carolyn said and hung up.

Faith stood still holding the receiver, shocked—and angry. How dare Carolyn hang up on her! They weren't even related! Then depression set in. If Ben had been his old self she wouldn't be feeling this way, but the new unimproved Ben was able to have the effect on her without even being in the same room. She replaced the phone and turned around intending to find out if Amy knew anything about what was going on, but the kitchen was as empty as the milk glass and plate where her daughter had been sitting. Faith would have to wait for Ben to come home. The prospect was not a happy one.

She was tempted to call Pix for moral support, but she was driving her mother, Ursula, to a lecture at the Massachusetts Historical Society in Boston. It had something to do with the Lymans—Ursula's maiden name—and both mother and daughter were interested in the topic. A skeleton in the closet had apparently popped out, Pix had said.

This took Faith back to the Ganley. She wondered if Charley would be in the mood to trade information. She could report on the meeting—not that there was much to say—and he might come across with the M.E.'s results.

She reached him at home, and he was in an expansive mood. His sister up on Cape Breton in Nova Scotia kept him supplied with oatcakes and two new tins had arrived the day before.

"Still no clue as to her identity. We sent her prints off and found out she's never committed a crime or been in the military. The NCIC, you know, the National Crime Information Center, has everything we've discovered so far, and maybe we'll get some hits from there."

Faith remembered a body that was found hanging in a tree in Aleford's conservation land, a suicide. It took a few years, but finally he was identified from the information on file with the NCIC. Charley told her after the man's identity became known—he'd been a drifter from Colorado—that they'd gotten leads a few times a year, and he figured they'd just be patient until one panned out. One finally did. At the time Faith had been struck by how much police work consisted of simply waiting it out. She hoped it wasn't going to be the case with the Ganley corpse.

"She was dead before she was put in the tank. She didn't drown—no water in her lungs. The official cause of death has been listed as suffocation."

"Suffocation! Any bruising? Signs of struggle?"

"None. And she hadn't been violated. But she did have a high blood alcohol level. They didn't find any other drugs, though."

"So, she probably passed out, which would have made the killer's job easier."

Faith heard a crunch as Charley bit into one of the oatcakes—they *were* delicious. He'd given the Fairchilds a tin after a visit back home several summers ago. The recipe was a family secret, of course, but Faith suspected oats, flour, brown sugar, and plenty of butter. She never could understand these family-secret recipes. When she made something special, she wanted everyone to know how to make it, too. And oatcakes—or sticky buns— were not exactly corporate secrets. We're not talking the ingredients in Coca-Cola here, she said to herself.

"The local papers are running two computer-generated pictures tomorrow morning. Dunne's furious that they didn't run today, and I don't blame him. The sooner we get her identified the sooner we can catch who did this. It doesn't take long to make up these pictures, but it being a Saturday, nobody sent them over to Dunne's office. When he finally figured out the problem, it was too late for the papers. So, how did the meeting go? We had a helluva job getting the tank out. Maybe someday you can tell me why it's art, by the way."

Faith heard more crunching.

"The basic message of the meeting had to do with damage control. Zip your lips. Don't talk to anybody from the media. Don't talk to anybody period."

"As if that will work." Charley laughed. "The media, okay, but as for the rest, well, it's Aleford. I'm sure Millicent knows as much as I do."

Faith had to agree. She saw Ben coming through the Millers' backyard and said a hasty good-bye to Charley.

She had time to wake up Tom. She wasn't tackling this one alone, and by the time Ben came through the door, affecting an air of nonchalance, both parents were waiting. They ushered him into the living room where they all sat down.

"Ben," Tom said, "why didn't you wake me up and tell me you wanted to go out?"

"I didn't want to disturb you." An angelic response. It didn't work.

Tom shook his head. "You didn't wake me up because you knew I'd say no."

"It's not a school night," Ben said angrily. "I'm allowed to go out on weekends and this is like a weekend."

"You didn't go to Josh's. I spoke to his mother. Where did you go?" Faith asked.

"You had no right to call Mrs. Walker!" Ben stood up.

"Calm down, son, and let's talk about this. Where did you go?"

"Just to a friend's, and I wasn't gone long. You would have still been asleep if Mom hadn't come home early."

"And that would have made everything okay?" Faith tried to say it gently.

Ben retreated into stony silence.

"Who is this friend? A new one? The boy who was at the soccer game yesterday?"

"What do you care? And it's none of your business!"

He was up the stairs before they could say, "You're grounded."

Faith sighed. "I know we'll live, but will he? At the moment I could kill him!" Words said every day in everyday homes, but she wished them back on this particular day. "You know what I mean."

Tom moved over on the couch and drew her close to him. "I do. Were we this awful? I'll have to ask my mother."

"Please don't. I like the grandparents to have the illusion that we're in charge here raising their perfect little darlings.

"We have to find out who this boy is," she continued, "and why Ben isn't friends with Josh anymore."

"Agreed, but easier said than done. What I do remember about being Ben's age is not telling my parents anything. Of course in my case, it was building less than seaworthy rafts and taking them on the North River and raiding our neighbor's orchard for apples."

"Oh, you rascal, you 'barefoot boy with cheek of tan,' " Faith teased.

Ben appeared for dinner, was studiously polite, and for the moment his parents were happy to let the matter slide with the mention that he was grounded indefinitely. They had enough on their plates.

Her face stared up at Faith from the front page of the *Boston Globe.* Two faces, one with short hair, a cap cut close to her head, the other with shoulder-length tresses. Her eyes were open, and she looked so alive that Faith had trouble believing that the photos had been taken of a corpse. The *Globe* had run them in color just above the fold with the headline in bold: "Ganley Murder Victim: Who Was She?" A smaller second line read: "Police Seek Help in Identifying Jane Doe."

Faith took the paper with her and drove to the catering kitchen where Niki had today's Ganley café food ready to go. Together they loaded the van, and Faith got behind the wheel. She wanted to see what if anything was going on at the museum. It was early, before any visitors would be allowed in, but she was curious to hear what the staff might have to say. Many of them had formed the habit of coming to the café for coffee and a muffin or bagel before the real work of the day started.

As she left, Faith put the newspaper on the counter in front of Niki.

"She was beautiful," Niki said. "Not just a pretty face, but gorgeous. Do you think that's what got her killed? A jealous girlfriend, wife?"

"Until we know who she was, anything's possible."

"I always wanted red hair like that," Niki said. "And her eyes, at least in the picture, look like that pale green jade collectors flip for. Well, the police won't have any trouble identifying her now. This is a face nobody would be likely to forget."

Unless they wanted to, Faith thought as she drove the short distance to the museum. It wasn't a face she would ever forget. Niki was right. The woman had a rare beauty that came through even in the computer composites—deep auburn hair and those gemstone eyes. It was the kind of face the Pre-Raphaelites—and

Theodore Ganley—adored, Jane Morris in modern dress.

Channing was waiting outside with the cart. He hadn't bothered to put on a jacket and was noticeably shivering. Usually he waited inside the door.

"Channing, you're freezing," Faith said as she got out of the van. She was about to tell him to go back and put something warm on when she realized that he was not her child, and in any case, too old to be told what to wear. As she got closer, she almost stepped back. He stank—a hungover sour smell with the contents of an ashtray thrown in for added flavor. He must have come straight to work from an all-nighter.

"You have to go home, shower, and change. Help me get everything upstairs and I'll take over until you come back."

"What are you talking about? I'm fine."

"You're *not* fine. There's no other way to put this; you stink and we can't have our customers put off their food by the man who's dishing it up."

He glared at her and started to pile things on the cart.

Faith tried to keep her voice light. "It must have been some party. Please go home. Take the van if you want." Channing normally walked the short distance to work. "I'll hold the fort until you come back."

"Okay," he said. The fight went out of him all at once, like a punctured balloon. He scarcely seemed to have enough energy to push the cart through the doors, up the ramp, and into the elevator.

Both the curator and assistant curator were waiting in the hall, hovering at the entrance to the café, obviously in need of caffeine.

"Hi. Channing has to run out for a bit; could you help me unload? Coffee's on me."

Maddy's assistant, Kelly Burton, Thomas the security guard, and two men, who had both been in attendance at yesterday's meeting, soon arrived. Faith recalled that someone had referred to one of the men, the tall one with the neatly trimmed beard, as Roland. Last night she'd checked the museum school's fall catalog, and a Roland Phillips was offering several painting classes. His bio stated that he was a graduate of Oberlin and the Massachusetts College of Art. After she had started the coffee and put out the baked goods, it took Faith a while to fill the various counters with the salads, sandwiches, wraps, and other offerings Niki had put together. All that remained was to transfer the soups—Hungarian mushroom and chorizo, cannelini, and kale—to their containers and the chili—vegetarian today—to its.

The group was seated together at one of the large round tables in the center of the café. There was an empty seat. Faith grabbed a cranberry Snapple and sat down.

"Phew. That's done. We're ready for the hoards of 'ghouls' Joseph Sargeant predicted would be coming. I wonder if he was right?" She was deliberately steering the conversation, which had been about the unseasonably warm weather, to what she assumed everyone was really thinking about.

"By the way, I'm Faith Fairchild. I run the restaurant here and cater other events." She put her hand out to Roland Phillips. He shook it, although the way he grasped it suggested he might kiss it. Could Phillips be a French name? Faith wondered.

"I'm Roland Phillips, and I teach painting and drawing at the school."

He released her hand, and Faith offered it to the man next to him.

"Oh, I know who you are. Everybody does. And we love what you've done with the place." He gave her hand a quick shake and gestured around the room. "Too horrible before. The old tum-tum couldn't even take the coffee. Sorry, I'm Glen Elroy. I teach sculpture and some of the clay classes."

"I imagine you all must have seen the paper today," Faith said. "Seeing a photograph should make it seem more real, but in a way I find it even more hard to believe. How could such a thing have happened? And here of all places."

She didn't see how she could send out any more feelers without getting completely tangled up in them.

No one said a word. Several people looked away. Roland's eyes were staring at the ceiling. It was as if she had farted or committed some other embarrassing faux pas.

Finally Elizabeth Canning spoke. "Actually I haven't seen the morning paper. They have a picture of the, um, person?"

"Two computer-generated ones that added hair and eye color. Pale green eyes and red hair."

Glen Elroy knocked his coffee over, sending the steaming liquid cascading over the edge of the table. Roland yelped and stood up, dabbing at his pants leg with a paper napkin. Elizabeth and Kelly quickly supplied more while Glen apologized profusely for his clumsiness.

"Can't take me anywhere," he said, directing his words at Faith.

The subject of the body in the gallery was firmly closed. Channing arrived, hair still wet, and everyone scattered. Faith left, too.

There are no accidents, she reminded herself. What had triggered this one? She was pretty sure it was the words *red hair.*

Not a single person at the table had seen the morning paper? She sincerely doubted that. In fact, there was a great deal about the Ganley that she doubted.

Maddy was coming up the stairs as Faith was leaving. The director had a folded newspaper under her arm. Faith had to step to one side to avoid colliding with her.

"Oh, sorry. I didn't see you."

Maddy had looked understandably drawn and tense at yesterday's meeting. Today she looked worse. The paper slipped out, falling to the floor, where it opened to the front page. Both women bent down to pick it up. Maddy grabbed it first, squashing it, obliterating the photos that had briefly stared up at them. Faith stood up and said good-bye. She'd been face-to-face with Maddy as they both sought to retrieve the paper. The woman looked completely terrified.

Pix was off in a corner catching up on her bookkeeping chores when Faith got back, and Niki was putting together a dessert buffet for a local library event that they were catering this afternoon. The library was honoring patrons who were veterans, particularly a WAVE from World War II who had just published her memoirs. Niki was having fun putting together a Red, White, and Blue buffet. The centerpiece was a Red

Velvet cake (see recipe, p. 388) that she had trimmed with flags. Niki made a mean Red Velvet cake with mascarpone cheese added to the cream cheese frosting. It was almost as good as Norma Darden's at Miss Maude's on Lenox Avenue in Harlem, one of Faith's favorite restaurants. Norma's fried chicken and BBQ were poetry, but aside from the cake—and the banana pudding—it was the restaurant's vegetables that made Faith's mouth water just thinking about them—the collards, rice, and black-eyed peas, plantains and yams. It was time for a trip home. She could certainly use Norma's comfort food now.

"What do you think?" Niki asked, stepping back from her creation.

"I think it's gorgeous and I *know* it's scrumptious," Faith said. She'd been serving it long before it became the current craze in Manhattan. She loved the deep, red mahogany color produced by a judicious amount of food coloring. The subtle chocolately cocoa flavoring of the cake was a perfect match for the rich cream cheese frosting. Niki's variation—substituting half mascarpone for half the cream cheese—wasn't strictly speaking traditional. Faith could never decide which recipe she preferred, and was glad she didn't have to choose. There was world enough and time for all manner of cakes. Red Velvet cake, especially this three-layered one, always reminded her of that wonderful adage, "Too much is just fine."

"May I lick the frosting bowl?" Pix asked, standing up, stretching, and walking toward them. "I bear good news, so I think I deserve it. Despite fewer catering jobs, because of the Ganley, we're ahead of where we were this time last year."

Niki handed her the bowl and a rubber scraper.

"Go for it!"

Faith thought they were doing all right, but it was good to have Pix spell it out.

"So that's the girl," Pix said. She stopped eating and pulled the paper toward her. "She's so young. She looks about Samantha's age. What kind of a world are we living in?" She put the scraper back in the bowl. There was still a lot of icing left.

"What did you think about the meeting yesterday?" Faith asked her. She'd told Niki about it earlier.

"It was hard to get much of an impression. Aside from Lynne Hollister and Joseph, everyone was quiet, whether from shock or guilt I couldn't say."

"That suggests you think one of them killed her," Niki said.

"No. I really can't believe a Ganley trustee would commit murder—oh, I know what you're going to say, Faith. Anyone is capable, even a group of mostly

Yankee bluebloods like that one. What I mean by guilt is that one or more of them have to know who she is, or rather was. She wasn't placed in the museum by accident. There *has* to be a connection with someone here, and they were all gathered in that room yesterday."

Faith nodded. "I agree, but we're no closer to a solution than before. Not that I expected someone to jump up and confess, but I thought there might be some body language. Some sort of clue."

"Lynne, whom I don't really know since she lives in Concord, kept fidgeting, doodling on the pad and fooling with her purse. And she came out with that blunt whodunit statement at the end."

"She seems so self-consciously theatrical," Faith said. "The way she dresses, even the way she walks— as if she expects to be the center of attention."

"So how do you get on this board? You said she was young. Why would she join up with a lot of oldsters from Aleford?" Niki asked.

Faith had talked about this with Patsy. "The board is no longer made up of Aleford oldsters. Maddy has tried to diversify it in terms of race, age, ethnicity."

"But not dollars," Pix interjected.

"True. If you accept a position on the board, except for the seat appointed by the Aleford Board of Selectmen, you have to have a generous amount of disposable income and be prepared to dispose of a goodly amount to the Ganley. But all these people, according to Patsy, are sincerely interested in the mission of the museum, and I quote, 'to showcase contemporary art with a special focus on New England artists, and to educate individuals of all ages.' "

"After I left yesterday," Pix said, "I took Ursula to a lecture at the Massachusetts Historical Society, and on the way into town we talked about the Ganley. Not just the murder, but the museum itself. She pointed out that a great deal of the resentment Maddy faced, and faces, is because Aleford has always thought of the Ganley as *their* museum, their own private institution. You'd be surprised at the number of people who really don't want to increase the museum's attendance. They are happy to keep it just for themselves and don't want outsiders coming into town."

"Same reason they don't fix the damn potholes," Niki said with a wry expression on her face. She'd had two flats on her Mini Cooper this fall alone.

"Exactly," Pix said.

"Did Ursula have anything else to say? What about the board?" Faith asked.

Pix paused. "Not really. We talked a little about Harriett. She's a member of the Historical Society, too, and Ursula had called her to see if she wanted to come with us, but she said she was tired. I told Mother I wasn't surprised what with all this, but Mother said she was. That she had known Harriett all her life and this was the first time she'd ever heard her admit to fatigue."

"She didn't look tired at the meeting," Faith said. "She looked annoyed."

"Well, she usually is," Pix said. "Poor Channing. He's between Mark and Samantha, so when he was growing up I'd seen him around."

"Why do you say 'poor Channing'?" Niki asked.

"He wasn't neglected—far from it. If anything his grandmother spoiled him. The sun has always risen and set on his head as far as she's concerned. She'd been quite the martinet with Channing's father, and you know how that turned out. I think she must have been afraid she'd lose him, too, the way she had his father and grandfather. Potter men had always gone to Deerfield, but Harriett kept her grandson home. He went to BB&N in Cambridge. I remember he asked me if I would speak to her because he wanted to go to Camp Chewonki when he was about twelve. Mark was a CIT and lots of kids from Aleford went. Harriett insisted on day camp here."

"And he's still living at home! I'd have been out of there long ago," Niki said.

Pix smiled. "Haven't you ever heard of a golden cage?"

"I still would have left."

"But Channing hasn't."

"Anything else?" Faith prodded.

"Ursula did say that she had taken a drawing class at the school some years ago. I didn't remember until she brought it up. The teacher was someone named Roland Phillips, and Ursula didn't like him at all. He'd come over and draw on her work, correcting it. She thought he was very full of himself and dropped out."

Faith sighed. Nothing much here, but what had she expected?

The phone rang and Niki answered it.

Faith and Pix heard her say, "I'm not surprised. I'll be right over," before hanging up.

"Speak of the devil, that was Channing himself. He said he's never seen so many people at the museum. We're already out of baked goods and it isn't even lunchtime!"

Joseph Sargeant had been right. It was the equivalent of slowdowns at highway accidents.

"Too bad we didn't think to get bags of Pepperidge Farm Goldfish. We'd be making a fortune. Sorry, that's not funny," Niki said.

"But true. Fortunately we have plenty of muffins, bagels, coffee cake, and cookies. I'll make more while you're gone. Better take the vat of split pea soup and those cheddar rolls from the freezer. If lunch sells out, people will have to content themselves with bread and soup."

Niki was soon on her way, and Faith started assembling ingredients for more muffins.

"I'm sorry to leave you in the lurch, not that I could do anything but stir," Pix said. "I have a dentist's appointment, and it's so hard to get one with Dr. D . . ."

"Say no more," Faith said. The Millers had introduced the Fairchilds to "Dr. D," a woman whose touch was so light and manner so warm that none of them experienced even a hint of dental anxiety when it was time for a visit. But she was very popular, and scheduling an appointment with her and her equally talented hygienist, Ann, was a coup on a par with scoring season Patriots tickets.

Several dozen muffins were on their way out of the oven when the phone rang again.

"Have Faith Catering," Faith said.

"Is this Mrs. Fairchild?"

"Yes, this is Faith Fairchild speaking. How may I help you?"

"I know who she is. The body you found."

Chapter 6

The voice continued. "I'm pretty sure it's Tess. She was my roommate." The voice, which sounded like a young woman's, stopped and Faith heard what she thought was a sob.

"Tell me where you are. I'll come right away," she said quickly.

"It's so horrible. I should be calling the police, but I just can't. I'd have to see her, wouldn't I? Then a few minutes ago I thought of you. I kind of know you."

"Know me?"

"You catered my cousin Stephanie Bullock's wedding a while ago. I was still living in Wyoming. That's where I'm from, but I was in the wedding and everybody was talking about how you were the one who, well, you know . . ."

Faith did know. She had unmasked a merciless killer hours before the ceremony much to her own peril. She remembered the feeling of total unreality she'd experienced at the reception, serving poached salmon with hollandaise when she was supposed to be dead. Tom had taken her straight to their house in Maine after the job—which she'd insisted on completing—was over.

A young girl's face, Stephanie's junior bridesmaid, began to take shape, and then a whole scene popped into Faith's mind. During the rehearsal dinner, the teenager had come into the kitchen and was soon confessing how out of place she felt at this sophisticated Boston Brahmin wedding. Niki had assured her that since the sophisticates were at present throwing dinner rolls at one another, she needn't worry about not fitting in. The girl had shown them a postcard that she was carrying in her evening bag, probably for moral support. It was a reproduction of the painting *Cliffs of Green River* by the late-nineteenth-century artist Thomas Moran. She told them she lived there, close to the spot where John Wesley Powell and his expedition had launched their boats, eventually coming upon the Grand Canyon. And it was just as beautiful today as then, she'd added. Before gathering up her courage to return to her place at the table, she told them her dream was to be an artist, too. The next day Faith had winked at her as she walked down the aisle in the ceremony in Trinity Church and had been rewarded with a grin and wink back.

"You were the bridesmaid who came and talked to us in the kitchen. I'm sorry I don't remember your name," Faith said, while the question she wanted to ask most—"Tess who?"—was echoing just behind her spoken words.

"Sarah. Sarah Newcomb Cummings." She said her name hurriedly. It wasn't what mattered. "Look, can you really come here? I don't have a car, but I guess I could take the T and meet you." Her voice trailed off. She sounded in no condition to take any kind of transportation.

"Of course I'll come. Tell me where you are," Faith said.

Sarah lived on Mission Hill in Boston, and Faith told her she would leave right away. It shouldn't take more than half an hour.

"Mrs. Fairchild? I know I shouldn't say this, but will you promise me not to tell the police until later? I don't think I could bear having them show up without someone here. I keep trying to believe that Tess is dead—murdered—but I can't, and I'm afraid I'd go to pieces if I was alone with them."

Faith promised. There really wasn't any choice if she was going to find anything out. She'd be telling the police, specifically John Dunne, as soon as possible, she reasoned. Besides, he probably knew by now. Tess's face was unforgettable. The number in the paper must be ringing off the hook.

Sarah was in shock and afraid. Her reaction was a normal one. Faith told her to make herself a cup of tea or coffee with plenty of sugar while she waited.

She hung up the phone and checked caller ID, adding Sarah's number to the directions. Bless the phone company for this now indispensable tool. On the way to the car she called Niki, but didn't get an answer. When, oh, when would Aleford admit that it was the twenty-first century and install some more cell towers? Tasteful, discreet, clothed in greenery, but capable of providing actual service? She left a message and told Niki to call her. That something had come up. She didn't need to phone home. Tom had decided to take the holiday off and had loaded his and the kids' bikes for a day on the South Shore, a nostalgic ramble through whatever byways of his youth that remained untouched by the Massachusetts Department of Transportation or developers, culminating in an early dinner at his parents' house in Norwell. Having their father all to themselves for a whole day was a rare treat. Happily, Ben had been sitting in the car with his helmet already strapped on waiting impatiently when Faith had left.

Faith had no difficulty finding Sarah's apartment building on Delle Avenue. Finding a parking place was another matter, but eventually she pushed the button next to Sarah's name and was buzzed in.

An older version of the teenager Faith remembered was waiting with the door open at her apartment. She was much taller, but had the same thick, shoulder-length light brown hair and dark brown eyes. Those eyes were red-rimmed now, and her lower lip was trembling. She was wearing jeans, a turtleneck, and a heavy wool cardigan that she was hugging close to her body.

"Thanks. Thanks for coming." She stepped back, and Faith followed her into a large room—Design Within Reach meets DIY. The sunny space boasted an Eames chair, a leather sofa, a flame-colored area rug, an old steamer trunk serving as a coffee table, floor pillows covered in oriental carpet remnants, and in front of the bow window, a Philippe Starck Ghost chair. Faith was beginning to feel haunted by them. A bookshelf created from cinderblocks and planks of wood leaned unsteadily against one wall. Curtains had been fashioned from sheeting.

Sarah sank onto the sofa. Faith sat next to her. The leather was soft and the pillows filled with down. Not a street or thrift store find.

"I'm sure this has been a terrific shock for you."

Sarah nodded. "I don't usually get the paper. I read the news online, but when I went out to the store this morning, there she was on the front page. Tess. It's so strange. I mean, that a person can be alive one minute and dead the next." Sarah started to cry. She pulled a ragged piece of Kleenex from her pocket, and Faith jumped up in search of a box. There was one on the floor next to a half-empty mug of coffee.

"Thanks," Sarah said, her voice muffled.

It was time to get a little further along.

"Why don't you tell me what you know about Tess? How did you know her?"

They were the right questions. Sarah sat up straighter.

"I came East over a year ago to go to the Massachusetts College of Art. I thought I wanted to be a painter, but I fell in love with photography, and that's what I'm doing." She gestured to several framed prints. "I found this apartment. It was partially furnished, which was a plus, but the rent was too much, so I needed to find a roommate. I put up notices at school and some other places where I knew students would see them, and Tess was the first one to call. She came over right away."

"Hi, I'm Tess Auchincloss. You must be Sarah."

She was so beautiful. Sarah could hardly keep herself from running to get her camera. Tess stepped into the apartment, and a shaft of sunlight struck her hair. It was red—not bright red, but a garnet red shot with gold. Her face was pale, like ivory. Not a single freckle marred the smooth surface of her skin. And her eyes, they kept changing color—now the color of celadon china, then a darker green, like an antique glass bottle. She looked around the room, walked past Sarah into the rest of the apartment, and came back quickly.

"Okay," she said, sitting on the bow window's wide sill. "This will do fine." She laughed and put out her hand to shake Sarah's. "So will you—but we'll have to do something about the furniture."

She left to get her things, saying she'd be back, and did Sarah have a spare key? An hour later the bell rang. Deliverymen struggled up the narrow staircase with an Eames chair complete with ottoman, a soft leather sofa, and a Philippe Starck Plexiglas Ghost chair. Soon after, another store delivered a beautiful rug virtually the color of Tess's hair, unpacked the furniture and arranged it. Sarah was pleased, but a little apprehensive. Obviously Tess had money and planned to entertain at the apartment in style. What would that mean for her? Would she be included or would she be spending more time in the library? The money part was confirmed when Tess arrived a few hours later with Vuitton luggage and an old steamer trunk carried by two extremely good-looking young men. Tess had changed from the jeans she had been wearing before into pencil-leg black pants like Audrey Hepburn wore and a sheer white shirt over a plain camisole. Sarah thought it was the kind of outfit that would look nondescript or like some kind of waiter's uniform on anyone else. She also noticed that Tess wasn't wearing any jewelry, just a Cartier Tank watch. The men left saying they'd catch Tess later, and Sarah offered to help her new roommate unpack, an offer that was promptly accepted. "But first put this in the fridge," she said, handing Sarah a bottle of Dom Pérignon. "Unpacking is thirsty work."

Money yes, parties no. The two men who moved her in and the two who moved her out were the only visitors Tess ever had. Dates would arrive downstairs, but she never invited them up. Sarah would watch her get into a Porsche, BMW, or some other fancy car. There seemed to be a never-ending variety—the same for the men.

"Sarah, let me get you some fresh coffee." The girl had completely withdrawn into herself, stopping abruptly in the middle of talking about Tess.

"Sorry." She shook her head. "I was thinking about the day she moved in. I'm okay."

"When was this?"

"Last September. Over a year ago."

"Why did she move out?" Sarah seemed best with direct questions. Less apt to zone out, Faith hoped.

"We didn't have a fight, if that's what you mean. We never did. She was very apologetic about leaving and insisted on giving me an extra month's rent. Plus she left the furniture she'd bought." She smiled ruefully. "All the expensive pieces. She said if she ever needed them she knew where they were. She was going into a furnished place. I'd gotten a job waiting tables at the restaurant at the Museum of Fine Arts and the tips are good enough that I can swing the rent on my own. Plus I've been selling some of my work."

But Sarah hadn't really answered Faith's question. She tried again.

"Where did she go? Did she stay in Boston? Was she leaving because she was relocating?"

"I don't know. Tess was a very private person. She didn't even get mail here. She had a post office box someplace. I didn't really ask her why she was leaving and she didn't say. I got the feeling she might be moving in with a guy, but we weren't the kind of friends who tell each other everything."

Or anything, Faith thought.

"When did you see her last?"

"Early this month at an opening at Gallery Kayafas on Harrison Avenue in the South End. There was a photographer's work I wanted to see, and it was a First Friday when all the galleries have receptions, so it's like one big party. The place was jammed and we couldn't talk, so we went outside. It was so warm. More like summer than November."

"Did she seem worried about anything?" Something that might get her killed, Faith added to herself.

Sarah shook her head. "No, the opposite. She said she was in a very good place in her life. That a lot of things were going her way, and one in particular was going to be bearing fruit soon. Those were her words, 'bearing fruit.' "

"Was she with someone? She must have had a lot of men interested in her."

"She was on her own that night, but it's true. She attracted men wherever she went. We'd come home from a night out and there would be all these notes and cards in her jacket pockets. She thought it was funny. Everything was funny to Tess. She didn't take life, or herself, seriously. And when you were with her, at least when *I* was with her, you thought she was right. I'm not really shy and don't think I'm hideous, but at first the other students at Mass Art were very intimidating. Everyone seemed so much cooler than I was. Tess helped me see that they were all just as scared and even more so than I was. We'd go to parties or gallery openings and she'd whisper stuff to me about everyone, so that soon I'd be laughing, and even if I didn't believe what she was saying, it made me feel at ease. Of course when you were with Tess, everybody came over to you, everybody wanted to be your friend."

And when you weren't? Faith made a note to herself.

"Was she from Boston?"

"Oh, no! She was a New Yorker. From a very old family. The Auchinclosses, you know, Jacqueline Kennedy Onassis's family? Her stepfather was an Auchincloss, and she was married to JFK at his estate in Newport. Tess was very proud of the connection, but she was estranged from her mother, who was pretty much her only immediate family. Her father, whom she adored, died several years ago, and her mother had remarried—a 'total asshole,' she called him. She didn't have any brothers or sisters, although she had some cousins she liked."

Faith knew about the Auchinclosses, including the author, Louis. She'd ask her sister, Hope, to find out about Tess's branch.

"Was she a student, too?"

"No, not now anyway. She'd been at Barnard for a while, but dropped out. And she'd gone to boarding school, Miss Porter's. She'd tried to break into modeling in New York, but she wasn't tall enough. She thought they wouldn't be so picky in Boston, and she was right. That's what she did for a living, and I think she had money from her father in some kind of trust. She also wanted to leave New York to get away from her mother, who apparently never really loved her. It was so sad. She told me she could never do anything right as far as her mother was concerned. My mother—and father—have been the opposite, encouraging me every step of the way."

Faith's eyes strayed to the wall where the photographs were hanging.

"Some are mine and others are by friends. The larger one is one of Abelardo Morrell's—he's a professor at Mass College and an incredible photographer, one of the big reasons I switched from painting." Faith got up and went over to look more closely. The black-and-white print was deceptively simple, a costume draped against a piece of staging covered with black cloth. It was extremely moving. A dress in waiting. The fabrics created a series of textures and colors. There seemed to be a limitless number of grays in the sheen of the skirt and the shadows of the folds. "It was taken backstage at the Metropolitan Opera. It's a costume from *Figaro*. The one next to it is one of mine. A picture of Tess, kind of my Sally Mann period."

Tess was staring straight into the camera with a child's unselfconscious gaze. Her hair framed her face, and she was sitting in the Ghost chair with her hands around one knee wearing lacey underwear. But the overall effect was not so much sexual as psychological. Tess seemed to be about to impart a secret or perhaps tell a joke. Her lips were slightly parted, and you could see the tip of her tongue. The energy of her mouth was in contrast to the languid pose. She wasn't going anywhere—but she did have something to say. Faith turned away from the photograph.

Sarah's color was better, and she no longer seemed about to break into tears. It was time to tell her that Faith had been the one who'd found Tess and it was time to go to the police.

Faith had decided they should take their chances and go directly to Dunne's office without calling first. With Sarah beside her, it would perhaps pass unnoticed—or at least unremarked upon for now— that Faith was once more in the middle of one of his investigations. They were in luck and the detective was in, coming out to the front desk as soon as he heard why they were there. The office he ushered them into had not changed in all the years Faith had known Dunne. A cliché—something straight from the pages of an unimaginative detective novel. Same gunmetal-gray desk, battered file cabinets, pale green linoleum, and uncomfortable, only slightly padded metal chairs. It boasted two windows, but they were covered by venetian blinds. The half-open dusty slits offered a glimpse of the parking lot and several large Dumpsters whose contents Faith preferred not to speculate on.

Dunne waved to two of the chairs directly across the desk from his. They all sat down. Sarah scraped hers closer to Faith.

"We appreciate your coming forward, Miss Cummings. We've had a number of calls this morning, but no one seemed sure of the victim's last name."

Sarah had given Dunne Tess's full name immediately, and he'd left them briefly. Faith assumed he was setting whatever wheels in motion might be necessary to inform her next of kin—her mother—and start the painstaking police work that would be necessary to trace her final hours, who she might have been with, who might have seen her.

Sarah related the story of how Tess had answered her roommate ad and went on to tell Dunne what she had already told Faith, including her impression that Tess was more than fine the last time she'd seen her only about a week ago.

"And you have no idea where she was living or with whom?"

Sarah shook her head. "I didn't have to forward any mail because of the PO box. I did think once or twice that she'd call to invite me over, but she never did." She looked at Faith, who took her hand. It was cold and slightly damp. "Tess always seemed like a person with chapters in her life. One chapter ended and a new one would start fresh. When I thought about it I guess I thought I was in the chapter that was over and she was on to the next."

Faith noticed that Dunne was letting Sarah talk without interruption. It was what she would have done, too. Sarah's second recitation hadn't provided much new information so far, but with every word Tess was taking on a reality she hadn't had for Faith up to this point. It was still impossible to connect the woman in the photograph Sarah had shown her with the body in the tank. As Sarah herself had put it, how could a person like Tess be alive one minute and dead the next? Somewhere buried in Sarah's words Faith hoped they would find an answer—or at least a direction.

"I wasn't hurt—maybe a little. I found a scarf of hers that I knew she liked a lot—Hermès. It was very expensive and an older one. Maybe it was her mother's. Yes, it was, because she was laughing about it one time when she was putting it on, telling me how she had filched it from her mother's drawer when she was leaving New York. The scarf and one of her mother's Birkin bags.

"I called her on her cell. She told me to keep the scarf. I thought she might ask me to come see her new place, but when she didn't, I tried to make excuses for her—that maybe she wasn't even in Boston. Maybe she was back in New York. It had been exciting to be in her life, and then suddenly I wasn't. But I found out pretty soon that she was in or near Boston, because I'd see her from time to time—once in July on Newbury Street and we had lunch at the Armani Café. Tess liked their desserts."

She looked away from Faith and at Dunne. "I know I'm kind of going off on a tangent, but maybe you'll be able to figure out who did this from what I'm saying, so it's important. The person who killed her is walking around out there." She pointed to the window. "A lot of Tess's life was, well, a mystery. She was a very private person . . ." Her voice trailed off. "I'm sorry . . ." Her eyes were filling up again.

"Miss Cummings, you have been and will be an enormous help. We are much closer now to knowing who did this to your friend. You have nothing to be sorry about."

" 'My friend.' Yes, Tess *was* my friend." She stopped short.

Dunne gave her a moment and then asked, "Can you think of any reason why Tess Auchincloss would have been at the Ganley Museum Friday night? Might she have been meeting someone there?"

"No, I can't think why she would be there. I think it's pretty hard to get to without a car. I've been to some of their shows, but somebody always drove. Mrs. Fairchild said Tess wasn't at the opening. If she had been, she might have stayed for some reason, but . . . it just doesn't make any sense." She looked at Faith, as if, Faith thought, searching for an answer, for reassurance that the universe was still a beneficent place.

The phone on Dunne's desk rang. He picked it up immediately.

"Dunne here."

There was silence as he listened.

"You're sure?"

More silence.

"Get on to the family, then."

He replaced the receiver. The phone, unlike the rest of the office, which looked like a stage set for a Mickey Spillane novel, was brand new.

"Did your friend own a car?"

"No, not that I know of. Why?"

"Do you have a car?"

"No. I don't need one. I can walk to school and work. I take the T everywhere else. I have one back in Wyoming, but thought it would be too expensive to bring it here."

Where was he going? Faith wondered.

"Did you ever see Tess Auchincloss drive someone else's car, or a rental?"

It was the first time he had used her name. She had a full-blown identity now.

"No, but why are you asking me about Tess and cars? The men she dated picked her up or, like me, she took public transportation."

"She didn't have a driver's license. Not here or in New York. We're checking other states now. And we haven't been able to locate her Social Security number, either. Was 'Tess' her full name?"

"That I do know." Sarah seemed to cheer up. "It was because we rented an old Katharine Hepburn movie, *Woman of the Year*, one time and she said she'd been named for the character Hepburn played. Her father loved the actress and the movie. He wanted his 'own little Tess'—those were her exact words. It wasn't short for Tessa or Theresa. She might have a middle name, but I don't know it. Wait! Her luggage was mono-grammed, and the middle initial was an *F*."

Dunne picked up the phone, told the person on the other end to run "Tess F. Auchincloss," and hung up.

"Did she ever mention her mother's married name or where she lived in New York?"

Again, Sarah shook her head. "She didn't like to talk about her mother."

"Okay. You've mentioned she went to Miss Porter's in Connecticut, so there will be a record there and also at Barnard. She modeled locally, so we'll check the agencies. How about her bank? Do you remember seeing its name on her checks? I'm presuming since you were there first, the lease is in your name and she paid you."

"Yes, but she always paid in cash. I don't think she had a checking account. Anyway, I never saw a checkbook."

"Was her credit card Visa, MasterCard, American Express, or something else?"

"I never thought it was odd until now, but she didn't have any credit cards. I just assumed she didn't want to run the risk of maxing them out. She had very expensive tastes."

"So she always paid cash. For everything?"

"Everything. And she always seemed to have enough."

The phone rang again.

"Uh-huh," Dunne said and hung up quickly.

"There's no listing for 'Tess Auchincloss' or 'T. Auchincloss' in any New England telephone directory. And we've checked with the phone company. She didn't have an unlisted number."

Faith broke in. "That's not a surprise. She had a cell and wouldn't need a land line. Most people her age just use their cell phones. Probably Sarah doesn't have a phone in the apartment, either."

"I had it taken out when I moved in. Mrs. Fairchild is right. Most people I know use their cells or PDAs."

"Can you give me Tess Auchincloss's cell phone number?"

"Sure. I have it right here." She dug into her purse and pulled out her phone, pushed some buttons, and said, "617-178-2593."

As Dunne wrote the numbers down, Sarah hit a button on her cell. She had Tess on speed dial. Her face crumpled, and Faith handed her a tissue. Sarah took it, mopped her eyes, hit redial, and handed the phone to Faith.

"Hi, this is Tess. You know what to do. Bye."

It wasn't a particularly distinctive voice. It was devoid of any regional accent, which was what Faith would have expected from a girl brought up if not to the manor born then to the town house or duplex on the

East Side. A pleasant voice, low, but not like Bacall's. Nothing cutesy, just matter-of-fact. "You know what to do." The more she learned about Tess, the more Faith was convinced that the young woman herself knew what to do—until the end, that is.

Sarah Cummings was fine. Faith had insisted on coming up after driving her home. She'd made Sarah a tuna fish sandwich and watched her eat it. Sarah had shown her more photographs of Tess, and Faith had told Sarah the police would probably be asking for them if they didn't turn up a portfolio on file at one of the modeling agencies. "You never shot her in color?" she'd asked, and Sarah said aside from some snapshots that a friend had taken at a surprise birthday party he'd given for Sarah, she didn't have any color pictures of Tess. The friend had e-mailed them to her and she'd pointed to the one that they'd stuck on the fridge. She and Tess were wearing those little cone-shaped kid's birthday hats. Tess's had slipped forward and looked like a unicorn's horn. They were both laughing. Faith asked her if she could print out a copy for her and she had. She'd asked Sarah what they had done for Tess's birthday, and Sarah had admitted that they hadn't done anything, that when she'd asked Tess, that night particularly, when her birthday was, she'd always said the same thing, "Never."

It was a relief to be alone. Not that she wasn't grateful to Faith, but the last minutes before she'd left, Sarah had felt so tired she wasn't sure she could stand up to let her out. But she was fine. All she needed was a nap.

She went into her bedroom, pulled back the covers, and just before she slid between the sheets, she went over to her dresser and took Tess's scarf out. It still smelled like her perfume. A blend she had had made up just for her, she'd told Sarah. It was subtle, but unmistakable—woodsy, spicy, but with an underlying floral scent like jasmine. Tess said it was a *chypre*— French for the island of Cyprus—parfum.

Sarah spread the scarf over her pillow, got into bed, rested her cheek against the silk, and almost instantly fell into a deep sleep.

"She doesn't exist." It was John Dunne. Faith had come back to find Niki gone. She'd left a note on the counter explaining that she was delivering and setting up the dessert buffet while Pix had gone over to the Ganley with the muffins Faith had baked and a load of cookies that Niki had unearthed. It was obviously a record-breaking day for museum attendance—but for a very wrong reason.

"You mean 'Tess Auchincloss' doesn't exist." Faith had come to the same conclusion after calling her sister.

Hope had never heard of her, and she and Quentin traveled in those circles. She'd told Faith she'd ask Quentin and a friend who would have been at Miss Porter's at the same time—Faith had told Hope she thought Tess had been in her midtwenties. When the phone had rung, Faith had been expecting Hope's voice—her sister was very efficient, and when she said she'd get on something right away, she did.

"Were you able to get anything more out of the girl?"

"Sarah?" Faith almost added, "She has a name," but the somber note in Dunne's voice stopped her. He'd come to a dead end. A very dead end.

She told him that aside from the color picture of Tess—she couldn't think of what else to call her even if that wasn't her name. Miss X?—she hadn't learned anything more.

"From everything Sarah has said I believe this was someone who didn't want anyone to know anything about her and went to great lengths to ensure it."

"Can you fax the picture over? I don't want to bother Miss Cummings"—so he did know, of course—"again so soon. She's had a pretty brutal shock."

"Give me the number again."

Faith wrote it down and said, "I'm planning to call Sarah later to see how she's doing. She may have thought of something else."

"She's comfortable with you. Try to find out if she can remember anything that would give us a lead on who this Tess might really be. And what connection she might have with the Ganley. We'll take the new photo out there again and send it to the media and the FBI, then post it on the Internet, which will bring in the crazies and just maybe a lead.

"She was never a student at Miss Porter's or Barnard, and she wasn't listed with any of the modeling agencies in Boston. We went further afield and she wasn't listed with any in New England, either. She had to be living here, since she was seen around town—and so recently. The calls we've been getting are from people who saw her at everything from a storefront poetry slam to the opening of Symphony."

"I just remembered. Sarah said Tess would never tell her when her birthday was, so we don't even have a birthdate."

"It's very hard to disappear. People always mess up and leave some kind of trail—credit cards, banks, jobs. This lady seems to have left nothing."

"Not even her footprints in the sand."

"Now don't you go getting all poetic on me, Faith. This is a murder case."

"I know. Believe me I know."

Faith left work at 4:30 after Channing had brought back the empty containers from the café and helped her wash up. She was glad the museum would be closed, as usual, the next day. Channing was more excited than she had ever seen him, almost manic. It was in marked contrast to his demeanor—and appearance—that morning.

"They were lined up out the door! When we ran out of stuff, I could have sold them the packets of sugar, salt, and pepper! You should have seen it!"

Faith was glad she hadn't, thanked him, and sent him home to grandma.

Tom and the kids weren't back yet. She hadn't expected them. Patsy called and Faith filled her in on the day's events.

"I still don't see how this ties in with the Bearden collage, but it has to," Patsy said. "Was this Tess artistic? Could she have fabricated the fake? Sounds like she was in with the art crowd."

"I don't think so. Sarah would have mentioned if Tess had been a painter. She wasn't in school. I know that. But she *was* part of the art scene and there could be a tie-in there."

They agreed that it didn't make sense to go to the police until they had more information, particularly on the Ganley end.

After she said good-bye, Faith wandered into the kitchen and pulled out some leftover broccoli risotto with pesto to heat up. She poured herself a glass of Rosemount Shiraz—the Australians were producing some great wines—and sat at the kitchen table. She loved her kitchen. It was not the one she'd come to as a bride. That had been designed for someone whose crowning culinary achievement was Welsh rarebit. There had been almost no counter space, some tiny glass-fronted cabinets, a malfunctioning electric stove, a fridge with a freezer that hadn't been defrosted since it had replaced an icebox, and no dishwasher. On the plus side, there was a good-sized pantry and the room itself was big. A large paned window overlooked the backyard, which was lovely in the daytime, but at night with one forlorn fluorescent fixture appeared to be rows of black holes. Faith had drawn from Have Faith's profits to install a Wolf range with a hood, Miele dishwasher, Sub-Zero refrigerator, plenty of recessed lighting, custom cabinets that matched what was there—she'd liked the old ones—and above all, miles of easy-to-clean, white Formica counters with a marble insert for making pastry. A few years ago she'd replaced the Souleiado Provençal fabric she'd originally used, instead covering the chair cushions and window seat with more durable, kid-friendly canvas from a boat supply company. It was bright red. Red. Tess's hair was red. Why had the murderer shaved it off? The killer had to have done it. No woman in her right mind with hair like that would ever get rid of it.

Tess had had good taste. Looking around at her kitchen reminded Faith of the apartment's décor. Contemporary. Tess had been interested in twentieth-century design. Except for the trunk. Whose trunk was it? A piece of glass had been cut to size and placed on top. Tess's idea or Sarah's? Faith reached for the phone. She'd planned to call the girl anyway.

"Hi, Sarah? It's Faith. Faith Fairchild. I just wanted to see how you were doing."

"I'm okay. I mean not okay, but . . ." Her voice sounded sleepy.

"I'm so sorry! Did I wake you up?"

"Oh, no. I was up."

Why was it, Faith reflected, that people always denied being awakened, whether it was 5 A.M. or P.M.? Some vestige of Puritanism that makes it a sin to be asleep—ever.

"I was wondering if that trunk you use as a coffee table was yours or Tess's?"

If Sarah thought the question odd, she didn't let on.

"Tess's. She brought it with her when she moved in, but said she didn't have a place for it when she left."

Faith was kicking herself. A trunk. The kind with labels.

"Could you take a good look and see if there are any labels on it?"

"Like a name and address!" Sarah sounded excited. There was a brief pause as she walked over to examine it.

"There's a decal from the Fontainebleau in Miami Beach. It looks pretty old. And part of a label from the Union Pacific Railroad, but sorry, that's all. No address—or name. Not even initials."

"It was worth a try." Faith was terribly disappointed. She'd envisioned Tess's real name and address in block letters. Dunne said people always mess up, leave a trail, overlook something. Tess hadn't.

She recalled what Dunne had said about trying to connect Tess with the Ganley.

"You're sure you're all right? Is there a friend you can call to spend time with tonight?" Faith wanted to ease into the subject; besides, she was worried about Sarah being on her own.

"I'm going to call my friend. The one who gave me the party."

A boyfriend. Good.

"I know we asked you this before, but if you can think of anything that might tie Tess to the Ganley, please give me a call and I'll let Detective Dunne know." They were partners again. Today had made that clear.

"I will, but other than her modeling for some classes out there, I can't think of anything."

"Tess modeled for classes at the museum?"

"Yes, there and other schools around here. I guess I should have mentioned this before," she said in a very small voice.

Dunne wasn't in his office. Faith left a message for him to call and tried his cell, leaving a message there, too. She had better luck with Charley, who told her he'd get on it immediately.

"And not a peep from any of them," he said in a disgusted tone, adding, "Keep this to yourself now, Faith. You can get me a list of the teachers and what they teach. That's all."

Charley had a fax at home. When she'd discovered that, Faith had felt for the first time that it really was a new millennium. She took the list of the staff and school faculty with their extensions that had come from Kelly Burton in a packet of information about the museum, added what each teacher taught, using the current course catalog as a guide, and faxed it to the chief. Roland Phillips and Glen Elroy were most likely to have used Tess as a model—Roland for his life drawing classes and Glen for the figurative clay sculpture ones.

The kitchen door opened and her family rushed in, cheeks glowing from the day's exercise and eyes sparkling from being with their adored and adoring grandparents.

"Look what Grandpa gave me!" Amy squealed. "It's a real spyglass. Like they used to use in olden times on sailing ships." She held out the brass hand telescope for Faith to examine.

"And he gave me this chess set. It belonged to his dad, my *great*-grandfather." Ben's voice was filled with awe as he set the inlaid wooden box on the table and opened it to form the board, sliding back a panel to reveal the intricately carved set.

Faith kissed her husband. "I take it you had a good day."

"A great day! And Mom sent something for you. They're cleaning the attic."

Faith had heard this many times before, but the fact that Marian and Dick were allowing items to actually leave the trunks and boxes under their eaves was new.

"Be careful, Mom," Amy said. "It's fragile."

Faith unwrapped the newspaper and found a lovely Rose Medallion covered jar that may have held tea leaves at some point. It was beautiful, and she resolved to both thank Marian immediately and ask about its history—one of Marian's yard sale finds or something that had been handed down. Both sources probably long-ago ballast on a China trade clipper ship.

"That was very sweet of your mother. What did you have for dinner? Are you hungry?"

Her mother-in-law, having fed a family of five for so many years, day after day, had quite sensibly given up any pretense to what she called "gourmet meals" some time ago for quick and easy, good, plain fare.

"Baked scrod, boiled potatoes, and green beans with almonds, although, as usual Dad kept taking 'a taste' as she was sautéing the nuts, so they were a little sparse. Then chocolate pudding and whipped cream for dessert. My-T-Fine."

Tom had tried to get Faith to stock boxes of his childhood favorite, but she'd told him there were limits to what she would do, even for love.

"Are you both set for school tomorrow?" she asked. "No last-minute homework?"

Amy said no and Ben looked at the ceiling.

Correctly interpreting the gesture, Faith sent him upstairs, and Amy settled down in a corner of the window seat to examine her new treasure.

"Coffee?" Faith asked.

"Nope. How about a dram of something?"

There was still some Laphroaig scotch left in the bottle that Tom's brother Robert and his partner had brought the last time they came to dinner. Amy was now outside looking at the stars; Tom and Faith moved into the living room. Tom lit the fire. Faith could just barely hear the tapping of Ben's computer keys. Pix had warned her that the homework load wouldn't merely double, but triple when he hit middle school—and Aleford parents wanted it this way, all the better to skip down the yellow brick road to the Ivies. Sixth grade in Aleford used to mean "the dreaded leaf project," which kept students busy the entire semester collecting the requisite examples and writing lengthy reports, all of which had to be bound in "an attractive portfolio." A few years ago a new earth science teacher had cottoned onto the well-known fact that with prior leaf projects floating about, not only from older siblings, but their parents as well, the exercise might not be producing the kind of independent learning Aleford schools were meant to foster. The new project involved an in-depth study of one's own backyard— literally. Students tested soil, made rain gauges and kept track of precipitation, listed and identified every last bit of flora and recorded visits by fauna, excepting *Homo sapiens*. They had to keep a daily log recording all this plus the temperature and make sketches of any changes they noted—the transition from trees fully leafed out to the current bare branches. Ben was keeping his log on the computer, which was permissible, and using a drawing program to make his sketches. Faith was pretty sure that was what he was working on now. She'd go see in a moment. Or maybe a few minutes. It was wonderful to sit with Tom, the fire warming her face, the scotch warming her inside from head to toe, and Tom—warm memories and warm anticipation. The kids had looked tired. They'd fall asleep early.

"Should I put another log on?" Tom asked after a while.

Faith shook her head. He must be tired, too, and she didn't want him to be *too* tired.

"Would you put the glasses in the dishwasher and turn off the kitchen lights? I'm going to check on the kids."

Amy had put herself to bed; clutching the spyglass, she was sound asleep.

Slightly muzzy from the drink, Faith walked into Ben's room without knocking. What was on his computer screen wasn't his big backyard, but a row of pictures, pictures of kids his age. A few faces looked familiar. The screen also displayed some text, which she was too far away to read.

"Mom! Get out! Just get out!" he yelled, plunging the screen into darkness.

"Ben, I will not have you talk to me this way! What was that on your computer?"

"Just get out. It's nothing. And none of your business."

Tom appeared at the door.

"What's going on? Benjamin?"

He was red-faced and looked close to tears.

"I thought you were going to 'respect my privacy' and then *she* comes barging in without even knocking."

"I'm sorry, Ben, but I want to know what you were doing. What kind of Web site was that?"

"*Nothing!* Can't you get it?"

Tom and Faith looked at each other. With Ben in this state they wouldn't get anywhere. Now was not the time. For anything, Faith thought dismally. Now she was tired. The day came crashing down around her.

"Go to bed. We'll talk about this another time," Faith said.

Her son didn't say a word.

"**Hello.** My name is Mrs. Whitman Polk. I'm sorry to bother you, and I'm sure it's nothing, but I promised my children I'd call the police if she wasn't back today."

"What seems to be the problem, ma'am?"

"Well, it's silly, but they're worried about our neighbor's fish. Her apartment is on the floor above ours. I'm sure she has someone coming in to feed them and we just have missed whoever it is, and in any case, can't fish survive for quite a while on their own? As long as they're in water, of course."

The sergeant had started to fill out a report. He put his pen down.

"You have a neighbor who's on vacation, is that it?"

"I don't know if she's on vacation, but she's away. It could be a family emergency or something else. But the fish. The children were in the hall when she came in with them and I suppose they feel protective, like some sort of aquatic rangers—they learn so much about caring for the environment in school these days. She let them name them. She's always very sweet when we run into her, which isn't all that often. Charlie and Goldie."

"And they would be . . . ?"

"The fish. Charlie like the tuna in the ad and Goldie because they're goldfish—very orange goldfish, though."

"And what exactly can we do for you, Mrs. Polk?"

"I know you can't enter her apartment, and it's hopeless to try to get the landlord to ever do anything, let alone something like this. I thought that if I put my son—his name is Tristan—on the phone, you could reassure him about Tess's fish."

The sergeant grabbed for his pen.

"Tess?"

"Yes, that's my neighbor's name. First name anyway. I'm not sure what her last name is. We've always been 'Tess' and 'Lila'—that's my name."

"What color hair does this Tess have?"

"What on earth does that have to do with her fish! If you must know, she has red hair. Very lovely red hair."

Chapter 7

Mrs. Whitman Polk didn't read any Boston papers—only the *New York Times*—and when her husband left her, he'd taken the TV, which she'd planned to get rid of in any case. Much better for the children, who were prodigious readers—which explained why they were so much more advanced than the other children in their classes. Troubling because what was a good mother to do without alienating them from their peers, but the gifted always suffer? Heavy sigh.

Faith imagined the sigh after hearing Charley's almost total word-for-word rendition of the Beacon Hill matron's monologue, as relayed by the desk sergeant. The recitation was occurring in the catering kitchen. He was filling Faith in on the discovery of Tess's last address, but Faith had the feeling this was not the real reason for his visit. This could be to consume some fresh-from-the-oven Red Velvet cupcakes (see recipe, p. 388) intended for the Ganley café—they weren't even iced yet—but he would have had to be clairvoyant to know that. Charley was sharp, and even prescient on occasion, but Faith doubted he had any gifts in the supernatural department. No, it was something else. She bided her time and listened as he explained that he had been in Dunne's office—they were sifting through the responses that had come in online, some sad, many crazy, and none viable—when the call from the Boston police had come through. They sped down Route 2 and had soon arrived at the town house on Pinckney Street.

"The girl lived in the top-floor apartment. The Polks below, then there's a basement apartment that's being renovated. It's empty at present. Dunne's getting on to the building's owner. A management company on the Hill takes care of things. We got their name from Mrs. Polk. She referred to them as the 'landlord.' Anyway, someone from the office came with a key, and we went in. He didn't know anything about the owner, or if he did he was keeping his mouth shut."

Faith knew Pinckney Street. It was the street that divided the desirable sunny south slope of Beacon Hill, which included Mt. Vernon Street, whose addresses Henry James called "the only respectable street in America," from the north slope. Part of Pinckney bordered a small private park, Louisburg Square. She pictured the house where Tess had lived as one of those lovely early-nineteenth-century brick Greek Revivals, perhaps boasting some of the Hill's famed purple panes, the result of the sun's rays on the manganese dioxide used to form the glass. From what Sarah had said, and Tess's taste in furniture and fashion, though, Faith wondered how such a "swinging single" had ended up in such a staid location.

"Had to take Mrs. Polk off to Mass General. She took a nasty turn when she heard the news, so I didn't get into the apartment for a while. It's small, and what with all the guys doing what needed to be done, I was about to leave when John said to have a look."

Faith shoved another cupcake his way.

"Nice place. Nice stuff. All antiques. Cost a pretty penny from the look of things, and you know what those rents are like. The whole setup was running her a lot each month. But here's the thing."

He paused and looked straight at Faith.

"She cut her own hair. Shaved her own head. There was a thick braid lying on top of the mantel in the living room. Tied with a ribbon at each end. In the bathroom, there was hair in the wastebasket, clippings from a shaver. The shaver was on the sink counter. They're checking it for prints, but everything in the place was neat as pie. No one held her down to give her the haircut."

He took a bite of the cupcake. Most of it disappeared.

Faith was stunned. Why would Tess shave her head? She thought of a few other baldies: Sinead O'Connor, but that was years ago and some kind of religio-political act; and Samantha in *Sex and the City*, but her hair was falling out because of chemo. Faith was sure Tess didn't fall into either of those categories, so why? She wanted to see the braid. She wanted to see the apartment.

"Did anyone have any theories about it? Maybe the neighbor knows?"

Charley shook his head. "Not a clue. Dunne got onto MGH and she'd been sedated by then, but not completely out of it. The last time she saw Tess, which was Thursday afternoon, the young woman had a full head of hair. Spent the night in her apartment, too, because Mrs. Polk could hear her moving around."

"Alone?"

"Pretty sure not alone, but she doesn't know who was with her."

"What about the fish?"

"Oh, they were goners, all right. Ordinary goldfish, like the kind from the dime store. These weren't in one of those glass bowls, though."

Faith knew what Charley was going to say.

"They were in something that looked like the piece in the show, right?"

"Yup. Right down to the turquoise-blue water. Got some milk to go with these?"

It took another cupcake and a refill of milk before Charley got around to the real reason he'd come. Faith had been grateful, but suspicious at the amount of information he'd been sharing so freely. Even with her old friend Charley, it was usually tit for tat.

"We went back to the Ganley with the new picture."

Dunne had faxed it to the chief so he could show it to the staff. Sarah had been cut out and Tess's party hat removed. The detective wanted to be sure none of them had seen her at the opening of New England Rocks! or any other Ganley events. Nobody had.

"Pretty much everybody connected with the school remembered seeing her around, and two of the teachers, Phillips and Elroy, had used her as a model for a few of their classes. But not this last semester. Maddy Harper says she never saw her, and only one of the trustees had—Jack Winston, but not at the Ganley. At some art thing in town."

"This suggests that she didn't have anything to do with the museum except for the modeling," Faith said. "The school is housed in separate buildings, so she may never have been to anything in the main part of the Ganley."

"That's what John and I think, too, except . . . well, we'd like you to keep your eyes and ears open. A couple of the people who claim they've never seen her were very quick to say so and very definite."

"Too quick and too definite?"

"Maybe. Now, we don't want you to do anything except let us know if anything strikes you. Don't be going off and asking a lot of questions yourself. However, you're there; we're not."

Faith had heard this sort of warning before, if not from Charley then from Dunne. The murder had occurred in the early hours of Saturday morning. It was Tuesday, and aside from finally identifying the victim and locating her most recent place of residence, they didn't have anything—not even her real name.

The phone rang. Charley had been about to leave. He'd stood up and reached for the heavy Hudson's Bay wool jacket he donned when the temperature dropped below thirty degrees. He sat back down, jacket in hand.

"Have Faith Catering, Faith Fairchild speaking."

It was Trisha Phelan, Scott's wife. Faith listened, told her not to worry, she'd be right there, and hung up.

"Are you and Dunne out of your minds!" She was furious. "Did you know that Scott was going to be taken in for questioning?"

Charley had the grace to blush very slightly.

"We talked about it, but nothing was definite."

Faith was grabbing her coat and purse. She, Scott, and his wife were the only ones who knew Scott was alone in the museum that night. Except for the murderer, that is.

"Come on, Faith. We got a call. We needed to check it out."

She was holding the door open for him to leave, so she could lock up.

"I'll follow you," he said.

Faith reached Dunne's office in Framingham well before Charley and was taken to the detective lieutenant's office immediately. The only person in the room who did not seem to have cartoonlike steam billowing from his ears was Scott. He stood up and pulled a chair over for Faith to sit on.

"Why didn't you tell us that Mr. Phelan was not only the last person out of the museum on Friday night, but also alone there for a considerable period of time?"

"I think that's obvious!" Faith waved her hand around the room. "I knew if I mentioned it, this is exactly what would happen, and you wouldn't look for the real killer. Besides, you never asked me."

"Mr. Phelan's well-rehearsed answer as well. Damn it, Faith. The fact that the two of you didn't mention it makes him look all the more guilty."

"What do you mean, 'all the more'? He's not one iota guilty!" Faith wasn't sure that was the correct way to phrase what she meant, but it's what came out. "He's never laid eyes on the girl. What possible motive could he have!"

Scott had been watching the two of them go back and forth, a spectator at a Ping-Pong match, his face expressionless. Just someone keeping score.

"Do I need a lawyer?" he asked.

"Do you think you need a lawyer?" Dunne said.

"Don't answer that! They always say that." Faith stood up and walked close to Dunne's desk. She leaned over, trying to decipher the upside-down words on the file in front of him. "Are you charging him with anything?"

"You've been watching too much TV or reading too many mysteries," Dunne said, closing the folder. "Believe me, I have no hidden agenda here. We are not charging Mr. Phelan. It was merely a simple question."

"And he's only here to assist the police in their inquiries, I suppose," Faith shot back at him.

"Sit down, Faith," Scott said quietly. "To answer your question, no, I don't think I need a lawyer. You answer mine and we can start talking. If you don't object, I'd like my employer to stay. As you know, she and I go back a long time."

"And so does he." Faith pointed at Dunne in a "j'accuse" manner.

Scott smiled. It was a thousand-watt Tom Cruise smile without any of the star's nuttiness. "Let the man answer."

"I don't think you need a lawyer, although of course I have to add 'at this time.' Just tell me what happened Friday night, okay?"

Scott went through the entire evening, ending with his firmly closing the back entrance at the museum. He hadn't seen another car—or person—anywhere on the Ganley grounds.

"But you have all this on the surveillance tape. That's how you got on to me, right? Except"—he looked puzzled—"why did it take you guys so long to haul me in?"

Dunne looked grim.

"I can answer that," Faith said. "The Ganley's surveillance is nonexistent. The tapes in the cameras haven't been replaced in years—that's if the cameras are even operational."

John Dunne was looking at her in a speculative manner. "You seem to have learned a great deal about the inner workings of the museum in your short time there. Care to tell me how you came by this information?"

Isn't Scott the one getting the third degree here? Faith almost said, annoyed with herself for shooting her mouth off.

It was Scott who came to her rescue. The smile was gone, and he was frowning deeply. "Only three people knew I was there alone late, and none of them would have mentioned it to you. How is it that you got on to me?"

Dunne never looked uncomfortable, even when—in Faith's opinion—he should. Charley had said there had been a call. She was about to say so, should have said it before, when Dunne answered.

"A phone call."

"A phone call?"

"From whom? You're not saying, because you don't know. Anonymous, right?" Faith said. Aleford had its band of stalwart rumormongers, led by Millicent herself, but they were open about the source of whatever information they decided to impart—proud of their encyclopedic, insider knowledge. Not for Miss

McKinley the handkerchief stretched across a phone or the mouthful of peanut butter.

Scott shook his head. "It doesn't matter, really. There's no way I could have had time to go off and kill the girl, bring her body back to the Ganley, dump her into the tank, and been home thirty minutes after Faith left. Unless you believe that the *two* of us plotted to off a complete stranger, shave her head, and make her a mermaid."

"Your wife will verify the time you arrived home, I'm sure," Dunne said dryly.

"My wife and the babysitter," Scott said.

Faith glanced over at him, but kept her mouth tightly closed this time. Trisha had left early to take the sitter home. Faith remembered Scott's quip about the lengths they would go to keep the girl happy and willing to work for them.

"Boyfriend troubles and my wife has a very sympathetic ear. When I got home the two of them were having a cup of tea in the kitchen, and Trisha had just managed to get Amber to the 'all men are pigs' stage before moving to 'more fish in the sea.' Strike that. Don't want to be thinking of fish and any kind of sea now."

Waves of relief washed over Faith. She knew what she was feeling and how it was defined, but despite the reference, this watery image was a welcome one.

But who had made the call?

"**Don't you** have somewhere to go? Little ones to tend to? Banquets to cater?"

"Was the call local?"

"Phone booth in Boston. Right by the Common."

"It was the murderer. He saw Scott leave. Was watching the museum and waiting for his chance to deposit the body in the tank. It must have been in something. Scott says he didn't see a car, but you can park outside the grounds and come in on any number of trails. You should look to see if there are any marks from some kind of cart. They all have those big two-wheeled garden carts in Aleford to move their compost heaps around or stack wood in."

"We've gone over the museum grounds and surrounding area, but unfortunately our job was hampered by the rain early Saturday morning. Not a heavy downpour, but enough to obliterate any traces from a cart or other form of conveyance."

"What about her apartment? Aside from the hair. Any books? People put their names, real names, in books. Or tuck letters, postcards inside."

"We're still going over the place, but nothing so far. There are a few books, but the young lady's reading material tended toward fashion magazines."

"Will you let me go in once it's unsealed? Remember, I knew about the clothes and you didn't." She was about to add that Dunne owed her for putting Scott through this ordeal, but decided not to go there, since it would bring up the question again of why she hadn't mentioned that Scott was the last to leave the museum.

"I'll think about it."

"And I'll think about letting you and Charley know what I overhear at the museum."

"No need to get snotty about this. I've thought about it, and when it's unsealed, I'll take you in."

Faith pulled on her coat, put out her hand, and they shook.

Faith got home just before the kids were due back from school. Tom's mother wasn't the only one who could have cookies waiting, she thought, and took some oatmeal cookie dough from the freezer. The recipe made thin, crispy nutlike cookies. The secret was in the generous amount of butter called for. Julia would have loved it.

The phone rang as she was walking over to preheat the oven. Normally the sound was one she greeted with anticipation. These days it triggered apprehension. The caller ID showed that it was the middle school, and apprehension immediately became alarm.

"Hello?"

"Mrs. Fairchild? It's Mr. Danson."

Mr. Danson was the vice principal. It wasn't the nurse. Ben was alive and well, but Faith's heartbeats didn't slow appreciably. Mr. Danson was in charge of scheduling—and discipline.

"Ben has been involved in an altercation with another student. He's here in my office and I'd like a parent to come over right away, if possible, so we can clear this up."

"An altercation? A fight? Ben's been fighting?"

Ben had never been in a fight in his life to Faith's knowledge. The whole thing was as alien as if Mr. Danson had said that Ben was tap-dancing on the school roof. No, that might be in the realm of possibility. This wasn't. She quickly became aware from the dead silence that the vice principal was waiting for an answer.

"His father is out at the VA hospital. It's the day he spends as chaplain there, but I can come. I just have to wait until my daughter's bus gets here. It won't be long."

"Good. I look forward to seeing you shortly. Good-bye."

"Good-bye."

Faith wasn't looking forward to seeing him—or her son.

She put the dough back in the freezer, put her coat on, and waited for Amy, who came running across the yard and into the kitchen a few minutes later. When Faith told her she had to go up to Ben's school and no, it wasn't because he missed his bus, Amy's eyes widened.

"Why? What's happened?"

It would come out eventually, Faith decided. "He's been in a fight with someone." She had a sudden thought. "He hasn't mentioned anything to you about having problems with another student at school, has he?"

Amy looked away. "Not really."

Faith moved to the door. She had to get going. She'd talk with Miss Amy later. Obviously her daughter knew more about what was going on with Ben than she was saying.

Ben was sitting on one of the benches outside the main office. The halls were empty and had that peculiar after-school smell of floor wax and sweat. The bulletin board behind him was covered with the same kinds of inspirational posters that had graced the bulletin boards at his elementary school. There were three of them: the ubiquitous and maddening WHEN LIFE GIVES YOU LEMONS, MAKE LEMONADE, the mystifying NO NEVER COULD, and worst of all, especially for the poor kitty dangling from the high bar, HANG IN THERE!

Did a student exist anywhere in the U.S. who'd glanced at these and thought, "Gosh darn it! I will get that A in math, break the school record for the mile, *and* raise a million dollars from my paper route to give to the poor!"? She walked in front of her son.

"What's going on?" she said.

He stood up. He looked very small. Given that both his parents were tall, as were the grands, once Ben hit a growth spurt, he'd join those of his classmates for whom this longed-for event had already occurred. At present, he was profoundly dissatisfied with his height and always made up for the as-yet-missing inches by standing very straight. But he looked small now. His shoulders were hunched over and his chin was on his chest. He'd had a bloody nose. She could see the crusted remains. Much as she longed to give him a hug—he looked so wretched—she decided to wait until she had all the facts.

"What happened?" She repeated the query.

"Nothing," Ben said.

Before she had a chance to probe further, and she intended to probe *much* further, Mr. Danson stepped out of the doorway.

"Good, you're here, Mrs. Fairchild. Perhaps you and Benjamin would like to step into my office." It was not a question.

Sitting in one of the chairs placed opposite the vice principal's desk, Faith realized that this was fast becoming an all too frequent position. Danson was occupying the power seat, the one intended to intimidate, that Dunne had assumed earlier. She was back in middle school herself trying to explain to her headmistress why she was tardy so often when her sister—living in the same apartment—never was.

Mr. Danson made a tent with his fingers. His hands were huge.

"I've heard Joshua's side, Benjamin. Now I want to hear from you. Tell me what was going on."

"Joshua? Josh?" Faith blurted out. "Josh Walker is Ben's best friend."

Mr. Danson's eyebrows rose. "Rolling around on the floor in the boys' locker room after school while a group of classmates are shouting, 'Fight, fight,' is not how best friends normally behave. Now, Ben, what do you have to say?"

"It was an accident."

"An accident?"

"Yes. We tripped over each other and kids thought we were fighting, but we weren't."

"Hmmm. An accident?" Mr. Danson's expression was easy to read: "If I buy this one, I'll bet you've got a bridge in Brooklyn up for sale, too."

"Yes," Ben said.

Faith looked at her son. She knew the tone. No one was going to get anything more out of him. His mouth was clamped shut, and he was looking at the floor.

Mr. Danson wrote something on a piece of paper and stood up, looming over mother and son.

"We do not tolerate this kind of behavior at Adams Middle School. I seriously advise that whatever is going on between these two 'best' friends get straightened out immediately. In the meantime, both will serve a week of in-school suspension."

Faith wasn't sure she knew what that was.

"Could you explain to me what this means?"

"We've found that suspending students is counterproductive. For some it's a welcome vacation, in fact. In-school suspension means that miscreants report thirty minutes before school for detention, are escorted to their academic classes, and spend every other part of the day in detention, including forty-five minutes after school. They may do their schoolwork, of course, but are allowed no other diversions. We don't make them wear orange jumpsuits, but it's not pleasant."

It was clear why this man's job was handling discipline. Faith hadn't done anything, and she found her stomach in knots. Miscreants? Orange jumpsuits? Where had the man trained—Walpole?

"I understand." She nodded.

"See you bright and early tomorrow morning, Benjamin." The interview was over.

As they walked out of the building, Faith was—for once—at a total loss for words. Ben fighting with Josh? With a few well-chosen phrases the vice principal had conjured up the entire picture of what had occurred in the locker room, and it wasn't a pretty one.

"Did you hurt Josh?"

Ben shook his head.

"I can see you had a nosebleed. Are you hurt anywhere else?"

Ben shook his head again.

The two boys were the same size and not exactly Rocky Balboas. Their biceps were more suggestive of linguine al dente than iron. It was something to be thankful for in all of this.

They met Ben's English teacher in the parking lot. She was struggling to open her car door without dropping her books and papers. Ben stepped forward to rescue the precarious load.

Not totally gone, Faith thought, grateful for any sign of the Ben she thought she knew.

"Thank you," she said, and turning to Faith, added, "I'm so sorry to hear about your father-in-law. Take all the time you need, Ben, to get your book report in."

"It's almost done. I'll have it to you by class tomorrow."

"That's good—and thanks again for the help." She slid into the driver's seat and was backing out before Faith could say anything such as asking her what might be wrong with Tom's hale-and-hearty father.

She looked at her son. "Could things get any worse?" was writ large on his face.

"We'll talk at home," Faith said, fearful of what might come out of her mouth before she could stop herself. She was furious with him.

Ben's new schedule was an annoyance for everyone, since it meant his father or mother had to drive him to school early and pick him up late. They could make him walk the five miles, shades of neither of their childhoods trudging lengthy journeys through blizzards, but it would be too cruel. Faith was impressed by Mr. Danson's obvious strategy. Making the student's punishment as inconvenient for the parents as for the child really brought the infraction home. Faith dropped Ben off with a curt, "I'll see you later." "Don't you *ever* do anything like this again" was unnecessary this morning. Both she and Tom must have said it twenty times the night before in what she was forced to concede were fruitless efforts to get through to their son. She'd also asked him, as soon as they had gotten home, "For my information, what exactly have you been telling your teachers is wrong with Grandpa?" He'd mumbled that it was only the one teacher, that the assignment was dumb, and that he'd just said his grandfather, his dad's dad, was sick, nothing specific. "You couldn't say the dog ate your homework like everybody else?" Faith had retorted and had gone on from there. She'd left a message on Tom's cell with the particulars, so he picked up where she left off when he came home. They'd always thought of Ben as basically truthful, and this was a shocker. After he'd gone to bed they debated about making him tell his teacher he'd lied, but he was facing so many consequences that they decided they'd deal with it by grounding him at home, adding on to the sentence he was already serving. At this rate it could be June before he was free. They were afraid, too, that given the way word spreads in a school, as elsewhere, Ben would be a marked man among the faculty and staff for the rest of his years at Adams. They told themselves this was a one-time error in judgment.

It was a relief to be at work, thought Faith. Niki had delivered the food to the Ganley and helped Channing set up. Now Faith and she were getting ready for the rest of the week. Besides the café, they had a bat mitzvah and a bridal shower next weekend. Not a heavy load. Bookings were down, as they were for the other caterers Faith knew—the ones who would admit it. She was happy to have the museum job.

"You know he really is an amazing artist."

"Channing?"

"Yes. He brought his portfolio to show me. That's what took me so long."

"What's his stuff like?" Faith was picturing School of Heavy Metal meets Salvador Dalí.

"Nothing like what I expected. Traditional. Some pastel landscapes. A lot of pen and ink sketches. There was one of an old moss-covered stone wall I really loved. Just the wall floating on a large sheet of paper. It made you look at it harder than if it had been part of a larger landscape, or on a smaller piece of paper. And figure drawings—some charcoal and others pastel."

"So for once a grandmother's claims to genius may be right."

"I don't know about genius, but he's very good and is only going to get better with age. Like a fine wine." She laughed. "Anyway, he's been drawing all his life, he said. I think he must have had a pretty lonely childhood in that big house, plus this Harriett sounds very controlling. Art was an escape—something she couldn't monitor. Yet also something she wouldn't put a stop to."

Faith was measuring heavy cream for the shrimp and corn chowder they'd be featuring at the museum tomorrow. She'd add just a hint of curry spices to give it a little kick.

Listening to Niki's analysis, Faith commented, "You're going to be a very good mother—whenever." As she spoke, the thought that she might not be doing such a great job on that front right now floated in and out of her mind. Earlier she'd told Niki about Ben's fisticuffs, and her assistant had offered some sage advice: "Find out who's replaced Josh." Faith had immediately thought of the boy Ben had been with at the soccer game.

"'Whenever' being the operative word here." Niki was folding layered phyllo dough like a flag around a teaspoon of ricotta and prosciutto. The flakey triangles froze well, and with the more traditional spinach and feta fillings plus a mushroom mixture, would be making the rounds at both events this weekend. "Thirty is still a speck on the horizon, like New Jersey in that Saul Steinberg *New Yorker* cover. I want to get used to being married for a while. Knock wood—because you can imagine how many 'I told you so's' my mother would hurl at me, accompanied by the dreaded finger shake—I don't see why I should have any trouble getting pregnant. I've spent all these years trying *not* to, so when I get around to it I'm bound to be Fertile Myrtle."

"Who's 'Fertile Myrtle'?" Patsy Avery walked in. She was dressed for work. She often stopped by on her way into town for a quick cup of coffee. Faith had a feeling that today, after what had been happening at the museum, her friend was here for more than a caffeine fix.

There was an awkward moment of silence. Niki, too, knew how hard—and long—the Averys had been trying to conceive. Patsy herself filled the empty air.

"It's okay, Niki. If you're pregnant, I'm happy for you. I'm happy for *anybody* who can manage it. I stopped crying at the Pampers ads on TV a year ago."

"I'm *not* pregnant. We were just talking about my mother's campaign for grandchildren."

Faith handed Patsy a mug of coffee and put a plate with a warm cranberry orange scone on it in front of her.

"I know you've been married for less than a year, but don't wait too long. If you want kids, go for it as soon as possible. At least see a doctor and make sure that putting it off isn't going to mean never."

She took a gulp of coffee, and Faith could see her eyes were teary. It wasn't an ad for diapers with all those adorable babies, but Niki's words that had been another reminder of the Averys' infertility. Faith had read that next to cancer, couples went to the most lengths—and expense—to find a "cure." She gave Patsy a quick hug, Niki nodded solemnly, and they changed the subject. First Faith filled Patsy in on Ben. Patsy worked with juveniles, and she, too, weighed in with some sound advice.

"In adolescence kids are constantly reinventing themselves, influenced by the media, but mostly by peers. You need to find out who this new Ben is, who or what he's modeling himself on, and most important, how comfortable he is with it all."

"I know we're not," Faith said.

"Yeah, but he may like himself just fine."

Patsy had come to ask Faith what was going on with the investigation. The police had not been in touch with Patsy, except to show her the new photograph, and Maddy had said that was the only contact she'd had, too, when Patsy called her. If the director knew anything more she wasn't sharing it. Faith told her about Scott, and Patsy said, "They had to check him out, but the trail is definitely getting cold. Who identified the body, by the way? The roommate?"

"Fortunately Sarah Cummings didn't have to—she really, really didn't want to go through that, and who could blame her—because the police got on to the

Polks. They lived in the same building—the wife and kids still do. Mr. Polk didn't move out until July, so he'd seen Tess and could make a positive ID."

"What about this guy? Tess moves in, his marriage breaks up, and he moves out? Coincidence?" Niki said.

"Dunne thought of this, too, but Charley said Mr. Polk's alibi is as ironclad as they come. He was in China at that hour addressing a trade convention. He's at MIT's Sloan School of Management. I think that's why he was so willing to cooperate. There was no way he could be involved. Although apparently anybody who's met his soon-to-be-ex-wife wonders why he stuck around for as many years as he did."

Patsy got up to leave. "So what's next?"

"I get to see the apartment. When I returned from the debacle at Ben's school, Amy had left a note on the table that Mr. Dunne—spelled 'Done'—had called and said I could meet him today in Boston at eleven. They'd had a nice chat apparently. I wasn't to call him back, and I'd know what he meant." Faith pictured the note. Amy had very precise handwriting, as if she drew each letter separately. Ben's was an illegible scrawl. They'd worried about this until his first-grade teacher pointed out he'd never have to attempt more than his signature and promptly started teaching him to "keyboard." Not "type." At the time, Faith had felt very old. She'd had a class called "penmanship" at school, and they'd used fountain pens—the kind she saw in flea markets and antique shops now.

Detective Lieutenant John Dunne was unable to escort Faith to Tess Auchincloss's apartment—that was the name the management agency had been given, and until Faith heard it wasn't the real one, it was the name she used when she thought about the girl. A uniformed officer accompanied Faith inside, taking a seat by the door and telling her he was in no rush to be someplace else. Faith got the message—light duty, something that didn't happen all that often and, when it did, something to stretch out as long as possible.

The apartment on Mission Hill had been tastefully furnished, albeit sparsely. In contrast, this apartment was Aladdin's cave. The wood floors were covered with jewel-toned Orientals. Heavy silk damask drapes framed the living and adjoining dining room windows, the tasseled tiebacks pooled in studied disarray on the floor. There were carved marble fireplaces in both rooms. Someone had selected the furniture with an eye for style *and* comfort. The only indication that anything was amiss was the fingerprint powder left on the polished surfaces of tables, a lovely Queen Anne sideboard, and a Victorian lady's desk that had been placed in front of one of the windows overlooking Louisburg Square. A quick glance at a large bookcase inlaid with an intricate design of flowers and vines revealed Tess's interest in art. The books were expensive ones—Annie Leibovitz's *A Photographer's Life* and Joel Smith's *Saul Steinberg: Illuminations*. There were a few pictures on the walls—nineteenth-century landscapes and a small still life of fruit done in the manner of the seventeenth-century Dutch painters. A large Rose Medallion Chinese export bowl graced the sideboard—Faith thought of the piece Marian had just given her and how much her mother-in-law would have admired, and coveted, this example.

She sat on the couch, sinking into the cushions, and stared at the fireplace with its precise stack of logs, brightly polished brass fender, and gleaming tools. So far the apartment was a beautiful space, but an impersonal one. She drew a breath and thought she could smell a lingering fragrance, one similar to Faith's favorite perfume, Guerlain's Mitsouko, a chypre. It was the only hint so far that someone had actually lived here. Dunne had mentioned fashion magazines. They weren't on the coffee table in front of the couch. There was nothing on the coffee table except the powder the police had used that Faith knew from experience was a pain to get off.

She got up and went into the kitchen through one of the doors in the dining room. It was small, but must have been recently updated. All the trends were represented—granite countertops, stainless steel appliances, a small refrigerated wine closet, shiny deep red lacquered walls and a black-and-white-checkerboard marble tile floor. The frosted-glass cupboards were filled with expensive china, glassware, and cookware. None of it looked as if it had ever been used. The dishwasher was empty, unless the police had removed whatever was in it as evidence. But of what? Tess went in for chardonnays, good ones, and stocked plenty of champagne, particularly Perrier-Jouët in the Art Nouveau bottles. There was a container of half-and-half in the fridge, a container of Breakstone's whipped cream cheese, a lemon, and some Odwalla orange juice. The freezer boasted Starbucks coffee beans, a package of plain bagels, and a loaf of Iggy's seven-grain bread.

Tess was obviously no cook. But she did eat breakfast.

A small pantry closet held a few cleaning supplies, some Warholian cans of tomato soup, a package of Carr's water biscuits, and fish food. Faith didn't expect to come across the remains of the fish in their container and so far hadn't seen a place where the objet d'art cum pets would go. There was a broad sill at the kitchen window. Perhaps there. How close a replica had the tank been to the one at the Ganley? If an intentional duplicate, it was macabre. The murderer giving Tess a gift of her tomb. She shuddered.

Faith had pinned all her hopes on the bedroom, leaving it, and the adjoining bath, to last. Everything was white—the silk canopy draped above the king-sized bed, the spread, the pillows, the carpet, the chaise longue with the fashion magazines tucked neatly in a hanging pocket, and the long muslin curtains at the window—a curiously old-fashioned look for an other-wise early-Hollywood starlet bower, complete with Art Deco dressing table and mirror. It was here that Faith at last found an indication that Tess had occupied the space. The cut-glass Lalique scent bottle contained her signature fragrance. And one of Sarah's photographs of Tess had been framed in silver and occupied pride of place next to a sterling dresser set. It was a head-shot, like a publicity still. Tess looked straight into the camera's lens, her generous mouth closed, but curv-ing slightly upward as if she were about to smile more broadly. Could someone have such flawless skin and could eyes sparkle like this in a photo that hadn't been retouched? Faith couldn't see Sarah doing that and was stunned anew by the beauty of this remarkable face. The picture was a black-and-white print, but somehow

it managed to suggest Tess's deep auburn hair—hair
that surrounded her face in a nimbus. She put the photo
down with a feeling of unbearable sadness.

The bathroom contained a deep oval tub, steam
shower, toilet, bidet, and an elegant sink that looked
more serviceable as a fountain than a place to brush
one's teeth. There was no medicine cabinet, but a small
faux-finish malachite chest held towels, soaps, sham-
poos, and the like—plus a generous supply of condoms.
The whole apartment had felt like a love nest from the
moment Faith walked in. A study in perfection for a
mistress who was herself a study in perfection.

All that remained was Tess's closet, and upon opening one of the built-in drawers Faith could see why the
young woman hadn't needed to go back to her earlier
apartment to fetch a Hermès scarf. She had them here
by the dozens, also Missonis and Roberto Cavallis.
Either or both Tess and her lover had a shoe fetish.
There were dozens of pairs ranging from Christian
Louboutins to Alexander McQueens—all works of
art in and of themselves with dizzyingly high heels.
The Birkin bag Sarah had mentioned was here, along
with plenty of Tod's and Lanvin. Faith was sure they
had been thoroughly searched, but opened several at
random. They were stuffed with tissue to keep their
shapes, nothing else. Faith started in on the hanging

garments. Again there was nothing from H&M. Tess was going in for Shanghai Tang in a big way. Also Dolce & Gabbana. Some vintage stuff—Chanel and Balenciaga. There was something odd, though, and something she bet the police hadn't picked up on. Many of the labels had been cut out—and this was a woman who shopped labels. She opened one of the larger drawers. It contained Tess's lingerie. Faith had been envious before, and now as she examined the silken contents, she was totally jealous. She recognized La Perla, Vera Wang, and others, but again the labels had been neatly snipped off. She had a sudden thought and stepped out of the closet to call Sarah. She was home and had the answer Faith had begun to suspect.

"Tess had a very delicate complexion. She was constantly looking for new moisturizers. It drove her crazy to have any sort of tag next to her skin."

They talked a moment more. Sarah asked how the investigation was going, and Faith could hear the disappointment, and fear, in Sarah's voice once Faith said, "Slowly."

After hanging up with Ms. Cummings, Faith left a message about the tags on Dunne's machine. They were zero for zero now. The killer hadn't sought to hide Tess's real identity by shaving her head and removing the labels from her clothing. But, Faith added, picturing the rows of shoes and bags a few feet away, both of these items had been taken. Tess would certainly not have gone barefoot on a night like that—or probably anytime except on the beach—and she would never have left home without a signature bag.

She went through the dressing table, the closet, and the bathroom drawers again. Tess had very expensive tastes, but the only jewelry Faith turned up was a diamond Piaget watch and a David Yurman bracelet. Did she have a safe deposit box at some bank? Everything about her suggested that men showered her with diamonds. Where were they? It was another question for Sarah—the question of Tess's lack of bijoux. Sarah the roommate. So far the person who knew her best. Sarah the roommate. What had their relationship been like from Tess's point of view? Sarah was adoring—or so it seemed.

Wandering back to the dining and living rooms, Faith felt unsatisfied. She was not much further along than she had been when she arrived.

"Just a few minutes more," she told the officer.

"Take your time," he said.

She opened the drawers in the sideboard. Christofle silver, some linens. The desk had been emptied—or was empty. Dunne had said they had checked all the books. No names on the flyleaves, no missives hidden inside. She was about to give up when she took a closer look at the drawing to the left of the bookcase. A Degas reproduction surely chosen with Tess in mind. A young woman was stepping into her bath—milky white skin and startling red hair softened by the pastels the artist had used. It was an intimate picture. One almost felt like a voyeur, and Faith was reminded of Degas's description of his work, "I want to look through the keyhole." Faith admired it, as she had admired it before when she saw it in Maddy Harper's office, one of the Ganley acquisitions that Maddy's predecessor, and she, had kept. Both the images and the frames were exactly the same. Faith took it off the wall, but there was nothing on the back. She walked over to the policeman.

"I think we need to take this with us and give it to Detective Dunne. It may be very valuable and may tie into something at the Ganley Museum."

"Can't remove anything from the premises. Sorry. But I'll call and tell them what you said."

"I'll get in touch with him, too. It may be nothing or it may be—"

"Something," he finished for her. "That's usually how it goes."

Faith returned the drawing to its place on the wall. There had been a book on Degas in Tess's collection, but Faith doubted this piece would have been included.

Degas did so many of these sketches. She reached for the book anyway, flipping to the subject index. As she did so, she noticed a slim volume next to it. She put the Degas book back and reached for the one next to it instead.

It was a book of poetry, privately published, printed on a hand press and bound in soft cerulean-blue leather with a ribbon of the same color to mark the reader's place. She didn't have to look inside for the title or author. Number five of the limited edition was in the Fairchilds' own library. Inside this one on the title page there was an inscription from the author, just as there was in theirs, but the sentiments were quite different. This read, "To my darling Tess from her devoted JoJo." He'd drawn a line through his printed name to indicate the closeness of the relation. The name "Joseph Sargeant" was bisected first from last. Joseph Sargeant—poet, First Parish parishioner, Ganley trustee, and sugar daddy.

Chapter 8

Faith slipped the book into her bag and walked toward the door.

"I'm done," she said.

Driving back to Aleford, she pondered her phrase. She really was done in the sense of not being able to undo what she had done. In the clear light of day—with the book burning a hole through the leather of her purse—she wasn't sure it had been such a good idea to take the item from the apartment. It wasn't a crime scene, but it was close to it, and the nice policeman *had* told her nothing could be removed. Her action had been a reflex. She saw the book and took it. She could have left it, called Dunne, and told him what she'd found. That would have been the correct way to proceed.

But this wasn't a stranger who was involved. It was Joseph Sargeant. She pictured him at the Harvest Festival lustily singing "If I Had a Hammer." The image was immediately followed by the more recent one of Joseph in his tuxedo at the New England Rocks! opening reception. There had been an empty place next to him at the table, and she remembered noticing the way he'd watched the entrance and scanned the crowd. He'd left the room several times, and it was obvious that he had been waiting for someone. Waiting for Tess? As the evening had worn on, his face had taken on a slightly grim look at odds with the art- and wine-induced glow of those around him. Faith thought he might have slipped away before dessert, but she wasn't sure.

Had the lovers quarreled? Joseph was wealthy enough to have set Tess up in the apartment and provided every woman's dream clothing allowance. Why would Tess have put all that in jeopardy, if in fact she had? She might have been held up at another engagement, another opening. And if there had been a falling-out, how serious might it have been? Serious enough for murder?

Faith turned off Route 2 and passed Wilson's Farm—a small family-owned stand that had morphed into a major business, a local Whole Foods competitor. It was still family owned and one of her favorite places to shop. She

248 • KATHERINE HALL PAGE

pulled in and quickly picked up some snow peas, black mushrooms, bok choy, and other veggies to stir-fry with some scallops she had in the freezer for dinner. She added some of their mesclun mix for salad and a large bunch of the red grapes the kids liked. On the way to the register, she grabbed an assortment of peppers to roast. The sights and smells were calming in their familiarity and promise of meals to come. Her focus cleared. She knew she had done the right thing. Joseph Sargeant would have to go to the police, but he wouldn't have to go alone. It was time to tell Tom everything, or mostly everything. He'd seen Joseph through his wife's terrible illness and he'd see him through this. Whatever JoJo had done.

As soon as Faith got home and put the food away, she called Tom.

"Hi, honey," he said, sounding surprised. She rarely called him at work. "Everything okay?"

"Yes and no. Could you grab an hour for a walk? I want to tell you something." As she spoke, Faith realized she had raised red flags. Pix took walks on the spur of the moment. Faith did not. And then those words no man ever wants to hear, "I have something to tell you." No woman, either, for that matter. She hastened to reassure him.

"Don't worry. I'm not running away with the milkman or developed a sudden desire to visit the Taj Mahal.

It's just time I told you some stuff and it's such a beautiful day, I thought we could talk outdoors." Maybe she thought that Tom's reaction would be better contained by a wide-open space than the parsonage living room. No maybe. Faith tried to be honest with herself. It was the plan.

"Why don't you come over here and we'll go out to Slocum's Woods?" He still sounded worried—and slightly dubious.

"Great. I'll be right there."

Pausing only to make a thermos of Tom's favorite, Peet's Russian Caravan tea, and put it and some shortbread cookies in a day pack with light jackets for them both—Tom had headed for work without one—Faith threaded her way through the tombstones in the cemetery to the church. Not *cemetery* she corrected herself as she passed a stone that sported an exceptionally lugubrious carving—a skull with wings—*burial ground*. The Unitarians coined *cemetery* from the Greek for "place of sleep" for Mt. Auburn much later in the early 1800s. First Parish's burial ground was not the kind of place one wanted to linger, let alone sleep, and soon Faith was at Tom's office.

The unseasonable weather had continued and it was as warm as a day in May, although in New England that could feel more like November, or what November was *supposed* to feel like. The Fairchilds walked along the trail that the Aleford Conservation Commission maintained, hand in hand. Faith imagined how they would look to a passerby. Like two figures from one of Watteau's bucolic fantasies minus the frills. Tom was holding her hand a bit more tightly than usual, but she ascribed that to the stress uncertainty produced.

"Let's stop here," she suggested when they reached a clearing with some less-than-comfy-looking boulders. "I have tea and cookies."

Tom took the pack from her, spread out his jacket, and motioned for her to sit down.

"Teatime can wait."

Faith was tempted to start at the beginning with the fake Bearden, but it would make for a terribly long story, and she wasn't sure that it was relevant yet. She'd know when she heard from Dunne about the authenticity of the Degas. Plenty of time. Joseph Sargeant was what mattered now, and she described what she'd observed the night of the opening up to the present, slipping the book out of the pack.

Tom was quiet for a moment or two, examining the inscription. He handed the book back to his wife.

"I don't know what to say." He paused again. "Yes, I do. I'd have done what you did, even though it's going to cause problems with John." Tom and Dunne had been on a first-name basis almost from the beginning. With Faith, it fluctuated.

"Poor Joseph," Tom said. "I was worried about him even before Celia passed away. His wife was not only everything in the world to him, but also his job for so many years. He took an early retirement—he'd been a stockbroker—to care for her and kept her at home. Eventually round-the-clock care. He never needed to work—money from both sides—but he'd enjoyed it. When Celia did die, I thought he'd go back, but he told me he'd gotten out of the habit and was too old in any case. 'It's a young man's game, Tom,' he said, and he was probably right."

"I don't know him well," Faith said. "He's involved in some church activities, but I've seen more of him since I've been at the Ganley than all of last year. It's been my impression, though, that he has his routines. I always see him running, rain or shine, at the same times. He has his poetry, the folk music group. But basically he's a loner."

"Celia was the sociable one and more active in the church. So, what do we do?"

Faith was surprised. She'd assumed Tom would take it from here.

"I thought *you'd* have a plan." She started to say that's why she'd told him, but decided it would not be in her best interest.

"Well, I guess the best thing to do is for you to tell John about finding the book and ask him if he'll let me come in with Joseph to talk about his relationship with the girl, rather than have them go and bring in Joseph by himself. I'll go over to Joseph's now and wait there until I hear from you."

Faith nodded. Tom couldn't tell Joseph about this over the phone, nor having told him, leave him alone. Besides how the police might view this—leaving a possible suspect alone and subject to flight or covering up incriminating evidence—there was another implication. If Joseph was guilty, his remorse might lead to another death—his own.

"I don't want to call Dunne until you've told Joseph, though," Faith said. "Why don't you go over there and call me when you're ready?"

Tom agreed, and as they put the thermos and jackets in the pack, he added, "But your involvement with all this ends with the call, okay?"

"Well, fancy meeting you two here! How nice to see you're able to leave your parish duties for a woodland walk with your wife, Reverend."

They were both startled to hear the familiar voice and see the equally familiar figure emerging from behind a large pine. It was Millicent Revere McKinley, and there was no telling how much she'd overheard.

Faith decided she'd stick around for a while in what she knew was probably the vain hope of finding out, but it was worth a try since it would take Tom a while to get to Joseph Sargeant's house. Tom gave her a look that seemed to indicate he'd read her thoughts, confirmed by his words.

"Hi, Millicent. I *have* been playing hooky. Such a lovely day. But I have to get back now. No reason for you to rush off, though, Faith."

"Well, toodle-oo. Faith can give me a hand. I'm collecting pinecones for my wreaths."

Faith had been so surprised by Millicent's sudden appearance that it had barely registered that the woman was carrying the kind of backpack mountaineers attempting Everest went in for. Millicent's wreaths were a staple of her church's holiday fair, and Faith had seen her at work, the dining room table a mass of cones, Millicent wielding her glue gun with a vengeance. Now, besides noticing what Millicent was carrying, she also registered that the woman seemed to be wearing some kind of a dirndl—a Von Trapp at one with the sounds of nature.

"I'd be happy to help for a while," she said.

Millicent set the pack on the ground, pulling the bottom brace out so it stood up. Faith was relieved to see it was almost full.

"Now, no sap stains and only perfectly intact ones. There should be plenty to pick from under those trees." Millicent moved toward a row of pines off to the left, and Faith obediently followed her.

"Tom so rarely gets a free moment. I took a chance and called him to see if he could break away for a quick walk."

"And talk," Millicent said, rapidly piling a bunch of cones on top of her cache.

So, she *had* heard!

"Well, yes, talk, of course." Faith had a mischievous thought of what they might have been doing in the secluded woods—Tom had always been a great outdoorsman—and was happy for the moment that talking had been all they'd been doing.

"We were talking about my job at the Ganley. It's been interesting. I was telling you about it the other day. I enjoy working with the people there. The trustees . . ." She let her voice trail off. She wasn't sure where she was going. She handed Millicent some pine-cones for approval. Millicent threw most of them to the ground and added the rest to the collection.

"Ganley? Trustees? I thought you might be talking about young Benjamin and his new friend. I saw them; let me think when was it—a week ago Saturday waiting for the bus. I assume they were waiting for the bus. They were at the bus stop, or rather the other boy was. His family moved in over the summer from one of those places in the Midwest"—Millicent made it sound like Outer Mongolia. "Travis—a popular name I'm told—Beale, but I doubt it's our Beales."

"Our Beales?" Faith was trying to think back two Saturdays ago and where she might have been. She was also struck by the encyclopedic nature of Millicent's knowledge concerning any and all Aleford residents.

Millicent straightened up and gave Faith a disapproving look. "The Beales were one of Aleford's original families. Their farm was where the Friendly's ice cream place is on the road to Bedford."

"Oh, those Beales. Of course," Faith fibbed. "But you saw Ben waiting for the bus?"

Millicent was enjoying herself. "As I said, I *assumed* he was because his little friend was standing at the stop. Benjamin seemed to be crouching behind those junipers in front of the library. The bus came and they weren't there when it left, so they could have gotten on, but then again I wouldn't want to say. They could also have run off someplace entirely different. Children do such odd things."

And so do adults, Faith reflected, looking at the octogenarian Heidi/Edmund Hillary in front of her. The backpack was as vintage as the woman hoisting it, the woman playing mind games with Faith. Millicent wouldn't come right out and say what she obviously thought: what was Ben Fairchild doing getting on the bus to the Alewife T stop in Cambridge—that being the only one that went through Aleford Center—with a boy Millicent hadn't seen him with before and on a day earmarked by most Alefordians for soccer and family fun? The game part for Millicent was in knowing something Faith didn't know and by innuendo suggesting much more.

Ben wasn't allowed to go to Cambridge, namely Harvard Square, alone on the T. In the past, the Fairchilds or Josh's parents had dropped the two boys off to go to Million Year Picnic, the venerable comic-book store where they had started with Tintin and were now moving on to Art Spiegelman, picking them up at a specified time. It wasn't that Harvard Square was such a dangerous place, but the boys were simply too young to hang out there. Teenagers, especially suburban teens, had been heeding the square's siren call for decades, and for every innocuous guitar-strumming neohippie or Socialist Workers Party hawking news vendor, there was someone who had paradise to sell in his or her pocket.

The pine trees felt as if they were closing in on her, and Faith had to take a deep breath. Thoughts of the murdered girl, stolen art, and what Joseph Sargeant may or may not have had to do with it all leaped into the backseat with Ben now riding shotgun. Faith wanted to get home immediately. It was too early to pick Ben up, but she'd be waiting outside the school.

Millicent gave her a pitying look. "I'm afraid these won't do at all, Faith dear."

Faith let the cones she'd gathered fall to the ground and looked at her hands. They were covered with sap.

Millicent had kept up a steady stream of chat about various Aleford individuals and events. Town elections had come and gone. Most of the offices had been unopposed, but there had been a hotly contested school committee race.

"Handing out pencils with your name on it! Think of the expenditure! Who in their right mind would vote for him? There's waste enough in the schools. Maybe he thought people would donate the pencils after the election."

While Faith had not approved of the electioneering tactic—she could have told him Aleford wouldn't go for the pencils any more than they'd gone for the lollipops with the candidate's name, followed by "Lick" whoever his opponent had been a few years before—she had approved of the candidate's positions and voted for him. She let Millicent talk on—and on—conserving her energy and barely listening. The election was over, and while, in Tip O'Neill's immortal phrase, "all politics is local," the Aleford School Committee was not the election on her mind.

She'd offered to carry the pack, but Millicent refused, suggesting in her carefully worded response that she intended to get the cones back to her house in one piece, and Faith was not to be trusted with the delicate task. Millicent admitted to eighty-five now, since the birthday party Ursula had given her several years ago that Faith had catered. She stood straight as the muskets carried by her forebears and had the strength—and keen eyesight—to wield one handily. Just looking at her was making Faith feel very, very tired. As they approached the parsonage, she thanked Millicent for what she knew not and made her way into the kitchen where she brewed herself a very strong cup of coffee. Tom called ten minutes later. He'd spoken with Joseph and they'd leave as soon as they heard back from Faith. I should have fortified myself with something stronger, Faith thought, as she dialed Detective Lieutenant John Dunne's number.

As it turned out, his reproof was brief. He was eager to get a plausible suspect to question, but his tone did indicate he'd deal with her action later. Faith called

Tom's cell and told him Dunne was waiting. Someone from his department was coming to the parsonage to pick up the book, she told Tom, so Joseph shouldn't be surprised at seeing it in the hands of the police.

It was Detective Ted Sullivan, "Sully," Dunne's right-hand man, and he was in a hurry, only saying, "I don't know whether to hug you or lock you up and my boss feels the same. We can't get a break here—not with who she is—nothing. Whatever she had in the way of IDs were in her purse, which the perp has to have destroyed. No letters, not even bills in her apartment. No phone, which is not unusual these days. They all use their cells, and she must have had it with her, so no calls to trace. Tess Auchincloss doesn't exist. This guy Sargeant is our first real lead. Maybe hug you wins." And he did.

Faith took Amy to pick Ben up. Amy had always displayed a kind of radar, registering the slightest blip in the mood of the Fairchild household even when she was an infant. She'd followed her mother out to the car and got in without a word. Faith didn't want to go into Ben's Cambridge jaunt in front of his sister. She also wanted to talk to Tom first. After getting in the car, Ben was in the backseat literally and figuratively. Faith's thoughts had returned to the body in the gallery. The hideous discovery that was never far away from her mind. The murder being discussed now in Dunne's office.

She knew she had to find out more about Ben's new friend, Travis. Both Patsy and Niki had been clear about locating the model for the new Ben, and Faith was positive it was this boy. But another time. Now she merely told the kids that she'd give them an early dinner and they should get to their homework in the meantime.

And then she waited.

She saw the headlights in the driveway at 9:30. Amy was asleep and Ben had dropped off, too. She'd stood outside his door and heard his slow, regular breathing before venturing in to turn off his light and put his book away. It was *Swallows and Amazons*, a childhood favorite. He'd looked like a child, and she was glad that he hadn't put aside his childish things completely, whatever mirror he might be looking into. She'd drawn his duvet up over his shoulders, knowing he'd kick it off by morning, and returned to her post.

Joseph was with Tom. The Ganley trustee looked ghastly. His face was as white as his hair—hair so white it looked as if he used peroxide, hair that had turned early and always suited his bright blue eyes. He was a handsome man, she realized, never having thought about it much before. She thought he was in his late fifties, but his lean runner's body was that of a much younger man, as was his unlined face. She could see faint traces on his cheeks—Joseph Sargeant had been crying.

"Could you rustle up some food? I've eaten, but I'm sure Joseph must be hungry," Tom said.

It was what Faith did best.

"I'm fine," Joseph said. "And I don't really know why I'm here bothering you at this time of night."

Born and bred in Aleford, Mr. Sargeant would consider any hour past nine the middle of the night and not an appropriate time for eating or visiting.

"You're here for that drink I promised you, and Faith will be very put out if you don't eat some of her food."

Joseph managed a weak smile. "Well . . ."

"How does an omelet sound, with a little cheese?" This was not a man who wanted to tuck into a heavy steak dinner, and not only were omelets comfort food, but fast to prepare.

"That sounds great."

Faith pulled out a chair, and Joseph sat at the kitchen table. Tom left, returning with a bottle of bourbon and three glasses.

"This is your tipple if I remember correctly."

As Tom poured the drinks and added ice, Faith got out her omelet pan and started to heat it. The eggs wouldn't be at room temperature, but she doubted Joseph would notice the difference this would make in the finished product. She whisked them together with a little salt and pepper, put some slices of sourdough bread in the toaster, and tested the pan with butter. It sizzled, and she poured the mixture in. Meanwhile, she put out some wild strawberry jam and more butter, then slid the finished omelet onto a warmed plate, added the toast and set it in front of Joseph with a knife and fork. Before sitting down, she put together a small mixed green salad with some buttermilk dressing left-over from dinner and placed it within his reach.

For a while, Joseph was occupied with eating. Faith was happy to note that he *had* been hungry and went to get the remains of an angel food cake she'd made yesterday. That would go down easily, she thought. She cut a thick slice for Tom and told him there was some of that Ben & Jerry's Stephen Colbert's AmeriCone Dream flavor in the freezer. She was sticking to her bourbon and branch, but she knew from experience Tom could mix anything with cake. She wondered where he'd eaten dinner—nothing but Paleolithic vend-ing machines at Dunne's. It must have been fast food at the nearby strip mall. And why had Tom had time to eat and Joseph hadn't? She was desperately wishing that one or the other of the two men would clue her in on what had happened, but she couldn't say anything. Finally Joseph moved his plate to one side and took a long pull on his drink.

"I can't thank you enough for coming, Tom. I couldn't have faced it alone. Ever since I saw Tess's picture in the paper on Monday I've been trying to think what to do. Each time the phone rang, I was sure it was the police. I told myself that since I had nothing to do with her murder, there was nothing I could tell them. I guess I was a coward. But the real reason was that I didn't want to talk to them about her, didn't want what we had together cheapened. I knew how it all would seem."

Tom filled Faith in. "I'd told John how I knew Joseph and what his relationship to the young woman had been when I called to say we'd be coming in. Once we were there, both John and I advised him not to say anything more without an attorney present, which is why we're so late."

"My dealings with the firm I've used for many years have not included any that required one of their criminal lawyers. It never occurred to me that they *had* some. We had to wait for her to come out from town," Joseph said.

"Have you been charged with anything?" Faith couldn't keep still. She immediately realized how silly the question was. If he'd been charged, he would have been arrested and not sitting here at her kitchen table consuming cake and ice cream.

"No, not yet anyway. I'm not supposed to leave town, though. I'll be meeting with my attorney in the morning. She seems very good—and very smart."

"I went to grab a bite to eat while John questioned Joseph once she arrived," Tom said.

Faith nodded. She was still waiting for more details, though. Details about Tess. Joseph was visibly more relaxed, and his color was coming back. He pushed his chair back from the table.

"You saw the book. You know how I felt about her. We met last June at Art Basel. A group from the museum went."

Art Basel in Switzerland was the most important of all the art fairs showcasing twentieth- and twenty-first-century works, although the spin-off, Art Basel Miami, was nipping at its heels. Art Basel was huge, over two thousand artists had been represented, and a must for anyone serious about contemporary art or serious about being seen at the scene. Faith had read that there had been 150 private planes at the Basel-Mulhouse airport, which indicated the kind of change attendees had jiggling in their pockets.

"Jack Winston introduced us. He's a fellow Ganley trustee. I don't know if you've met him, but Faith, you have, right?" Joseph said.

"Yes," she replied, filing away for future contemplation the fact that the young trustee had known Tess better than she'd realized.

"Of course I was immediately struck by how beautiful she is, was," he amended, his voice breaking slightly. "Anyway, she seemed to know a great deal more about the art and artists than I did, and we ended up spending most of the time there together—skipping the whole thing the last day to be tourists. We went to the zoo and had dinner overlooking the Rhine at an Italian restaurant, Chez Donati. We laughed, because we'd booked thinking it was French. The next day my flight was earlier than hers—she'd come on someone's private plane—but she was there at the airport to say good-bye. We made a date for dinner the following night at Aujourd'hui, and that was it. Tess was smart, funny, and very caring. I never thought I'd find love again."

Faith got up and put the box of tissues she kept under the counter on the table. He mopped his eyes and blew his nose.

"You must think I'm a silly—or worse—old man."

"I think a wonderful thing happened to you—and you're certainly not old. What is it? Fifty is the new thirty?" Faith said. Fifty did seem a bit old to her, but she was sure once she got there, it wouldn't.

"Tess said the age thing didn't bother her, that it was just a number. I was the one who worried about it. Thought she should be with someone her age. 'Men my age are boring,' she told me, and I wanted to believe her. I own some property in Boston, and the apartment on Pinckney was vacant and had just been renovated. We had fun furnishing it. I knew she didn't make much money modeling and she'd quarreled with her family, so they'd stopped her allowance. I picked up the tab." He darted a look at Faith. "She liked nice things—was used to nice things—but she never asked me for anything. I bought her a necklace and a matching bracelet at Shreve's and she made me return them."

"What had Tess's father done? I gather he died and her mother remarried soon after."

"She didn't like to talk about her family, although she had been very fond of her father. I gather there was some kind of trust, but her mother had arranged things so Tess couldn't touch it until she was thirty. Pretty harsh, I thought. No siblings, like me. I wanted to marry her, but didn't dare ask. I kept on thinking I was too old for her—and I was afraid she'd say no, then our life together would end."

Faith had a fleeting thought—with a setup like the one Joseph had provided, it was unlikely Tess would do anything to change it, no matter how little she asked for outright. She hoped the young woman had been even half as much in love with Joseph as he was with her.

"We traveled a great deal—out to the West Coast a few times. A cruise in Alaska and a trip to the Grand Canyon. Tess had never seen it. We went on one of those rafts down the Colorado."

"And abroad?"

"No. Tess said she was tired of Paris, London, the 'usual places,' she called them. She had never explored her own country much. This fall we went all over New England, rented a spectacular house on Deer Isle in Maine for a week. Tess said she'd be content to live there forever—together. Maybe I was going to ask her to marry me. Maybe she would have said yes."

His eyes welled up with tears again.

"Time to get you home," Tom said. "You've got a rough day tomorrow."

"I know. My attorney is going to have to be a conjurer. I have absolutely no alibi. Tess was supposed to meet me at the museum that night. I kept trying her cell—there's no phone in the apartment. She said we didn't need one. I left the reception early and drove to Pinckney Street. She wasn't there."

"How did you know?" Faith asked.

"I had a set of keys and went as far as the door to the apartment. I knocked. There hadn't been lights on from the outside, but you can't see the ones in the rear from the street. I knocked, but she didn't answer. Maybe she had someone else, and he was there, but if so she didn't see much of him. We were always together. I'd even started running on the Esplanade instead of out here. I waited a while, thinking she might come in, then I went home and hoped she would call. I kept trying well past midnight. Tess liked to stay up late and sleep late."

"And those other people, the Polks? They didn't see you?"

"He moved out sometime last summer, I believe. I never ran into him much. Sometimes the wife and kids. They thought I was Tess's uncle. So, unfortunately, no one saw me, except passersby on the street. No one who could be found. It didn't occur to me that I'd have to account for my whereabouts, otherwise I'd have made a point to camp out in the middle of the green here," he finished bitterly.

"Come on." Tom shot a look at Faith that all but said "Shut up." He'd told her not to get involved and here she was bothering Joseph with a slew of questions. Faith flushed. She was trying to save the man from arrest and worse.

"Tom's right. You need to get some sleep."

"I wish I could," Joseph said.

"A hot bath and chamomile tea. I'll give you some."
Faith went to one of the cabinets and got out a box of
tea bags. Joseph wouldn't want to be fussing about
with leaves and strainers. The word *bath* had triggered
one more question, and Tom would have to lump it.
She waited until he was out of earshot, though, getting
their coats.

"There wasn't any contemporary art on the walls of
the apartment, but some other lovely pieces."

"They were mostly family things that Tess admired
when she was out at the house. She said Pinckney Street
wasn't the proper spot for modernity."

"So Tess didn't bring any artwork herself when she
moved in?"

"Tess was her own work of art. I mean the way she
dressed, wore her hair, as if she was a blank canvas.
She brought some very fetching"—Joseph was dating
himself now, Faith thought, the adjective was usually
followed by "a peach of a girl"—"clothes, a lovely photo
her former roommate, a photographer, had taken, and
one framed Degas reproduction."

"I remember it—a study for one of his bathers."

"Next to the bookcase in the living room, yes. A
woman with red hair stepping into the bath. When

Tess unpacked it, I told her it looked like her. She could have been the model." Joseph gave a little start and shot a glance at Faith. "Funny, now that I think of it, isn't the original . . . ?"

"Sorry to keep you waiting. Amy was having a bad dream. She went back to sleep right away, but keep an ear out, Faith," Tom said.

Amy almost never had nightmares. It was her radar again.

They left and Faith went upstairs, leaving the light on over the sink for Tom. She checked Amy and replaced Ben's cover, then got ready for bed herself, slipping in between the sheets with every intention of falling asleep quickly. Yet, she was still wide awake in the darkness when she heard Tom return. She thought she knew what Joseph Sargeant had been about to say. He'd seen that sketch before, presumably the original, just as Faith had, in Maddy's office.

Only a week until Thanksgiving. Tom's parents, brothers, and the Averys were coming. This was the year for Tom's sister to go to her in-laws, and Faith's family was gathering at her aunt Chat's in New Jersey, an act of courage that Faith's mother had already mentioned twice. "It's so far away!" "Yes," Faith had replied. "And you have to cross a great big river to get there."

Living in the wilderness herself, she could identify with her aunt, but like the rest of the family, she had never understood why Chat had given up her duplex in the San Remo on the West Side for acreage in Mendham.

Tom's mother would bring the sweet potato and marshmallow dish without which a Fairchild Thanksgiving gathering could not truly offer thanks. Patsy and Will were bringing pies, and Faith was adding a Red Velvet cake in honor of their Southern roots. Each year she tried to wean her father-in-law away from peas and string beans. Her last attempt—brussels sprouts with walnuts and brown butter—had been a success. This year she was going to try a parsnip puree, heavy on the cream (see recipe, p. 387), in the hope that he would take an ample portion thinking they were mashed potatoes and get hooked.

Although Thanksgiving marked the beginning of Tom's most stressful season—the merriest time of the year was in truth the saddest for many—it was Faith's favorite holiday. Not simply for the pause it offered to take stock and be grateful, but for its unvarying menu. She could tweak the stuffing, add some new twists to the veggies, but the meal was a simple and satisfying one—a guaranteed winner for every palate.

She pulled the van into the museum's back parking lot, got out, and rang the bell. Since the murder, security had been tightened—the alarm code changed and a directive issued stating that propping the door open would no longer be tolerated. Faith didn't know where they were hidden, but she'd also heard that new video cameras had been installed—with film.

Channing answered the door immediately, and they loaded the cart. He was wearing a white T-shirt for a change that stated fear no art, and his green apron was tied around his waist. Folding the bib under was a compromise that Faith was willing to accept. He'd been doing a good job, better than she'd expected from grandmama's little darling. She sent him up in the elevator and took the stairs, stopping off at the ladies' room. As she was about to leave, she heard voices in the hall and leaned against the door instead, creating a tiny opening. Glen Elroy and Roland Phillips were arguing.

"Forget about how they found out, but I'd like to know why you would tell them she modeled for me more than anyone else!"

"Because she did," Glen said. "And I had to say something. They kept coming back to the fact that I didn't identify her right away."

"They kept harping on that with me, too. I told them I wouldn't have known my own mother with her head shaved, which is the truth."

"You didn't recognize her?"

"No," he answered quickly. "Besides. I usually saw her without clothes."

"Yes, there's that. God, she was gorgeous. Demanding, though. She always wanted to be paid up front in cash. No checks. Same with you?"

"Yes. It was a pain, because I'd have to get reimbursed. I listed it under studio materials."

"Did you see a lot of her away from the museum? You get around more than I do."

"What are you suggesting?" Roland demanded. "I didn't kill her, if that's what you mean. And the person you should be quizzing, Sherlock, is Marvin, as you well know."

"Yes, Marvin . . ." Glen said slowly. "Maybe I will have a little talk with Marv."

"And stay away from that Fairchild woman. She's working for them, I hear. Some kind of Miss Marple."

"Oh, she's far too attractive for Miss Marple. But thanks for the warning."

Faith was flattered—and puzzled. The two men had clearly not been telling each other all they knew, about others on the staff and their own relationship to Tess. The cash part went along with everything else Faith had heard about Tess's financial arrangements. Unless she had obtained false IDs, she wouldn't be able to open a bank account—or she might not have wanted to leave any kind of paper trail if someone was trying to find her. Whoever she was. With murderous intent? Was *this* why Tess had created a new identity?

She waited until she was sure Elroy and Phillips had moved on, and then went into the café. Kelly Burton, Maddy's assistant, was waiting.

"Does two o'clock still work for you?"

"Yes," Faith said. Maddy was giving a dinner party at her home for some prospective and current large donors. Faith had thought she might cancel the event, but it was apparently business as usual. Not a bad idea. Presenting the Ganley as having weathered the storm with firm leadership at the helm was bound to impress people. Maddy wanted Faith to see the premises and finalize the menu.

"Good, she'll meet you there."

A thought struck Faith. "Are you still fish sitting?"

Kelly laughed. "The artist wanted his goldfish back immediately, and the police said I could give it back to him. Apparently he'd already received a commission for a duplicate with, if possible, the original fish. Someone who saw it at the opening."

"An art lover or someone more twisted?"

"I think it's someone who's a major collector and planned to purchase the piece when the show was over, but doesn't want it now that it's been in, well, police custody."

"Is Maddy in her office?"

"She was when I left."

"I'll go up with you and poke my head in. She likes these doughnut muffins. Why don't you take one, too?"

"I've gained three pounds since you took over, so I'll forgo the muffin much as I'm tempted. My boyfriend made a crack about love handles the other day—although he should talk."

Kelly looked at Channing as she spoke and Faith saw a look of total disgust cross his face. Whether it was at the guy's insensitivity or Kelly's weight gain—nonexistent as far as Faith could see, the girl was as slender as a reed—wasn't clear. Had Channing had a thing with Kelly? They seemed to be the same age. Was this the girlfriend who had dumped him?

So, little Swimmy was gone. Joseph had told Tess about Harriett's objection to the piece in the show, and as a joke, Tess had surprised him with a duplicate—she knew the artist's work. She thought just one fish would be lonely, though, and added a mate.

Maddy was on the phone, and Faith put the plate on her desk, mouthing, "See you later." The director nodded. On the way out, Faith paused to study the

Degas. She wished she could take it off the wall, but with Maddy a few feet away that was impossible. The piece looked identical to the one in Tess's apartment. Even the frames were the same—not the ornate gold plaster ones customary to Impressionist paintings and drawings, but a simple black ebony type with rounded corners like those often used for Japanese prints.

Back in her car, she opened a window and found she could get enough cell reception to make a call and phoned Dunne. He had gotten the message about the Degas and had dispatched someone to get it just a few minutes ago. He'd let her know if there was anything significant about the drawing.

"And Faith"—her first name, he couldn't be too mad about the book—"next time you remove a book or any other evidence, I'll throw it at you."

He was mad.

The red brick exterior of the former Ganley gatehouse that the first director had remodeled as his residence boasted two turrets and an oak plank door that would repel any number of barbarian hoards. Faith wondered what the inside looked like. The only windows she could see through without climbing over the shrubbery were to the left and right of the door—wavy leaded-glass ones that left much to the imagination.

She was sure there must have been a bellpull at some point, but a conventional doorbell had replaced it. She'd pressed it, heard a chime, but Maddy did not appear. Faith pressed it again and also lifted the heavy iron knocker extending from an MGM lion's mouth, letting it fall with a bang. Still no Maddy. She gave the knocker another try—it was fun—and when it still did not produce a result, went around to the side to see whether Maddy's car was behind the house by the garage. Perhaps she was napping. Recent days at the Ganley had certainly been exhausting.

No car. No sign of anyone. The garage was a large one, meant to hold both horseless and traditional carriages in the early days of the estate. Faith had heard that Maddy's husband had converted part of it into a studio, and she went and knocked on that door. No answer.

Feeling like Goldilocks—the whole place was a storybook illustration—she turned the knob and walked in. Perhaps Spence, intent on his work, hadn't heard her knock, she told herself, knowing she was trying to justify her entry—and snooping. The large room was empty. Skylights filled the area with sunshine and illuminated the piece on the easel that he was obviously working on. The fresh paint shone like newly minted coins. She walked over for a closer look.

Spencer Potter was a very good painter. Faith had never seen any of his work before. It was reminiscent of Henri Rousseau, the French postimpressionist whose spellbinding, enigmatic works, often set in jungles he never saw, went virtually unrecognized until after his death. Like Rousseau's, Spence's canvas was filled with precisely drawn lush vegetation, but unlike Le Douanier, as Rousseau, an employee of a Paris customshouse, was known, Spence's plants were even more oversized and otherworldly, totally alien flora. And the canvas, too, was enormous. It seemed to pulsate with sensuality. Other canvases were propped against the walls. He was prolific. Most were similar to the one on the easel. Some had birds, both recognizable—a blue heron, ravens—and fantastical. A coyotelike animal dominated one canvas, the face peering through a tangle of thorny bushes on an arid plain. Where did he show? she wondered. Somehow she'd consigned him to dabbler status, a hobbyist—not the serious painter he obviously was. Several canvases off in the corner had been turned toward the wall. Works in progress? Rejects? She carefully turned the first one around and gasped.

It was definitely an homage to Rousseau. To his most famous work, *The Dream*. Faith had stood before it many times at the Museum of Modern Art in Manhattan. A naked woman, posed like Manet's *Olympia* on a velvet-covered Victorian couch, dominates the jungle that surrounds her, beckoning to the lions, birds, and a flute-playing simian creature. Faith had noticed a similar couch when she came in, a prop, and she knew the model for this work, as well. Rousseau's woman had dark hair; Spence's woman had red-gold hair. It was Tess.

"What the hell!" The door flew open, and Spencer Potter stomped in, clearly upset at having his space invaded. "Oh, Mrs. Fairchild. Sorry, I didn't recognize the car."

"No, I'm the one who should be apologizing for barging in." Faith hoped the tremor in her voice was going unnoticed as she tried to turn the painting back to the wall without drawing attention to the act. "I was looking for Maddy. We have an appointment to discuss the dinner Saturday night. I thought you might know where she was, and then when I saw your work, I was drawn in—they're wonderful."

"Thank you." Spence was taking off his jacket as he came closer. Faith hadn't quite managed to replace the painting, but she stepped forward to meet him.

"I'll just be going now. If Maddy could give me a call? I'm happy to set up another time."

Spence stepped in front of her and looked over her shoulder at the canvas she'd been examining.

"No—I don't think you'll be leaving."

Chapter 9

"He was asleep in his bed all night. We can all swear to it!"

"We haven't come about Buster, Mrs. MacIlheny. It's about Florence. May we come in?"

"Florence? Well, she's not here for sure. Hasn't been for over five years. What do you want with her, anyway?"

"Want to let you know something. I'm afraid it's not good news."

"It never is in this life. All right, I guess you'd better come in."

Sheriff Boyd and his deputy stepped into the house. They knew from experience what they'd find. Mary MacIlheny kept everything as neat as a pin, but there wasn't much to keep, and what there was showed the signs of wear that had been inflicted by her six children. Four of the six were still at home. Their other progenitor, Mr. MacIlheny, had succumbed to lung cancer shortly after the birth of the youngest, and was presumably enjoying more peace now than he'd ever enjoyed in his earthly abode.

Mrs. MacIlheny stood in the living room, but did not ask the officers to sit down. A new sound system looked remarkably out of place, and Boyd exchanged a look with his deputy. Buster must be dealing again. The sheriff cleared his throat and took a sheet of paper from the manila envelope he'd been holding.

"Do you recognize the person in this photograph?" he asked, extending it toward her.

She grabbed it. "It's Florence. She hasn't been gone so long that I wouldn't know my own daughter. Her hair's different, is all. If she's in trouble, it's nothing to do with me. She was of legal age when she left. Left without a word to anyone. Just scrawled 'Good-bye' on the bathroom mirror in lipstick. Didn't think about who was going to have to clean it off."

Boyd interrupted the litany of complaint—he'd heard it about Buster, and Sharon the next in line. She was in the service now, where he hoped her salary was keeping her fingers from sticking to articles of clothing and cosmetics at the nearest mall. He had no doubt he'd be hearing the same words from their mother about the younger MacIlhenys in due course. Florence had been an exception. There always seemed to be one in a family like the MacIlhenys. He took a deep breath.

"I'm afraid she's dead. Maybe you ought to have a seat."

"Dead?" Mary MacIlheny backed up to the sofa and collapsed onto the middle cushion, the one that had the most stuffing left. "My little girl? Flo? Dead?" She started to wail.

The officers looked uncomfortable. It wasn't the kind of town where news like this got delivered very often.

"Can I get you a glass of water?" the sheriff asked.

She shook her head and dabbed at her eyes with a tissue she pulled from her pocket.

"Why? How?" she cried, as totally bereft as she had been defensive before.

"I'm afraid she was murdered. But according to the police in Massachusetts, she didn't suffer. There were no signs of any violence."

" 'No signs of any violence'? What do you call murder?" Mary sat up straight. "Now you'd better tell me all about it, and don't try to sugarcoat things."

Tess's photograph had been posted on the Internet, and *America's Most Wanted* had run a brief spot asking anyone with information about her identity to call the Massachusetts State Police. Dunne had expected results from the TV show, but the call came from someone who'd seen her face online. A high school classmate who told him it was definitely Florence MacIlheny. They'd gone to school together all their lives in a small Illinois town west of Danville. Sheriff Boyd had corroborated the identification and Tess Auchincloss vanished, replaced by the real identity she'd tried so hard to shed.

After listening to the sheriff, Mary MacIlheny got up and went into the hall. They could see her rummaging around in a closet, pulling a boot from the rear, and a bottle from the boot. She disappeared into the kitchen and returned with a jelly glass full of what appeared to be gin. She didn't offer any to the two men and it wasn't because she knew they were on duty. She took a hefty swallow and sat back down.

"She wanted to get away from here for as long as I can remember. It wasn't natural in a child so young. Always buying those fashion magazines. All her babysitting money went for those—and other ones. *Town & Country*—rich people riding horses." She drank deeply. "Rich people who *looked* like horses. You know what I mean? Long noses and chins. Tall. Skinny."

The two men exchanged glances. They didn't know where Mary MacIlheny was going. Boyd knew she was no fool, and it wasn't her fault that she was widowed with such a brood and the only money coming in to cover the mortgage what she made cleaning houses and as a cashier at the Walgreens in Danville. They waited.

"Got a passport just before she left. Came in the mail. I wanted to know what she needed one for. 'You never know when you might get a chance to go to Paris,' she said. As if a ticket was going to drop from the sky. Maybe it did for her. She was pretty. No, beautiful. I told her her face was her fortune and she said, 'I know, Ma. I know.'"

Mary drained the glass and went back for a refill. It was her own private wake.

She took up where she left off.

"Tell the police in Massachusetts that she didn't leave here because she came from a bad home. No one ever raised a hand to her. Not that she gave cause. She pulled her weight. Took care of the little ones while I was at work. She left because there was nothing here for her—and she didn't want to end up like me."

Mrs. MacIlheny was focusing on a spot on the opposite wall. It was as if she were watching a movie, a movie that had been shot a long time ago. She shook her head.

"Turned eighteen and took off while the kids were in school and I was at work. Missed her own high school graduation. Not that she cared. She was smart enough. She could have gone to college, gotten a scholarship probably, but that wasn't what she wanted."

"Did you or any other members of the family ever hear from her?" Boyd asked.

"Not directly. The day she left, she took all her money out of her savings account and a hundred and fifty dollars I kept in the flour canister in the pantry— she was the only one who knew about it. A few months later I got a big package. It was a set of new canisters, and there was three hundred dollars in cash in the one marked FLOUR."

"What was the return address?"

"There wasn't any, but it was postmarked 'New York City.' I figured that's where she'd go."

"How about the rest of the family? Was she closer to one of them more than the others? Buster? He's the next oldest, right? Could she have gotten in touch with him without your knowing?"

"Sheriff, you know Buster. Do you think Flo would keep in touch with him? Sorry, Florence. She hated us to call her by her nickname, and starting when she was about nine, wouldn't answer to it. No, if she'd gotten in touch with anyone in this house, I would have known about it."

"How about her friends? Friends from school?"

"She was a loner. All the boys—some of the teachers, too—were crazy to go out with her, but she wasn't interested. When she was sixteen she started taking waitressing jobs—always gave me half what she made. Worked Saturday nights—big tip nights, she said, guys wanting to impress their dates. She didn't even go to her proms and laughed when I asked her about them. Florence was a great one for laughing. 'Why on earth would I want to get all dressed up to go to the gym? It's the gym no matter how much crepe paper they hang or Kleenex carnations the committee makes.'"

"Did you ever hear her mention a family named 'Auchincloss'? Possibly from New York?"

"No. If she knew anybody outside of her own hometown, she kept it dark, but then she kept a lot of things dark. She wasn't sneaky. Not my girl. But she just didn't say. I guess there was a lot she just never talked about."

The gin hit with a wallop, and Mary MacIlheny started crying softly. It was sadder than her earlier outburst. Boyd's deputy, new on the job, thought it was the saddest thing he'd ever seen.

"Is there someone we can call to be with you?" Boyd asked.

She shook her head. "The kids will be back soon. Funny. Once in a blue moon, one of them will ask about her. I guess we all thought she'd stop by for a visit someday. Not to stay, of course, but just to say hi." She stood up and smoothed the front of her skirt down. "You go along now."

The officers stood up, too, and Boyd said, "I'm sorry to trouble you further, but can you think of anyone who might have done this? Might have had some kind of grudge against your daughter?"

The photograph had fallen to the floor, and Mary stooped down to pick it up, examining her daughter's face for an answer, a message.

"No. I have no idea why anyone would have wanted to kill Florence. Kill someone this beautiful. I guess her face wasn't her fortune after all."

Spencer Potter was possibly even better looking angry than he was when calm. And he was very angry now. Faith backed away from him in what she hoped was the direction of the door that led into the garage. She'd noticed it when she'd first come in. Come in! Why had she done such a stupid thing? But how wass she to know that Spencer was involved with Tess, too? She should have guessed. All roads led to the Ganley.

"Stop moving!" he shouted, and she did. She kept still, but not quiet.

In as conversational a tone as she could muster, Faith said, "I understand the girl did a great deal of modeling all over the Boston area. I'm sure you saw her at the school, and any artist would have wanted her to pose. She was lovely, and your painting captures that."

Of course her body wasn't found at any of those other art schools or museums. Faith didn't feel it was necessary to add that. All she wanted to do was get out of Spence's studio. A studio redolent of turpentine and oil paint. When she had first entered, she'd greeted the smell with pleasure—a reminder of friends' studios, an odor that presaged great works. Now the fumes were making her queasy. Extremely queasy.

"I think we should take a little walk—or maybe a drive," he said.

"Unfortunately I'll have to take a rain check," she said. It was one Faith did not intend to use. Potter was looking around the studio now. For what? A weapon? Rope? He removed the long scarf he'd been wearing around his neck and stepped closer. A garrote? A gag? "Rain check"? She'd made it sound as if she were at the market and they'd run out of coupons. But the impulse remained. Unless it rained for forty days and forty nights and Spence had the only means of transportation, she intended to get as far away from the man as possible and stay there. She wasn't going for any walks or drives. If she couldn't make her way out of his studio, she was going to stay there with her feet firmly planted on the paint-splattered floor. Some of the paint was red. Blood red. Maybe staying put wasn't the best idea. He wouldn't have to worry about covering up the evidence, she realized in alarm.

The outside door was flung open so hard it smacked against the wall with a bang. "Darling! I have to talk . . . Mrs. Fairchild? Weren't we supposed to meet at my office? I've been waiting—"

It was Madelyn Harper, and her husband smoothly cut her off.

"Mrs. Fairchild was interested in my work. Why don't you go back to the museum, and I'll send her along when I'm finished?"

Faith was surprised to see a look of fear cross Maddy's face. If anyone should be expressing fright it should be Faith herself, she thought, feeling vaguely annoyed at being co-opted.

"No," Maddy said quickly. "I need to get everything organized for the dinner Saturday night. She has to come with me."

Now it was Spence who looked apprehensive.

"Leave her here. How long could it take to decide between chicken and beef?"

Faith had seldom felt so sought after in her entire life. The popular girl. Yet, she wasn't enjoying the lime-light. The whole thing was too bizarre. Spencer seemed afraid to let her go off with his wife and Maddy seemed equally fearful of leaving Faith where she was—with good reason, Faith thought, but Maddy couldn't know what Faith had seen. Her head was spinning, and she walked to the door.

"Sorry to disappoint both of you, but I have to pick my son up at school. I'm already late. Maddy, I'll fax you a couple of menus and we can talk tomorrow. I know what the museum has served in the past, so there shouldn't be a problem even though we're running short of time. And you *did* tell me to meet you here, so I could see the premises, but that can wait." Wait until I can come with Niki, Pix, and anyone else I can think of, Faith added to herself, or be skipped entirely. She could just come a little early on Saturday. "And Spencer, we'll arrange another viewing. I'm sure my husband would love to see your work, too." Her husband—her 6'2", wiry but strong protector.

She hastened out lest either or both Harper-Potters made a sudden rush at her.

Ben was sitting on the curb in front of the school, scowling. She was indeed late. He jumped up and got in the front seat.

"What took you so long?"

"Nice to see you, too," Faith snapped back.

"It's not as if you had to come far."

"You're wrong there, sweetie. It was very far."

By the time John Dunne called, she had worked it all out—maybe. Spence had killed the young woman in a sudden fit of passion after she'd spurned his advances during a tryst he set up after the opening at the Ganley. He knew his wife would be worn out. Or maybe he'd put something in a nightcap to speed her on her way to dreamland. Maddy had been knocking back the wine, as Faith recalled, and it wouldn't have taken much to do the job. Or maybe the tryst was before the opening, because why would Tess have come all the way to Aleford at that time of night unless she was involved with Spence? He'd hidden the body someplace in his studio. There had been a large armoire, plus there was that couch. Easy enough to throw a dropcloth over the body and stash it behind the settee. Or maybe it wasn't being spurned—not at first. They could have been having a thing, and Tess decided to break it off, inciting Spencer to murder. The old "If I can't have her, nobody will."

There was no way to tell when the painting had been done. It could have been before she met Joseph Sargeant.

While Joseph had painted a portrait of a young woman who asked for naught, Faith was pretty sure that Tess's lifestyle required a sizable amount of largesse, which Spencer Potter, even with all his pedigrees, did not possess compared with Joseph. Faith was sure the key to this murder lay with the character of the victim, and she had been getting such contradictory impressions that it was impossible to reconstruct what Tess had actually been like. Sarah Cummings was in awe of her—and also more than a little jealous, Faith suspected. She had only Sarah's word that the roommates had parted on good terms. Tess turned heads. Had she turned Sarah's boyfriend's? Had it led to more?

Tess was spring to Joseph's winter, a kind of exalted, perfect virgin spring. And to Spencer? Tess as the embodiment of the Pre-Raphaelite's Lilith, the sensuous *belle dame sans merci*. And the others—Elroy and Phillips, the museum schoolteachers. Marvin Handler the curator. Jack Winston the trustee. Who was she to them? And to the women connected with them? What did they think of Tess?

The phone's ring put a momentary stop to her speculations.

"I thought you were supposed to be a big art expert, what with growing up on the Met's doorstep and all," Dunne said.

"I'm assuming you're calling to tell me the Degas was not an original. And for the record, you grew up if not on the Brooklyn Museum's doorstep, then in its backyard."

"True, which might explain that the moment I saw the masterpiece"—Faith could hear the quotation marks surrounding the word—"I knew it was a reproduction, and not a very good one at that. What I don't understand was why you thought it might be the real McCoy?"

Now would be the time to tell him all about the identical Degas in Maddy's office—and the Bearden. Yet she hadn't figured out how it could possibly tie in except as another example of things being rotten in the state of Ganley.

"What kind of frame does it have?"

Dunne described the same frame Faith had seen in the apartment and Maddy's office, one that had to have been custom-made. It wasn't the kind available at the frame-it-yourself places.

"And there were no signs that the apartment had been entered?"

"Come on, Faith, admit you made a mistake. Sargeant said it was the girl's and you wanted to make something out of it, that she had an original. No, to answer your question, there were no signs of forced or any other kind of entry. If someone switched the pictures, he or she would have had to have keys, and according to Sargeant only he and Tess had them, plus the management firm had one. And there are no balconies or fire escapes."

"Could I see it? Do you still have the picture or did someone put it back?"

"You just don't know when to quit. Yes, I still have it, but no you can't see it."

"Why not?"

"Because I'm not in a good mood today. Try me another time. Maybe."

He hung up before she could protest further.

She called Patsy immediately and caught her just as she was leaving for a conference with a client and her mother. Faith had told Patsy about the Degas, but not about Tess's relationship with Joseph. They'd speculated about Tess being the forger, but no one had mentioned that Tess was an artist, and you'd have to be very skilled to pull off such convincing fakes from such different artists. They'd agreed that it was more likely someone Tess knew. Someone who had let her keep the original as a loan or more permanently. Now the original wasn't an original, Faith told her friend, whose reaction was the same that Faith's had been.

"Somebody had to have switched them. It's not that obscure a print, I believe. Could have been someone on the force. How long was it in the property room?"

This was not a question, or issue, Faith was going to raise with the good detective lieutenant. Not if she ever wanted to work with the police again. They were more clannish than any Scots.

"I don't think it was around long, and think of the logistics—getting into the apartment, racing out to buy a print. I don't even know where one would go. It wouldn't be at the MFA, because it isn't in their collection. You could find it online, but that would take time for shipping."

"Then whoever it was has keys. Tess isn't around to tell us who she might have given a set to—and if she did, Joseph wouldn't know. We have to find X."

"I agree. I may not be Bernard Berenson, but I can tell a reproduction from an original, no matter what Dunne was implying."

"Of course you can. Now I have to run. I'm trying to keep this girl out of the clutches of the juvenile justice system. Her mother's a tough lady and loves her daughter very much, but she's at sea when it comes to raising a teenager. This is a first offense—and a minor one—and I'm connecting them with the EdLaw Project. I've told you about them. They advocate and intervene on behalf of low-income students, so they can get the kind of education all kids are entitled to in our communities."

Faith sympathized with the girl's mother. Ben wasn't a teen yet and she felt very much adrift. She had heard about EdLaw and the terrific job they were doing.

"I'll let you know if anything else happens."

"Okay. Good-bye for now. And Faith, Berenson had a white goatee. If I see any whiskers on your pretty little chin, I'll tell you."

Amy was at a friend's house and Ben was upstairs presumably doing homework. After a while, Faith went and knocked on his door to see if he wanted to come down for a snack. He had raced out of the car only to wait impatiently for her at the back door, then was off again to the sanctuary of his own room once she'd unlocked it. Three more days of in-school suspension. She knew he must be feeling humiliated. She hoped he was feeling chastened.

She knocked and went in.

"I thought you might be hungry. Want to come down and have some apple crisp? Amy's class went apple picking last week, and I made some for dinner—the kind you and Amy like with maple syrup."

Once again she saw some photographs of what looked like classmates on his screen, and once again, he literally pulled the plug on his iMac.

"Sure, why not," he said with studied nonchalance that didn't fool her for a minute.

"What was that you had up on your screen when I came in?"

"Nothing. It's not porn, if that's what you think."

"I could see it wasn't porn, but what was it?" They trusted Ben, and Amy, but both of the kids' computers had filters. It was too easy to mistype something and find yourself looking at a woman with such enormous breasts you had to wonder where she shopped for clothes, although clothes were apparently not important. You didn't even have to mistype. Innocuous words took on very different shades of meaning in cyberspace.

"It's well, kind of a yearbook," Ben said.

"Part of Facebook or just for your school?"

Ben seized upon her words like a drowning man reaching for a rope. "Our school. Me and some other kids are doing a Facebook just for us."

" 'Some other kids and I.' "

"Mom!"

Repressing the urge to tell him he'd thank her later when he interviewed for a job, she felt relieved. He wasn't into anything he shouldn't be, and he was certainly enthusiastic about it.

"Come down and tell me more about the project. Is Josh involved, too?"

Wrong question.

"I'm not that hungry after all. I'll wait until dinner."

Faith sighed. She'd fallen off the tightrope.

"Okay. I'm going to walk to the market and pick up some ice cream to go with the crisp and a few other things. I won't be gone long. Amy will be home in an hour, but I'll be back by then."

She'd been standing next to him. He reached up from his chair—he seemed to have grown several inches in the last week—and gave her an awkward hug. She kissed the top of his head and left. The lady or the tiger. You never knew which would emerge.

It was still unseasonably warm for November, and Faith was sorry she had worn a jacket. A sweater would have been sufficient. Her encounter with Spencer Potter had left her feeling on edge. She realized she had forgotten to tell Dunne about finding Tess's portrait there and Spence's subsequent behavior, which could only be described as menacing. Dunne might say the man had merely been annoyed at Faith's poking around where she shouldn't, but then again he might take it seriously, as was she. There was more than a working relationship between the victim and the artist, Faith was certain, and she intended to find out what it was. Tess just a model? Somehow she didn't think so. She'd call Dunne as soon as she got home. Somehow describing the incident on her cell in the middle of Aleford, especially since she was passing Millicent Revere McKinley's house, didn't seem like a good idea. As if to prove that if walls can talk they must have ears, Millicent sallied forth from her front door, market basket in hand.

"Just going to pick up a few odds and ends for dinner," she announced.

Mostly odds, Faith thought. They'd been invited to partake of this meal with Millicent twice over the years and the words *groaning board* took on a new meaning. Later in the wee hours of the morning—both Tom and Faith were groaning as well. One time it had been steak and kidney pie, a treasured recipe from a British friend, Millicent had proclaimed, adding that the "dear was really one of us, just born on the wrong side of the pond." There had been no discernible steak and a great deal of offal kidneys. The other time, the main course was a mystery. It could have been animal, vegetable, *or* mineral. What was certain was that the rice had been burned and, like the smell of singed hair, emitted an odor that killed the appetite before it even reached the table.

Faith matched her steps to Millicent's, which involved quickening her pace.

"Such news. I do feel so sorry for that poor family. All the way out in Illinois."

Faith made a sympathetic noise, a kind of extended *hmmm*. If she waited, Millicent might drop a few more hints and Faith might be able to discern what the hell she was talking about. Who did Millicent know in Illinois? She'd never been out of New England to Faith's certain knowledge. "Never needed to," she'd told her the first time they met.

"And so young." She was swinging her basket like a schoolgirl. She didn't have pigtails—Millicent's hairstyle was as rigid as her principles and had never strayed from the look adopted from Mamie Eisenhower—but pigtails were suggested. Millicent gave Faith a smug little smile. Whatever tidbit she was enjoying must be a delicious morsel indeed.

Faith made another sympathetic noise. This time an *aaah*.

"I'm sure they were puzzled about why she changed her name, though. I am as well. 'Florence' is a perfectly good name. I had a cousin Florence. Not a first cousin, one of the Higginsons. Mother's side."

Before Millicent could dig any deeper into her family's roots, Faith spoke up. She knew what Millicent was talking about, and she was stunned. It was Tess. It had to be. But how had the woman found out? Especially before Faith herself? Witchcraft?

"Are you referring to the young woman who was found at the Ganley?"

"*You* found, to be precise." Millicent regarded the minister's wife sternly. If Faith had not been where she probably shouldn't have, the whole thing wouldn't have happened. Millicent's illogic was staggering and unwavering.

"I found, yes. Is that whom you are talking about?" Faith was being very careful. She didn't want Millicent to leave the paths of genealogy for grammar just when Faith was getting her on the track she wanted—no mean feat.

"Yes. I was speaking to John about another matter. I saw a work crew repairing the potholes on Main Street and wanted the one left in front of my house as is. A complete waste of taxpayers' dollars! The crew wasn't from the Aleford DPW, so I knew it wouldn't do any good to call Charley. John is generally so much more amenable, anyway."

It was clear that filling in the speed trap made by the elements would destroy one of the ways Millicent gathered her information.

"And he told you about Tess?"

"That's not her name, dear. It's 'Florence' as I've just said. Florence MacIlheny from Illinois. They're not keeping it secret. I'm surprised he hasn't told you, but then John and I go way back."

As do I, Faith fumed. Could Dunne have known when they were talking this afternoon? She thought not. They were a team, weren't they? He'd have told her. But it was true that John and "Millie"—he was one of a handful privileged to use the nickname—did have a special relationship dating back to that memorable day when Ben was just a baby and Millicent saved both mother's and child's lives with Jenny Moore's thrown in for good measure.

"She left home when she was eighteen and came East." Millicent sounded approving, her tone suggesting that anyone with any sense would of course migrate in the direction of Plymouth Rock.

"Did Detective Dunne say where in the East she went? How she happened to come to Boston?" Faith had no problem asking Millicent questions in the service of knowledge, even though it was the equivalent of groveling.

"That's not clear. She probably went to New York City first. Her mother had some sort of package from there. The only peep out of her all these years." Millicent's tone was definitely *not* approving of the

Big Apple. Her first spring in town, Faith had worn a T-shirt emblazoned with the i love new york logo to the town's Memorial Day picnic. She'd been very homesick. When Millicent caught sight of it, she put her hand to her mouth. Faith might as well have pinned a big red letter *A* on her chest. Although that might have been preferable, what with its New England association.

"I wonder when she started using the name 'Tess Auchincloss'?" Faith mused. "Probably not in New York. Too many people would have known she wasn't part of the family. The whole thing reminds me of John Guare's play *Six Degrees of Separation*—based on the true story of the young man who told everyone he was Sidney Poitier's son and was believed—cared for, wined, dined. Up here she could have used the Auchincloss name in somewhat the same manner. It established her as 'one of us' if the us you wanted to be with was of a certain class."

Millicent looked irritated. She hadn't heard her own voice for almost a full minute, and they were at the market.

"From the sound of it, this was a young woman who got in over her head."

An unfortunate choice of words, Faith thought.

"She should have stayed home, married some nice boy, and not worried her family to death."

More unfortunate words.

"I'm treating myself to a nice, old-fashioned boiled dinner tonight. Mother's recipe. She always added rutabagas." And with that Millicent skipped through the door in search of her ingredients, leaving Faith gagging.

As she walked back to the parsonage, a new picture of Tess—she couldn't think of her by any other name—began to emerge. Faith saw her growing up, her beauty setting her apart from others in her small town. Millicent didn't say it was a small town, just Illinois, but Faith saw Tess escaping from that kind of life, not one in the Windy City, for instance. She couldn't have developed such a sense of style—and such expensive tastes—without *Vogue, Vanity Fair, Elle,* and other magazines. Faith imagined her leafing through the glossy pages, picturing herself there. Then she left home as soon as she was of age and transformed herself—becoming who she'd wanted to be for so many years. It was an act repeated by countless other young women and men across the country, and across the decades. Earlier she might have headed for Hollywood and Schwab's drugstore.

What had happened to her after she left home? What had happened on that journey from Florence to Tess, a journey that led to death?

Faith had reached the parsonage. She took the mail out of the mailbox and went in through the front door. Angry voices from upstairs greeted her. She stood still and listened.

"You have *got* to tell Mom and Dad! What is with you and this kid? He's like that guy Mom was telling us about, Swingolly. If Travis told you to jump off a bridge you'd do it!" Amy shouted.

"I would not!"

"Whatever, but if you don't tell them, I will!"

"You tell and I'll kill you!" Ben was screaming. He ran down the stairs. "Tell Mom I went to the library. And *nothing* else!"

His mom was waiting at the bottom of the stairs; Benjamin ran headlong into her outstretched arms.

"Why don't you tell her yourself?" Faith suggested in a calm voice, as Ben struggled free. She didn't try to hold on to him. Ben and Amy squabbled occasionally, but they rarely fought. This had to be major.

"Let's go into the living room. Amy," she called upstairs, "please come down and join us." Faith figured that since her daughter seemed to know everything about what was going on with Ben, she might as well be included in the conversation. She continued to keep her voice calm. If she started shouting, things would escalate and they'd get nowhere. She may not be up for Mother of the Year, but she had gleaned this much and it seemed to be working. Ben's face was less flushed, and as Amy joined them, Faith could see that her eyes were bright with angry tears, but the tears were staying put.

Each child took a wing chair and Faith sat on the couch. Stereo again, she thought, recalling her recent chat with Charley and John Dunne. None of that mattered now. Tess, the art forgeries. What mattered was her son.

She tried to think of a way to start the conversation, but after looking at his sister, Ben himself broke the ice.

"Mom, I may be in a lot of trouble."

"The kind of trouble that I should call Dad about and see if he can come over for a while?"

"Yeah," Ben said.

Miraculously Tom was free and fifteen minutes later took a seat next to his wife. He told Ben to start from the beginning, and the whole sorry mess came out.

Travis Beale didn't have a problem most new kids face. He was bigger than most of the other boys in the sixth grade, and he had made the JV football team. He thought soccer was for "wusses" and was soon making Ben's and Josh's lives a living hell. Then somehow he heard about Ben's technical skills. At this point in the recitation, Tom and Faith had exchanged knowing looks. When Ben went off to college, they'd never be able to fix a crashed computer, program a remote control, or reset the clocks on the phone, oven, microwave, and elsewhere after the power went out—a frequent occurrence in Aleford. The town wiring had been fine since Edison, why did it need upgrading?

At first Ben was so relieved to have Travis as a friend that he didn't think much about what the boy was asking him to do—mainly posting pictures of classmates on his computer at home that he had set up as a Web server. Sure, some of the pictures were pretty rude—ones Travis took in the boys' locker room, but you couldn't see any faces, and it was all just a joke. Then Travis had the idea of starting a site with everyone's class picture, and each week they'd post a different question, so Ben set up a forum. At first the questions were things like, Who's smart and who's not? The clique surrounding Travis could log in and rate people, plus add comments. Ben's ratings were great, and he didn't really think much about Josh until a lot of stuff appeared about Josh being a "faggot." Ben didn't actually say the word. He told them he couldn't, but his parents knew what he meant.

"Before he got to be my friend, kind of, Travis was always saying things about me and Josh.

"When kids started saying that word about Josh, I posted all these good things about him, but it didn't help. Josh got really mad at me and said I had to choose who was going to be my friend—him or Travis."

Ben's head sunk to his chest as he whispered, "I picked Travis. I didn't want to have the kids saying stuff. They would have if I picked Josh."

"Oh, Ben, I wish we had known about all of this sooner," Faith said.

"You can't get involved in this, Mom. You don't know what kids are like. I'll never be able to go to school again!" Ben's voice ended in a high note a diva would have envied.

This was a tough one, Faith thought. The school had a policy about bullying, but not, to her knowledge, this kind of online situation. Clearly what Ben, Travis, and others were engaged in was harassment, but it occurred away from school. They hadn't used the school's computers, but their own. In affluent Aleford, every kid was wired. But the school had to be told. And the site shut down.

"What do you think you need to do?" Tom asked.

"I shouldn't have done it in the first place. We posted a picture of Josh in a dress using Photoshop a while ago. I took it off right away and Travis told me to put it back, but I didn't. Josh called when it happened, and I think he was crying. He told me he never wanted to see me again. When I see his mom, she looks like she wants to kill me." Ben himself was starting to cry.

"This is hindsight, son. I want to know what you think ought to be done now?"

Ben wiped his eyes on his sleeve.

"I can shut the site down. Unsubscribe."

"So it will all just disappear, go away? What about Josh and other kids who've been taunted?" Tom asked.

"I guess I have to write something. About what a mistake it all was. An apology. Then shut it down."

Faith nodded. "And we have to go in tomorrow and tell the school what's been going on. I have a feeling it may provide the explanation for some of the things that have been happening this fall, starting with your fight with Josh."

Ben looked resigned. "I'll be on in-school suspension for the rest of the year."

"I hope it's only that," Tom said. "Using the Internet this way is a crime in many states."

Amy jumped out of her chair and ran over to her brother. "Do you mean they could arrest Ben?"

"I don't think so, but he—and this boy Travis—need to realize how serious this is."

"I can't tell the school about Travis. You don't know what he might do!" Ben sounded genuinely frightened.

"I think you can leave that part to us," Tom said.

Faith added, "You can always tell him your parents found out about everything. He'll be reading what you post now, and I wouldn't be surprised if you get a call. Which reminds me. He used a camera phone in the locker room, right?"

"Yeah. He has a really neat one."

"And he was sending these images to other kids from his phone?"

Ben looked puzzled.

"That's against the law, too," Tom explained as gently as he could. "Especially if he was using them in a threatening way. To get things from kids."

Amy sat up straight. "He gave you a lot of anime DVDs and you would never let me see them. I'll bet he was making other kids give him theirs or maybe money."

A little sleuth. Like mother, like daughter, Faith told herself proudly before turning her thoughts back to her son.

"I'd like to make another suggestion," Tom said. "There's plenty of room in my study, and I think we should make it the general home office. We'll clear some space for Ben's computer, and he can do his homework while I work on my sermons and other things." And keep an eye on Ben's screen, Faith said to herself; wondering at the same time where Tom was going to put the stuff he cleared. Every surface in Tom's study held stacks of books and papers. No one was allowed to clean in there, because he had a "system," and if one paper were to be put back in the wrong place, total chaos would ensue. To Faith it appeared that total chaos had ensued the day Tom moved in. But she'd help and find space for Ben.

"Will that be all right?" Tom said, his tone making it clear that Ben had no choice.

"I guess . . ."

"Good! Now why don't I go up with you and help compose your farewell message before dinner?"

The afternoon light had fled, and the Fairchild family was sitting in the dusk. It matched their mood.

The Fairchild men went upstairs and the women retreated into the kitchen, where Faith put the kettle on for tea. Amy was partial to Celestial Seasonings's Strawberry Fields.

"I knew Travis was bad. I should have told you," Amy said.

"It was better for Ben to tell us. You did the right thing," her mother assured her.

"But it's been going on almost since the beginning of school, and so many people got their feelings hurt. Ben's been getting Ds on his tests, too. He rips them up."

The boulder that Faith had pushed to the top of the hill promptly rolled to the bottom.

That night in bed, Tom and Faith continued the discussion they'd been having ever since the kids went to sleep.

"What the kids are doing is mimicking what they see on TV. Humiliating people in these reality shows is a form of entertainment. We may think it's sick and cruel, but look at the ratings," Faith said.

"I'm not fooling myself that Ben is going to be the hero of the sixth grade now. A lot of kids won't understand, and the kids who've been targeted may not feel inclined to flock to him even though he has repented."

"You sound terribly clerical," Faith said, moving closer to her husband.

"That's because I am, dear," he replied, the words slightly muffled by the way he was kissing her neck.

"I couldn't face Mr. Danson again alone. I'm glad you'll be with us," Faith said, adding, "You don't think this is going to be a pattern with Ben, do you? Influenced by people like this Travis to do things he knows are wrong? Going to Cambridge, for instance. What could he have been thinking of?"

Tom stopped what he was doing and sat up in bed.

"Cambridge? What are you talking about?"

Faith realized she had forgotten to tell Tom about Millicent's sighting, also Ben's late paper and his sick-grandfather excuse. By the time she finished, Tom was out of bed, pacing. Never a good sign.

"Ben has been sending signals all fall, and I didn't pick up on them! Starting with Josh. We should have known things were bad when kids who have been best friends all their lives suddenly don't want to be together."

"I know, I know," Faith said. She didn't want to join him. It was warm in bed, and although the weather had been mild during the day, the temperature had plummeted, and it was raining hard. "I'm afraid I've been so wrapped up in things at work and the Ganley that I missed the signals, too."

Tom stopped and said, "Maybe it's time to consider your priorities."

"What are you saying? That I'm neglecting the kids because of work? Do you think I should quit and stay home all day?"

"That's not for me to say."

"Oh, yes it is. You're making quite an accusation here."

"All right, then. I think you should quit."

Rolled over as far away from each other as possible, neither Fairchild slept much.

Breakfast was grim. Faith had put on a suit, a charcoal-gray Anne Klein that she mostly wore to funerals. Tom was dressed up, too. She had the feeling she was on her way to court—and she had already been judged. Ben, in contrast, wore a bright blue rugby shirt, and it seemed the weight of the world had been lifted from his shoulders. Travis *had* called and been furious after Ben posted his message saying the site was being removed. There had been a lot of e-mails—mostly anonymous and mostly supportive. He showed them to his parents. Faith felt somewhat relieved that Ben had supporters, although it remained unclear how vocal they would be in person. She was also reminded anew from the mistakes in the texts about what a bad idea invented spelling had been—one of those educational fads in vogue when Ben started elementary school.

Faith hurried the kids along and left the dishes for her return. They were leaving even earlier than Ben's in-school suspension required to drop Amy off and meet with the vice principal. Tom had left a message on Mr. Danson's machine the night before saying that they would be in with Ben to discuss a matter relating to the school.

They were closing the door when the phone rang.

"Don't get it, Tom. We'll be late. Whoever it is can leave a message."

"It may be Mr. Danson. Get in the car. I'll be right there."

But Tom didn't come out immediately, and when he did he told Faith she'd have to go on without him.

"Joseph Sargeant is dead. A suicide."

Chapter 10

Tom had been so distraught that he hadn't lowered his voice. He immediately turned to the kids and said he was sorry they had to hear it this way.

"Joseph was a wonderful person. I know you'll always remember how much he loved to sing and other things about him. He's had some difficulties lately, and they became too much for him."

Both Ben and Amy nodded, their faces serious. Faith could see them trying to grapple with the idea that life could be so hard that death would seem a welcome relief. As Preacher's Kids—PKs, just as she and Hope had been—they were not strangers to death, but suicide was very different.

"I'm going to my office to get some information for John," Tom said. "He's calling me back. I told him

Joseph didn't have any siblings, but I have the name of his lawyer. He gave it to me when he asked me to be his health-care proxy."

Faith got out of the car to move to the driver's seat, and Tom gave her a tight hug. He opened the rear door and hugged each of his children, as well. Faith knew what he was thinking. She was thinking it, too. Why hadn't either or both of them been able to do something? They knew Joseph was depressed. What they didn't know was the extent of it. The desperation. The pain.

What she also didn't know was whether the man had killed himself out of grief—or guilt.

At the elementary school Faith went in with Amy to let her teacher know that the family had had some sad news, and then she drove to the middle school with Ben. She was trying hard not to see Joseph Sargeant's face—exuberant as he sang out during the Harvest Festival, bewildered and sorrowful as he talked about Tess.

How was she going to be able to keep her mind clear? Maybe the vice principal wouldn't be able to meet with them, and she'd have some time to get used to this news. No, those weren't the right words. She'd never "get used to" the news of Joseph's death.

The vice principal was waiting for them in the main office, stepping away from the teachers checking their mailboxes, a few students handing in dismissal notes. He didn't have a prior appointment and ushered them straight into his office.

Last night they had talked with Ben about whether he wanted to tell Mr. Danson about what had been going on or whether he wanted his parents to describe the situation. Ben had bravely opted to tell his own story, and now as Faith listened to him, she was proud, but so nervous about the outcome that she could hardly sit still. Could he be expelled? Was it a police matter?

Danson listened gravely, interrupting only once to ask how long the site had been up. When Ben finished, he turned toward his mother. She knew that he was wishing time away. That it could be the beginning of the school year all over again and that he had never become involved in any of this. She knew, too, from the pleading look in his eyes that he wished she could make it all better. At the moment, he didn't want his independence and could care less about the necessity to separate in order to develop his own healthy ego, superego, what have you. He simply wanted Mommy the Wonder Woman to take care of him, preferably by swooping him up in her arms and flying away.

"Thank you for coming to me, Ben," Mr. Danson said. "I know it wasn't easy. Before we talk about where to go from here, I'll need to know the names of the other students involved, particularly the student who was your partner in this."

And that Ben would not do. He was polite, but adamant. Mr. Danson assured him that what he said would be kept strictly confidential, but finally Ben shook his head and said, "You can keep asking, but I'm not going to tell you."

He shot a warning look at Faith, and she gave a slight nod. Last night Tom and she had offered to be the bad guys, but now she realized it was Ben's decision. She knew what kids could be like and Travis's retribution was bound to be ugly. If Ben wasn't going to be a stoolie, neither was she.

Mr. Danson gave a slight smile. "It doesn't really matter. I'm certain I know who it is, whom you've been with exclusively for the last month or so, and when I speak to him, I'll make sure he understands I didn't get his name from you."

He was handling all this in a very sensitive manner. Faith's regard for him increased. She couldn't relax, though. What was coming next?

"Cyberbullying—that's the name for what you were engaged in—is different from face-to-face bullying. I'd venture to guess that some of the things you posted yourself or things others posted are remarks you would never make in person, especially since you could be identified as having said them."

Ben turned red. "No, sir."

"We are in the process of drawing up a policy on cyberbullying, whether it be online, through text-messaging on your phone, or any other of a number of ways. My problem now is that it's not in place. Plus your actions occurred off school property. You've already removed the site, which is what I would have requested. I can't impose any formal discipline here, but I have a suggestion."

"I'm sure Ben would be open to anything," Faith said. She certainly was as she bounced back and forth between feeling better—no formal punishment and the police wouldn't be notified—and feeling anxious—there needed to be some sort of consequence for her son's actions.

"I don't want you to think of what I have in mind as an unpleasant duty. I'm hoping it's something you will enjoy and continue for the rest of your years here. Mr. Bradley, one of our math teachers, is starting an after-school program to teach computer skills to Aleford's senior citizens using the equipment in our computer lab. I'd like Ben to be a volunteer."

Ben brightened visibly. "Sure. I could do that. I've already taught my grandparents how to use their Mac."

"All right, then. I'll give your name to Mr. Bradley, and the two of you can get together. He wants to start as soon as possible. The Council on Aging has about a dozen people signed up. Now, I believe you are due someplace else."

He stood up, so did Faith and Ben. At the door Danson asked, "Do you have a minute, Mrs. Fairchild?"

"Of course," she replied.

He said to Ben, "Don't worry. No secret plots. I just want to talk with your mother about this issue a little more. We'll be having a speaker come in after the holidays, and I want to get parents involved."

Ben left, and Faith took her seat again.

"I've worried about the kinds of sites Ben might be going to on the Internet," she said. "But I never thought he'd create one himself that would be a concern."

"The Internet is the new playground, not just for middle school students, but younger and older ones, too. I brought up the notion of face-to-face because that's where the real danger lies. What they say about someone doesn't feel real to kids when they hit a send button. They can't see how that person is reacting. Unless someone like Ben comes forward, or we hear from the parents of someone who is a target, we have no way of knowing what's going on or how much harm has been done. Anonymity is easy online. Kids can create accounts without using their own names, or even steal another kid's password, and post just about anything in his or her name on their site. The difference from old-fashioned playground bullying is that earlier the taunts were only heard in the schoolyard. Now they go global.

"What before was confined to one school or class ends up on YouTube and MySpace getting tens of thousands of hits a day. There's a new fad where kids film other kids doing crazy stunts or, worse, beating each other up. Anything for a laugh," he concluded bitterly.

Faith was stunned. "It's worse than I thought."

"There's a thin line between free speech and harassment. We need to start educating kids—and parents—around the issues early. We can only do so much here. Parents can do a great deal at home."

"We're moving Ben's computer from his bedroom into my husband's study for the foreseeable future. Ben is agreeable, at least he says he is."

"That's a good first step. You don't have to look over his shoulder every time he sits down, but just the presence of an adult makes a kid think twice about what he or she may be about to do or say online. There have been some tragic cases as a result of cyberbullying. This is a time when kids are very emotionally

vulnerable, particularly when it comes to sexual identity. A thirteen-year-old in Vermont committed suicide
after suffering a humiliating electronic campaign that
questioned his."

She was listening intently, but the moment Faith
heard the word *suicide*, she knew she had to leave
immediately. She thanked Mr. Danson, told him to
please let her—and her husband—know what they
could do to help, then left.

Kids were streaming off the buses and from carpools
into the front hall. It was pandemonium, and she realized, having gone to a small private school in Manhattan,
that she had never experienced what it was like in hall-
ways like these. The noise alone was disorienting, and
when it was paired with all the other elements that
made middle school so difficult—changing classrooms
and teachers, a ratcheting up of the pressure to get into
a "good" college that began in kindergarten in Aleford,
the hierarchical social groupings, and those totally out-
of-control hormones—Faith wondered how anyone
made it through the day unscathed.

Cherishing the silence in the car, she waited a few
minutes until she could summon enough energy to call
Tom to report on the meeting. There was no answer at
his office, at home, or on his cell, so she left messages
everywhere. Ben would be fine, but they would all be

facing hydralike situations for many years ahead. And then there was Amy.

Niki had called at six that morning answering the message Faith had left on the machine the night before. There was no problem covering things at the Ganley café, she'd said. Faith had given her the *Reader's Digest* Condensed version of Ben's exploits and said she'd go straight to the kitchens after the meeting at the middle school. Before hanging up, Niki told Faith that she and her husband had been at Niki's parents' for dinner and gone clubbing afterward. "It wasn't just the baby thing—my mother actually asked Phil what kind of underwear he wore—but the son-in-law worship was getting to me, and I had to make sure his wicked side still existed. If my mother could, she'd have a shrine to him complete with plaster statue—a Greek-American saint: college grad, very gainfully employed, loves children. All those things that made me say no in the beginning."

Driving to the catering kitchen from the school, Faith thought about the fight she'd had with Tom last night. He couldn't seriously want her to stop working, could he? He'd always been so supportive. As she drove through the center of town something Pix had said a long time ago resurfaced. That the time your children needed you most was in adolescence. "Anyone can read *Pat the Bunny* over and over again to a toddler, but to avoid drowning in the tsunamis of the teen years, a child needs a full-time navigator." Would this business with Ben have happened if she'd been a stay-at-home mom? She honestly didn't know, and it wasn't something she was ready to talk about with any of her female friends, even Pix. It wasn't that by doing so she'd be presenting the Reverend Fairchild in a negative way. She'd never pretended that Tom was a paragon all these years. That was the point of having women to talk to—they got it. They weren't men. No, it was that she wasn't sure what it said about her.

Niki was back from the museum.

"Kelly Burton called and said that Maddy's approved the Cornish game hen menu."

"Oh, dear. She can't have heard about Joseph. I'd better go up there and tell her in person. I'm sure she'll cancel."

"Joseph?"

"Joseph Sargeant killed himself sometime last night. His housecleaners found him early this morning."

Niki knew about Joseph and Tess. Faith had told her yesterday, planning to omit the part about removing the book, but Niki kept asking how Faith had found out, and eventually she'd told her. It hadn't bothered Niki; she was more interested in the relationship.

"What do the police think? That he killed Tess and now himself? A kind of delayed suicide pact? The situation was hopeless, so he put an end to it for both of them?"

"I don't know," Faith said. "Tom took the call, and as you know, I've been at Ben's school."

Niki went over and put her arms around Faith. "I can't believe all these things are happening to you at once. But don't worry about Ben. Be glad it's come out now. I was a little horror at that age, and look how well I turned out. We had these things called 'slam books' that we passed around. Each page would have a name at the top, and everyone would write awful things about the person. Our grandchildren will probably be doing all this by mental telepathy, brain waves."

"Grandchildren?" Faith smiled. She'd been close to sobbing on Niki's shoulder. Tom's words kept coming back to her, bouncing around between Ben's situation and Joseph's death. Quit work! It wasn't just that she'd be giving up a much-loved livelihood, she was realizing, but Niki and everyone else associated with Have Faith.

"Maybe what Patsy said the other day about not waiting too long made sense, and maybe we are going to start trying—such a funny way to phrase it. Have sex like bunnies is better. And no maybes—we are definitely not telling my family until I'm in my ninth month."

"Patsy! I have to let her know about Joseph, too," Faith said, at the same time envisioning slender Niki putting on pounds and kaftans, which wouldn't fool her mother for even as long as it takes to hum one bar of the theme song from *Zorba*.

"Things are fine here, especially since tomorrow night's dinner will be canceled. Patsy's probably already at work, so give her a call, then head up to the museum. You can take some more salads. It's so sunny today, that's what people will want to eat."

Faith called Patsy. She was shocked and saddened. She asked Faith to call again after telling Maddy, and Patsy would contact the rest of the board. They agreed to meet late in the afternoon at Faith's house. There was no way, Faith told herself, she would not be highly visible as the happy homemaker should Tom come home early.

At the museum, Kelly Burton told Faith to go right in, assuming she'd come to finalize the dinner plans. She told Faith she had to leave for a meeting with the education director at the museum school office, tucked in among the studios, but would be back in an hour.

"I'll be at the dinner, so let me know if there's anything you want me to do."

Faith didn't feel comfortable telling Kelly the news before the director, so she thanked her and said she would let her know.

Maddy got up from behind her desk to greet her.

"I know this has all been rushed, and I appreciate your work," she said.

"I'm afraid I have some sad news," Faith said. The best way to deliver tidings like this was to be direct.

"What is it? What's happened?" Maddy looked totally panicked.

"Joseph Sargeant is dead. A suicide."

Maddy's panic subsided, and Faith was startled to see a look that could only be described as relief cross the director's face.

"But why? He didn't seem depressed the last time I saw him. It was at the opening, just a week ago." She sat down in a chair by the window and Faith sat in another one, drawing it closer.

"It's not altogether clear, but he was possibly despondent over the death of the young woman found here. They were . . . involved."

"Joseph and Tess!"

So Maddy *did* know her name. She may have heard it this week, but the familiarity with which she uttered it indicated prior use.

"Her name was actually Florence MacIlheny. She was from Illinois. Her family has been notified. She left home at eighteen, and they haven't heard from her since."

Maddy was nodding and now the relief was even more apparent.

"How tragic! And Joseph. I never suspected it was, well, that he . . ." Her voice trailed off.

"I've told Patsy and when you give her the go-ahead, she'll get in touch with the rest of the board. I told her we would call after I broke the news to you. It will be in tomorrow's papers. And then, I thought you or Kelly would want to contact any of the dinner guests who aren't trustees to tell them it's being postponed."

"Postponed? I don't think Joseph would have wanted us to do that. When the idea of these small outreach dinners was proposed at one of the board meetings, he was most enthusiastic. He offered his home for one of them."

Faith wasn't sure. Yes, Joseph might have been a strong supporter, but on the other hand, the man was dead, and having what amounted to a party so soon after his demise seemed inappropriate.

Maddy, however, was carrying on with business as usual.

"I have to join the others at the education committee meeting, but afterward I'll call Patsy and help make the calls to tell those who haven't heard plus assure everyone that we're still on. We'll be gathering in Joseph's memory."

A cynical thought crossed Faith's mind. A wake of this nature might increase the pledge amounts. Was that what Madelyn Harper was thinking?

"I didn't place the order," Faith said. "I assumed you'd be calling the dinner off. If I can't get what I need, I'd suggest we go with the chicken Stroganoff menu—the ingredients are always readily available."

"Anything is fine. Whatever you think. Now I have to go."

Maddy opened a door to a closet and grabbed her jacket. As she hastily put it on, she appeared to remember why Faith had come in the first place.

"I was very fond of Joseph, and he was a loyal friend of the Ganley's all these years. He will be missed."

As a eulogy, it was a little terse.

"I'd like to call my assistant as soon as possible and my cell phone doesn't work here," Faith said. "Could I use your phone?"

"Of course. So inconvenient not having service."

And with that, Maddy left, a slight smile on her face and a spring to her step.

She thinks her husband killed Tess, Faith immediately thought to herself. It explained her reaction to Faith's presence in Spence's studio—did Maddy really think he would try to murder Faith? The second time is easy. Was that what was crossing her mind as she practically dragged Faith away? And now, everything was rosy. Joseph was the murderer as far as Maddy was concerned. As far as the police were, too, Faith was sure.

But what did she think?

She called Niki, and they decided to go with the Stroganoff. It was easier to eat than the hens, in any case. It was a wonderfully rich recipe—lots of sour cream (see recipe, p. 381). They'd serve it with wild rice and start with borscht made with golden beets as a first course. Niki thought strawberries Romanoff—that delectable combination of strawberries and threads of orange peel soaked in orange liqueur, then layered in a parfait glass with whipped cream—would continue the theme. She also suggested serving minibabkas with a variety of fillings. To many people dessert meant cake, no matter how tasty another offering was.

Faith was glad to let Niki take over. She was exhausted—mentally and physically. Her sleepless night was catching up with her. She picked up her purse and started to leave the office. At the door she stopped. There was Degas' bather, identical in every way to the one she had seen in the Pinckney Street apartment. She took it off the wall and turned it over. There was nothing written on the back, just as there had been nothing on that one. The brown paper looked the same, even down to a small tear Faith had noticed in one corner. But how—and when—had the drawing made its way to the Ganley? *Back* to the Ganley, she was positive. She thought about her conversation with Joseph the other night—her last conversation with Joseph. He was starting to say that the original drawing was in the museum's permanent collection, one of Theodore and Julia Ganley's purchases. If *he* had switched them—easy to do, he had keys to the apartment and he could slip into Maddy's office just as Faith was doing now—he wouldn't have made the comment. Her head was aching. She was about to hang the piece back on the wall when a voice from the outer office startled her.

"What do you think you're doing!"

It was Roland Phillips, teacher of drawing and painting at the school. A prime candidate for art forger.

Channing was just behind him, and after taking in the situation, he backed out of the room.

"I wanted to see it in better light," Faith said.

Roland looked skeptical.

"Degas is one of my favorites. Of course I love all the ones of the little ballerinas, what were they called, the '*petits rats*'? But his other subjects are perhaps even more compelling . . ." She was talking rapidly, aware that she wasn't sounding very coherent. She left Degas abruptly.

"I have to go now. I want to check in with Channing. Make sure all is well in the café."

"Where's Maddy?" Roland had his arms crossed in front of his chest and was blocking the door. What did he think? That Faith was about to abscond with the piece of art? Or was he angry because she had been examining it so intently?

"She's at a meeting down at the school, but will be back any minute." Faith suddenly realized that they were the only two people on the top floor. She also realized that she was still holding the Degas and quickly put it back in place. Roland moved to one side and Faith fled. It occurred to her as she hastened down the stairs that perhaps he'd been waiting for Faith to relinquish the masterpiece and nothing else.

What was the cliché that Dunne always seemed to utter at some point in every investigation? "Everybody's a suspect until nobody's a suspect"? That was it—and the suspects in this one could fill Radio City Music Hall.

She asked Channing for a cup of coffee. Caffeine was in order. She was slightly disconcerted by the suspicious glance he gave her. At least she thought it was suspicious. It could have been surly. The young man definitely needed to work on his social skills. Grandmother may have taught him how to navigate a place setting, but he hadn't learned the art of dinner table conversation—or any other kind, it seemed. Her judgment was tempered by the memory of something Niki had told her. Harriett Potter's apron strings were more like chains. Channing was free to go out any night of the week, but Friday nights belonged to Granny. She'd pick a movie—nothing X-rated—a play, or a concert. They'd eat out first, usually at one of her Boston clubs—the St. Botolph or Chilton. It was their "date" night. "How sick is that?" Niki had commented, and thinking about it now Faith thought it was more sad than sick—for both grandmother and grandson. She wondered what all those Boston Brahmins thought of Channing's attire. But then Harriett would inveigle him into a proper navy blue Brooks Brothers blazer and gray slacks with the correct club tie.

"I don't see how all this connects with my Bearden, but it has to," Patsy said. "Especially considering the Degas. Dunne may be questioning your eye, but I'm not."

"And how does it connect to Joseph's death?" Faith said. They were drinking tea again instead of coffee, suburbia's panacea, ubiquitous in times of joy and sorrow, stress and chilling out. This afternoon was a time of sorrow *and* stress; Faith had made a large pot of Lapsang souchong. Patsy hadn't touched any of the chocolate macadamia nut cookies Faith had put out. She must be very upset, Faith thought.

"Let's talk it out," Patsy said. "It's hard to believe that if Joseph did kill his girlfriend it was because he discovered she was involved in stealing artwork from the Ganley—and perhaps other museums—replacing them with fakes, and selling them. But it's a possibility."

"She was part of the Boston art scene, and it's a microcosm of the New York one, which means it runs the gamut from legitimate to pretty shady. He could have been so upset by this flaw in his goddess that he killed her, but I can't see Joseph behaving this way. He'd just have left her and withdrawn into his shell again."

"And we still have the problem of that sentence he didn't finish when he was talking to you. That would indicate that he *didn't* know what she was doing."

"Or didn't know that I knew," Faith said, starting to nibble on a cookie.

"Maybe she was cheating on him, he found out, felt totally used, and—" Patsy's new train of thought was interrupted.

Amy came bursting through the door. She'd been at a Brownie meeting. Patsy—and the chocolate cookies—

were favorites. Faith poured her daughter a glass of milk, and all talk of the Ganley and Joseph Sargeant came to a halt. She hadn't told Patsy about Tom's wish for Faith to morph into June Cleaver. That would have to wait, too.

Overnight, New England was plunged into a deep freeze and moved directly into winter without the usual chilly autumn days that served as a prologue. There was no question about turning on the heat, and Faith didn't have to surreptitiously nudge the setting higher. Tom did it himself.

Bundled into a down coat that made her look like the Michelin man's sister, Faith sat in the bleachers watching her children's final soccer games, wishing she'd had the forethought to put on three or four more pairs of socks. She hadn't been able to feel her toes since halftime. Tom was by her side, cheering enthusiastically, his cheeks as red as ripe apples. He wasn't wearing gloves, but she knew he was cold because he'd taken out an ancient cap his mother had knit—and continued to repair—from his pocket and pulled it down over his ears.

They were going to have to talk. She'd said as much after breakfast while the kids were getting ready and they were briefly alone. "Tom, we have to talk." The sentence that has sent grown men heading for the hills or the modern equivalent since Eve looked Adam in the eye.

Faith longed to be at work, helping Niki get ready for the dinner at Maddy Harper's: (a) she would be warm, (b) she wouldn't have to endure this spousal tension, and (c) she would be warm. It wasn't an option, though. Tonight's job had become a bone of contention. Tom thought Maddy should have canceled out of respect for Joseph, and further that Faith should have told her to find someone else to cook out of the same respect and also so she could stay home, pop popcorn, and watch *Happy Feet* with her family. While Faith had enjoyed the movie when she took Amy and two friends to see it in a theater, it wasn't one she was burning to see again. Tom's demand smacked of Harriett Potter's enforced "date nights" with Channing. It was fun to curl up with the kids and watch a DVD now and then, but if Tom's idea of fun was to stay home every Saturday night, he'd be doing it alone. Friday nights, he was almost always still writing the sermon he'd promised would be done earlier in the week.

He turned toward her, and she gave him a weak smile. He turned away.

Mercifully, both games were over at last, and the family headed for the car.

"Are you still planning to be out tonight?" Tom asked her as they pulled into the parsonage drive.

Faith sighed. "I accepted the job. It's what I do. I'm sorry. And I have to leave soon to help Niki. She's handling a fund-raiser for one of the libraries—Death and Desserts. Some local mystery writers are speaking while the audience consumes 'Devilish Chocolate Cake' and 'Mousse to Die For' among other things. We'll talk later."

He didn't say a word, and an hour later she was at work by herself starting to pack up for the dinner. Scott Phelan was meeting her and would help load the van. At Maddy's he'd serve, and they'd clean up together. She hoped she wouldn't give in to the impulse she had to cry on his very attractive shoulder.

The door opened and she called out, "Scott?"

"No, it's me—or I to be correct."

She hadn't seen John Dunne in a few days, and it was enough to soften the memory of his appearance. There was nothing softening it now as he filled the entire frame before stepping into the kitchen and closing the door behind him.

"You really should keep that locked when you're here, especially when you're alone."

"I never thought I had to in Aleford."

"You never thought you'd find a very dead bald mermaid here, either."

He sat down at the counter.

"Coffee?" Faith asked.

"Sure—and any baked goods you might have lying around. I haven't had anything since breakfast and I think breakfast was yesterday."

Wondering why he was here, and so apparently amiable, Faith cut a large wedge from one of the chocolate cakes Niki had rejected. It was ever so slightly tilted to one side. She poured coffee for both of them and thought about offering to make him a sandwich, but she would be leaving soon, and she wanted him to start talking.

"What's up?"

"Sargeant didn't kill himself."

"What!" Faith almost choked on the hot coffee she had just swallowed.

"The stuff was in a cup of cocoa. He made it himself. The pan was in the sink. One cup in front of him. He was on the floor in his own vomit. The chair had fallen on top of him. No fingerprints except his on the cup or saucer. This was a very fancy guy. No mugs. Wedgwood china. Only his prints on the chair. But here's where it gets funny. Nobody's prints on the kitchen doorknob leaving the room."

"And his should have been there since he must have used that door."

"Right. Plus none on the outside knob. His were on the front door—in and out—but it doesn't figure that in all the time he lived there he never used his back door."

"But his cleaners? They found him. Wouldn't theirs have been on the back door?"

Dunne shook his head. "The top half of the door is glass. They saw him and called 911 without going in."

Faith didn't want any more coffee. Or anything else of a comestible nature for a long time.

"Easy enough for his killer to join him for a warm drink, wash the cup, and leave once he was dead."

"It was cyanide, so it didn't take long."

Faith knew that it wasn't as hard to get cyanide as one might assume. It had been widely used as the major ingredient for insecticides years ago, and with the New Englanders' classic penchant for holding on to string too short to be saved, cans of the stuff were in basements and potting sheds all over town.

"The clincher, however," Dunne said, "was the traces of fresh mud we found on the floor just under the chair opposite him. We had a pretty heavy rain Thursday night."

Faith remembered the night only too well.

"There wasn't any dirt under Sargeant's chair, and at first glance, there wasn't any under the other one. The murderer was tidy, but not tidy enough."

"Who would possibly want to kill him?" Faith brushed away a strand of hair that had fallen across her face. She felt totally disheveled and totally distraught.

"That's what I want to know," Dunne said. "But right now I want to know everything you haven't been telling me. Starting with why you were so interested in that Degas."

"It actually starts with another piece of art from the Ganley, and I wasn't holding out on you. I honestly didn't see what it had to do with Tess's murder. I'm still not sure the crimes are related."

"Crime?"

"Theft. Forgery."

Faith told him everything, beginning with midnight at the Ganley. "We weren't *taking* anything, just *looking*," she'd said, and he'd interjected, "Yeah, that's what they all say."

She ended with yesterday in Maddy's office and Roland Phillip's arrival. Dunne had been particularly interested to learn that Spencer Potter had painted one portrait, and perhaps more, of the dead woman.

"I told Joseph I'd seen the drawing at the apartment. I don't think he'd made the connection with the one

at the Ganley until I mentioned seeing the other one."
Faith was overwhelmed with guilt. Would he still be
alive if she hadn't said anything?

"He must have voiced his suspicions to someone, and
that someone was afraid of what he knew," she said.

"Which was?"

"That genuine works of art were being replaced
with fakes. The one at Pinckney Street *was* real—at
least when I saw it. Tess either found out or was in on
it, so she was killed."

Dunne was giving Niki's cake a meaningful look.
Faith cut another slab for him, thinking once more that
all roads led to the Ganley.

Dunne ate his cake in two bites and got up.

"The guys are going over his house, particularly the
kitchen again. If anything turns up, I'll call you. And
Faith . . ."

"Yes?"

"Don't do this again. Tell your friend Patsy, too."

She started to protest that they hadn't wanted to
confuse things, but the impact of his words had hit
hard.

"I know. I'm sorry." She put her words in deeds by
telling him about the Ganley dinner tonight and that
Scott, who was walking into the room, would be there
with her.

"Watch everybody. Particularly the husband. You said you thought his wife suspected him. He's still a suspect. Everybody is until they aren't." She was cheered to hear him drag out the old chestnut. He couldn't be that mad if he wanted her to act for him and had said he'd let her know if they found anything more at the house.

He and Scott nodded in passing. Scott gave him a wide berth, both because Dunne needed it and because of what Faith knew to be Scott's innate aversion to the police in any form.

The van was soon loaded, and Scott took off. Faith was following in her car. She'd decided at the last minute to stop by the house and leave some dessert for her family. They wouldn't care that part of the cake had been consumed, especially since it had been consumed by Detective John Dunne.

While they'd been getting everything ready, Faith had let her mind roam free. She knew about Tess and Joseph. Who else did? Jack Winston, the Ganley trustee, for one. He'd introduced them. Who else from the Ganley was at Art Basel? The relationship hadn't been a secret one. Others would have seen them together at events around town. The New England Rocks! opening was apparently the first Ganley event for the two of them as a couple.

Faith glanced at the clock. In another life, before children, she'd hated wearing a watch and almost never did. She had one strapped to her wrist—a Movado, Tom's last birthday gift, she thought with a sudden stab, remembering how happy the day had been and how pleased Tom had been with the success of his choice. The habit of looking for the time on a wall persisted, though. For once she was early, and before leaving, she could make a quick call to Tess's roommate, Sarah.

The girl was home, but Faith was pretty sure she wasn't alone from her guarded answers. No, she had never heard Tess mention anyone named Joseph Sargeant. Faith reminded Sarah of the conversation she had reported—that Tess had said shortly before her death how happy she was. It had occurred to Faith that Sarah must have known why Tess was so happy. A wealthy, attentive new beau? Or something else? All Faith's attempts to get any information out of Sarah were fruitless. Either Tess hadn't shared or Sarah didn't want to.

"Look, I really didn't know her all that well," she said. "I mean we lived together, but she was a very private person. I'm getting on with my life now, and I don't want to think about her anymore!"

She hung up before Faith could say another word.

Tom was in the kitchen making hamburgers—his specialty—for dinner. Faith set the cake on the table and walked over to the stove for a quick hug.

"A peace offering?" he said, pointing to the dessert.

She flushed. This wasn't what she'd planned. A hug and kiss with the promise of something more later was what she'd had in mind.

It wasn't like Tom to be snide, and this was definitely a snide remark.

"You figure it out," she said and took off for her job.

Alexander Harvey, the Ganley's founding director, had done well for himself in his living arrangements. The roomy gatehouse had been gutted and reconfigured into three rooms downstairs and three up with a downstairs half bath and full bath up. He had definitely planned it with entertaining in mind. The spacious living room with plenty of wall space for artwork opened into a dining room that was almost the same size. As Maddy walked Faith through the rooms, she mentioned that they had kept most of the original furniture. Sandy had been an expert on twentieth-century design and left everything to the museum with the express hope that they would continue to be in use. Hence a Le Corbusier chaise, van der Rohe

346 • KATHERINE HALL PAGE

chairs, a Noguchi table and lamps, and a number of pieces by Saarinen. A sideboard displayed a colorful array of Russel Wright dinnerware. The large Jens Risom dining room table would easily seat tonight's twelve dinner guests.

"The only thing we changed significantly was the kitchen. Both Spence and I like to cook, and I'm assuming my predecessor didn't. There was little counter space, an ancient fridge, and no dishwasher, but a stove that was vintage and in mint condition. We were able to sell it to a couple who were duplicating a late fifties kitchen. It more than paid for this one." She pointed to the Viking range. "I'll leave you to it. I have to get dressed. Shout if you need anything."

Faith had debated telling the director about the new twist in the deceased trustee's case, but decided she'd learn more watching the invitees if they didn't know. Maddy would surely tell her husband and perhaps the others, although it would cast a definite pall over the evening and might keep those checkbooks firmly closed.

There had been no refusals, and Faith was able to watch the table from the pass-through, standing to one side so as not to attract attention. Scott was serving the soup. She recognized Maddy and Spence, of course, and Harriett Potter. Roland Phillips must cook for himself. He'd wolfed down hors d'oeuvres and now seemed intent on slurping up his soup quickly enough to request another portion. He hadn't even waited until everyone was served, earning a poisonous look from Harriett. He was not invited because of his deep pockets, but because he and the curator, Marvin Handler, were giving a short presentation on the Ganley's wish list for the museum and museum school after dinner. The only other trustees present were Jack Winston and Lynne Hollister. Lynne wasn't sporting a broken wineglass around her neck, but was imbibing a great deal from the intact one at her place. She was wearing a bright fuchsia body suit with what looked like a baby doll nightgown over it. She'd wound ropes of pearls around her pretty neck. The pearls shone in the candlelight. Faith was sure they were real. She'd learned the young woman was very wealthy. She and Jack made a nice couple. Had she known Tess? She seemed to be what Tess had aspired to—old money and plenty of it.

Harriett was wearing real jewels, too. Diamond earrings and a large diamond butterfly brooch that glittered against the black silk of her dress. What used to be called a cocktail dress and the kind of fashion that never went out of style. It must have cost a pretty penny at Charles Sumner when Harriett had bought it new, Faith was sure—affirming one of her core beliefs that buying "good" was an excellent investment and saved money in the long run. She paid for her clothes with her profits and the interest thrown off by a nice little trust her maternal grandparents had set up, so she'd never had to explain this to Tom, who would have been shocked at the price of a little black dress these days—or the shoes and bag one had to purchase to go with it.

Maddy was wearing black, too. Again her dress seemed to be made of sackcloth, but she was wearing wonderful Amie Louise Plante earrings from the museum's store—a dangling cascade of small green enamel and gold leaves.

Faith did not know the other five guests and presumed these were the targets for tonight's outreach. Kelly Burton had answered the door, greeting everyone and mingling during the first part of the evening before leaving discreetly through the kitchen. She was certainly Maddy's right-hand woman, Faith noted. She told Faith she'd be back for the presentation, which would be made in the living room over after-dinner coffee and liqueurs. She didn't tell Faith where she'd be until then.

The evening progressed smoothly. The wine and the food were producing a ruddy glow on the guests' faces. It had also created a pleasant ambience, and the snatches of conversation Faith overheard were positive.

It was going to be a fine night for the Ganley, and Maddy had been right not to cancel. The guests not associated with the museum all lived outside Aleford in Weston, Lincoln, and Lexington. None had known Joseph, but looked down respectfully when Maddy had said a few words in his memory at the beginning of the meal.

Kelly returned with a laptop for the presentation. The party moved into the living room, and Faith passed the coffee around while Scott took orders for drinks. She'd placed assortments of Burdick's chocolates about the room and watched as Roland homed in on one, pulling the Arne Jacobsen chair closer all the better to reach the plate.

When everyone was settled, Maddy stood up.

"Thank you so much for coming. It's been a lovely evening and I for one have enjoyed getting to know those of you who are new to us better. Marvin and Roland have prepared a brief presentation on the museum and our school, detailing some of our most pressing needs. I'd also like to announce that Joseph Sargeant, our dear friend, left us several bequests, one of them for a scholarship fund. We will of course be naming this after him and accepting contributions to it in his memory."

"Don't you think we should wait until the police find his murderer first?"

Lynne Hollister's conversational tone was completely at odds with her words. Marvin dropped the coffee cup he was lifting to his lips. Faith didn't rush to the kitchen for club soda and cloth to treat the stain that was spreading across the carpet. She didn't want to miss anything.

"What an earth are you talking about!" Maddy was furious. "Poor Joseph killed himself."

Lynne stood up and placed her drink on the table next to her. There was something feline in her movements. Faith half expected her to stretch. She certainly had claws.

"The police found some evidence that has caused them to revise their opinion as to the cause of death."

"I don't believe it," Harriett said with indignation. Who was this chit of a girl to spoil the evening? "How did you get this information?"

Lynne was moving toward the closet where the coats had been hung up. "Let's just say I have a friend who's in the state police loop. Believe it."

She put on her coat, not much more substantial than what she was wearing underneath, and said, "Coming, Jack?"

He shook his head, she shrugged her shoulders, and left.

"I'm sure this is a rumor Lynne has picked up," Maddy said, her voice shaking. "Please let's continue."

Marvin and Roland picked up on her cue and hastened toward her. She was standing in front of a wall that had earlier held one of Spence's large canvases—not one of Tess—and was now ready for projection.

"I'm afraid it's true," Faith said. She couldn't simply stand there, and the news would be out soon—it was out already. "The detective lieutenant in charge of the case told me they were treating it as a murder, not suicide."

Her words produced a virtual stampede for the door, especially among the donor prospects—those prospects looking very dim now. At the moment the Ganley was tainted.

"What do you want to do, Maddy?" Jack asked.

Only he and Kelly remained. Even Spence was gone—upstairs, Faith presumed.

"I can't think about this now. We'll talk tomorrow."

Jack left. Maddy ran upstairs and Faith went into the kitchen trailed by Kelly. Scott was waiting.

"You really know how to clear a room," he said.

Faith didn't know whether to laugh or cry.

Kelly Burton wasn't laughing. That was certain.

"I need to tell the police something. Or maybe you could tell them for me?" she said hopefully.

"What is it?" Faith asked, not making any promises.

"I didn't recognize the body when they first showed us the pictures, but I did when they put hair on her. I'd seen her in Maddy's office once. I told Maddy, and she first said I was mistaken, then that the girl had been there to pick up her fee for modeling at the school. I went along with her, because I needed this job. I don't have any experience, and this is helping my résumé a lot, plus I get health insurance. Maddy didn't come right out and say it, but I knew she'd find some sort of excuse to fire me if I told. I know how she operates."

Faith was beginning to get some idea of this, too.

"You do have to tell the police. I can arrange it for you, and I'm sure they will be glad you've come forward now. As for your job . . ."

"Oh, I'm leaving. I decided tonight right after Lynne spoke up. This isn't the right place for me."

Or a whole lot of other people, Faith thought.

To make room for the guests' cars, Maddy had asked her to park in the museum lot, a short walk away. Kelly left immediately after her confession, and Scott followed soon after. There hadn't been a peep from the director or her husband. The house was absolutely quiet.

Faith had forgotten that part of the well-worn path took her through the woods, but it was only for a short distance. Even so, she felt nervous. Her anxiety increased when she heard the same soft sound she'd heard the night she and Patsy had entered the Ganley. Something—or someone—shuffling in the leaves. When she stopped, the noise stopped. She speeded up and ran to her car, the only one in the lot. She opened the door, slid behind the wheel, and locked up. Even though the museum was closed the lights in the parking lot were on. She looked about. She was alone. She let out a sigh of relief. Nerves. That was all.

Then she realized that she was sitting on something. Something crumbly. She reached her hand underneath. Crackers. Someone had dumped crackers on the seat.

Goldfish crackers.

She put the car in gear and drove straight to the Aleford Police Station. Charley was at the desk speaking to the officer on duty. He had his coat on and looked as if he were heading for home. Faith held out her hand with the crackers, enough intact to show what she had been sitting on.

"And it could have been anyone at the dinner party! Obviously a warning! We have to call Dunne and tell him. We can probably eliminate the non-Ganley people, but the curator Marvin Handler was there; the director and her husband; Roland Phillips, the teacher at the school who used Tess as a model; and some trustees—Harriett Potter, Jack Winston, and Lynne Hollister." Faith took a deep breath. She was about to continue. She had to tell Chief MacIsaac about Lynne's announcement and Kelly's confession. But he spoke first.

"I think we can eliminate Harriett Potter. Somebody whacked her on the head as she was walking home, and she's at Emerson Hospital with a concussion."

Chapter 11

Harriett Spencer Potter had been a champion horsewoman in her time, and she was still as strong as a thoroughbred. When she came to, she'd managed to make it to her door, and her grandson had called for help. Before she was transported to the hospital, she'd told police she had no idea who hit her or when it had happened. The last thing she remembered was leaving the museum director's house.

The police had fanned out, searching the path through the woods from the Harpers' to Harriett's house and the surrounding area, which abutted the museum parking lot. They didn't find anything except evidence that Aleford's young people had partied there in the not so distant past.

Deputy Dale Warren drove Faith home. Her car was impounded until they'd had a chance to go over it. She was beginning to think of the Goldfish on her seat as a bizarre form of performance art. She told Charley that hers had been the only car in the lot when she left, but when she'd arrived both Spencer's and Madelyn Harper's cars had been moved there to make room for the guests' vehicles at the house. She assumed the others from the Ganley would have been instructed to park in the lot also.

She had called Tom from the station, so she was not surprised to find him waiting in the kitchen. He took her in his arms and she leaned into the safe haven. Then he murmured, "This has got to stop," and the haven was filled with rocky shoals.

"I'm fine," she said, pulling away. "It was just someone with a very sick sense of humor." This was what she had said to herself on the way to the police station, but had added, "Or it was a warning." She left that out now. If it was a warning, she considered herself warned, and there was no need to remind Tom.

"I told you not to go tonight."

"You're sounding awfully parental. And you've made your point. I'm going to take a long hot shower and go to bed."

"The kids are fine."

"I assumed that, otherwise you would have said something."

Stop, she said to herself. This was Tom. Her Tom. She started to walk toward him, to hold him close, but something in his face told her now was not the time, and she wearily headed upstairs.

There had been a light dusting of snow overnight, but the gray skies weren't making it sparkle. The kids, however, were excited, and Faith was happy to hear Ben talking about getting his board out. Josh was an equal enthusiast, and maybe a day at Wachusett Mountain would help heal the breach.

It was one of those Sundays when every pew was filled. This was partly due to Thanksgiving, only a few days away. Some college students were home early and occasional churchgoers were also out in force, feeling a need to give thanks or maybe hedge their bets. Yet, it was also a gathering of bereaved parishioners. Parishioners who had lost one of their own to a violent death. A bereaved—and frightened—congregation. The tension that filled the sanctuary was palpable.

"From lightning, and tempest; from plague, pestilence, and famine; from battle, and murder, and from death unprepared for." The Reverend Fairchild was speaking with unusual force, and his voice rose loudly above that of his flock at the litany's response, "Good Lord, deliver us."

It seemed to Faith that it was getting darker outside, too. That a tempest *was* near. As she stood to sing the Thanksgiving hymn, "We Gather Together," Pix, standing next to her, reached for her hand and gave it a squeeze. Faith hadn't seen much of her friend and neighbor lately, but yearned for the older woman's wise counsel. Pix's own marriage had been sorely tested, and she had raised three children who had made it through middle school and beyond. They were all present, filling out the row with their father, Sam, a bookend before the aisle. All were tall like their parents, but the rest of their features were a mix of this immediate ancestry and some other genes, resulting in only a slight resemblance to one another. Faith thought about Ben and Amy at this age, home from work or college. It seemed so far off, but she knew how quickly the years had passed since their first steps, their first words. Would Aleford still be home? Tom had questioned his calling as a parish minister several years ago and come to believe it was still his mission, but Faith knew the doubts surfaced when he had had a series of pointless meetings, petty phone calls.

Let thy congregation escape tribulation
Thy name be ever praised! O Lord, make us free!

Faith lowered her voice to listen to Pix's strong alto. Her empty nest had given Pix a freedom she had perhaps never had, her children arriving soon after her marriage, which had followed immediately upon college graduation. Faith knew she was enjoying the time with Sam, but also the new kind of relationships she had with her children. She traveled to Washington to see Mark, the oldest, and met Samantha, the middle child, who was working in Cambridge, often for lunch. Dan, the youngest, was at Clark University in Worcester, and Pix had taken to combining visits to the Worcester Art Museum, as an excuse, with exchanging clean for dirty laundry.

Tom was starting his sermon, and Faith tried to pay attention. Even with her husband's sermons, her mind tended to wander. Church had had this effect on her since she was a little girl. Her own thoughts often drowned out the message from the pulpit.

Freedom. If she quit work, would she be free to spend a different kind of time with her kids and friends? And Tom? She mostly saw Pix at work these days. That could change. But as for the others, her family, she thought it would be the same amount of time, but perhaps the quality would be different. She wouldn't be so stressed. But then she might be if she didn't have anything to do except chauffeur the kids and bake.

She had so much for which she was thankful. And— few things could be hidden from the eye of God—her job was one of them.

Tom was giving thanks for the life of Joseph Sargeant, and Faith bowed her head in prayer.

After the service at coffee hour, she filled Pix in on what had been happening and told her how out of touch she felt they had been.

"Don't worry," Pix said. "This happens with friends at times. We always pick up where we left off. I should probably be putting in more hours at work, anyway."

"The ghouls have moved on to some other trag- edy, so attendance at the museum and café is back to normal. I gave Niki tomorrow off, because she's been working so much overtime. We deserve a day off, too. After I bring everything to the museum why don't we do something? Go into town?"

Pix's idea of doing something generally involved a trip to the Audubon sanctuary or a hike up around Walden Pond, but she acquiesced.

"Why don't you call me when you're finished and we'll plan what to do?"

"It's a deal."

"And you can also tell me—if you want—what's going on between you and your husband."

Pix didn't miss much.

Faith woke up the next morning feeling ever so slightly flu-ey. The roots of her hair hurt when she brushed it, and it was an effort to perform even the simplest task like brush her teeth. She had no time to be sick with Thanksgiving no longer on the horizon, but galloping down the plain. At breakfast she told Tom she'd be doing something with Pix after a brief stop at work. He offered to drive Ben, but it was on Faith's way. The night before they'd all watched *Princess Mononoke*, another of Hayao Miyazaki's films. Ben told his parents he had returned the anime DVDs to Travis and told him he wouldn't be free to do anything with him. Faith was sure the exchange hadn't been as civil as Ben indicated, and Travis no doubt continued to have his followers. For the moment Ben was still finding his way. He continued to receive support for his actions in shutting the site down and apologizing, but it was from the second or third tier of kids in the pecking order. She hoped he would be satisfied with that and wished she could make him believe that the kids who were on top in middle and high school often ended up at the bottom of life— ex-prom-queen alcoholics, class-president telemarketers, and football-star identity thieves.

Channing was waiting at the door, and they loaded the cart with today's soups, salads, and sandwiches, plus a variety of desserts. He seemed uncharacteristically twitchy. Normally Faith had to look for the pulse in his skinny neck to detect movement. He was also dressed in a blue oxford-cloth button-down shirt and chinos—both well pressed.

She poured the soups into the urns and turned the heat to high. Channing had started coffee.

"Um. I'm not going to be able to stay."

Faith was annoyed.

"Why not? And why didn't you give me some notice? Niki has the day off, and I'm busy, too. I don't know who we can get at such short notice to cover for you."

"My grandmother and I are taking a trip. She always wanted to see those turtles. The Galápagos Islands."

"South America! You're leaving for South America?"

Faith had heard that Harriett had been released from Emerson yesterday morning. But would her brush with death send her packing so immediately?

Channing had his back to her as he restocked the refrigerated unit with salads and cold drinks.

Channing. His portfolio was by the door. Why would he be taking that?

"I never saw your work, Channing. Why don't you show me now?" Faith said coldly.

He turned around slowly. "Now is not a good time."

"I think it is."

Things were falling into place. She knew what she would find. Drawings of Tess. She modeled at the Museum School where Channing was a student. Maybe she would find other sketches, too. Preliminary sketches of artwork at the Ganley. Artwork that the talented Mr. Potter forged. Niki said he had been dumped. Dumped by someone at the Museum School who wasn't a fellow student. Dumped, Faith realized, by Tess. Tess whom he had been so much in love with that he gave her the original of one of his fakes. Tess would only have been satisfied with the real thing. All roads led to the Ganley. All roads led to Channing, who had easy access and a motive. The jealous rage of a spurned lover. And Joseph. Joseph had figured it out, too. It must have been a pleasure for Channing to kill his rival, a rival Joseph had underestimated.

"What's taking you so long?" Harriett called imperiously from the hall. "I have Boston Coach waiting. We'll miss our flight."

She walked into the café and stopped, casting an appraising eye on her grandson standing immobilized by the food cart and Faith equally still behind the counter. Channing came to life.

"She knows about me and Tess, Grandma."

Faith reached for the phone.

"Oh, no you don't! Your interference has caused enough problems," Harriett said as she dashed toward Faith, grabbed the receiver from her, and yanked the cord from the wall before the startled woman had a chance to dial.

"There must be some sort of twine or tape around, Channing dear. We need to tie Mrs. Fairchild up."

"What are you talking about, Mrs. Potter? I'm glad to see you are feeling so well, and Channing has been telling me about the exciting trip you're taking."

"It *will* be an exciting trip once I've disposed of you."

Channing was rummaging around behind the cash register. Faith knew there was a Scotch tape dispenser there, but nothing more substantial, thank goodness.

"There's a roll of duct tape in the utility closet. I'll get it," he said.

"Hurry, lovey, I don't want to have to pay the driver extra."

It was New England thrift with a vengeance.

"Please, Mrs. Potter, will you tell me what's going on?" Faith had no trouble pleading.

"You've figured things out, or some of them. Fortunately I know this museum inside and out—better than anyone except Sandy, and of course he's no longer with us. There are one or two little hidey-holes in the building where you will be secure. Theo adored the whole notion of them when he built his medieval castle."

Faith was not adoring the notion in any form. The idea of spending any time in an airless priest's hole, especially bound up, was extremely unattractive. Tom would assume she was at work. Niki was off, and Pix would think she got tied up—unaware of how true that was. No alarm would be raised for many hours and it could be much longer before she was found—if she was found.

Harriett knew her grandson had killed two people. Love had overridden any moral scruples. Could Faith appeal to that?

"Mrs. Potter, Harriett, don't you think it would be far better to try to get some help for Channing? I'm sure both murders were crimes of passion committed when he was not in his right mind."

"Channing? A murderer? Don't be silly. My grandson would never kill anyone. I killed them."

The idea of the hidey-hole was beginning to have an odd attraction. Faith's whole body ached, and she was sure she was running a fever. Sleep. A long sleep.

"Can you imagine? That strumpet appeared at my house demanding money. She said Channing had been taking works from the museum, copying them, and selling the originals on the Internet. I never thought that was a very good idea whatever Albert Gore said. And he comes from such a fine old family."

Harriett's words jolted her from her reverie. Not the reference to the former vice president, but the rest. She kept quiet, though, thankful that Channing was apparently having such difficulty locating the tape.

"Channing wasn't home, so I plied her with drink. Such a peculiar-looking girl. No hair at all. She was appearing in some sort of film, and the director had asked her to shave her head. Now, that tells you something about her right away.

"I heard him come in and called out that we had a visitor. She'd taken the train and was planning to attend the opening, where she told me she'd be informing Maddy and others about what Channing had done. She also planned to give an exclusive to the *Globe*. We couldn't have that."

She looked at Faith for a response, and Faith nodded. She had no choice. Harriett favored her with a "one of us" smile. Faith's response had been the correct thing to do.

"Once I ascertained from Channing that what she was saying was true, I told her to stay where she was while we changed for the reception and she needn't worry. There wouldn't be any problem. That satisfied her. She stretched out on my sofa—a Biedermeier—

without removing her shoes. Ridiculous affairs with heels so high it was a wonder she didn't fall over."

Channing was back for the finish with a large roll of duct tape in his hand. His grandmother flashed him an approving smile.

"With all that alcohol she'd drunk it was but the work of a moment to smother her with one of the cushions before we left. Then I told Channing we'd be very naughty and put the body in that dreadful monstrosity poor Maddy insisted was art. Now, that's enough. Channing, please be so kind as to help me. I'll hold her while you bind her wrists, but be sure to cover her mouth first. Only Thomas is here; we wouldn't want him to interrupt us."

During Harriett's tale of twisted love, Faith had held out a faint hope that Channing might be seeking a different kind of reinforcement—a straitjacket for his insane grandmother perhaps—but one look at the steely determination in his eyes when he returned convinced her she had hoped in vain.

The two Potters were moving toward her. The counter was between them, but not for long. It was on rollers and Channing had already seized a corner, to move it out of the way. Faith picked up the vat of Italian wedding soup bubbling merrily away by its insulated handles and flung the contents straight at him. Then she heaved the clam chowder at Harriett and pushed the counter with all her strength, pinning them to the opposite wall. She made for the door, their cries of pain and anger a welcome chorus. Thomas was racing toward her. She hadn't thought the man could sprint so fast. He took in the situation, slammed the door shut and locked it, while reaching for the walkie-talkie on his belt to press the alarm button.

"I never did care much for that Mrs. Potter," he said. "And her grandson isn't any better."

Faith was in the parsonage kitchen thinking about love. She had time. Her turkey was out of the oven resting, and everything else was done. The Averys had called saying they would be a little bit late and could Faith add two more places at the table? She could, and by the time she listened to the rest of what Patsy had to say, Faith was smiling broadly. There would be plenty of space.

She could hear the pleasant buzz of conversation from the other room. She'd firmly refused all offers of help, promising to call her father-in-law when it was time to carve, his time-honored job as head of the family.

But love. Maddy and Spence were very much in love. So much in love that they were desperately covering for each other. Maddy thought her husband had killed

Tess out of passion, or perhaps she was blackmailing him, and Spence thought his wife had out of jealousy. But there had never been anything between the artist and his model other than art. Spence didn't have the kind of money Tess needed, and besides, Spence was very much in love with his wife.

Had Tess loved Joseph? That was something no one would ever know. Faith wanted to believe she did and thought back to his description of their time in Switzerland. Tess had traveled on the passport with her real name on a private plane, a dream she couldn't turn down, and she must have arranged to be the last in line, so none of the others would see it. She couldn't take that chance just traveling alone with Joseph. And anyway, Florence was a ghost, the ghost of Tess's past life.

Harriett's love for her grandson was all-consuming, driving her to commit Nature's most heinous crime, that of murder. Joseph must have figured out that Tess's Degas had been switched with the one at the Ganley and may even have figured out that Channing was the most likely suspect. Joseph had known him all his life, so would have known of his artistic prowess. Even if Joseph hadn't gotten that far, he would have called Harriett to talk about what to do. The two of them had been involved with the museum the longest. So Harriett came calling and offered to make them a cozy cup of cocoa. Perhaps she'd even told Joseph about what her grandson had done. Made a plea for help for the wayward youth, content in the knowledge that the information would definitely go no further. Love, an all-consuming love. Channing was refusing to say anything against his grandmother, despite the lawyer's attempts to get him to agree to a plea bargain. What had Channing felt as he and Harriett loaded Tess into a wheelbarrow and trundled off to the Ganley that night? He had admitted to following Faith on several occasions, putting the fish in her car, and making the call about Scott. The Goldfish-cracker caper was a panicked response after he'd seen her looking at the Degas, which he'd switched back using the keys in Tess's purse. He'd heard about Faith's past investigations and hoped to frighten her off. Then he and his grandmother concocted the attack on Harriett to divert suspicion once and for all. The trip was a little extra insurance and yes, Harriett *had* always wanted to see those turtles.

But Channing had loved Tess, too. Or been obsessed with her. His portfolios contained literally hundreds of sketches of her. Her shoes, jacket, and purse were still in his closet. Faith was sure Harriett had told him to dispose of them, but he had kept them—talismans.

Faith loved her children. At the birth of each, she had been overwhelmed by the intensity of her feelings.

There was nothing she wouldn't do for them. Harriett felt that way. Love perverted. She'd refused to let Channing grow up. She'd created chains from her love and eventually those chains imprisoned them both.

Faith thought of Ben. Ties. Ties that bind, but never chains.

And Tom. He'd come straight to the museum and pushed his way through the crowd in Maddy's office—no mean feat with Dunne in the way—until he'd reached his wife and they had collapsed in each other's arms, tears flowing.

While she was at home in bed with Tylenol, which had effected a miraculous cure of her flu, he'd sat by her side.

"Can't you understand? I don't want to lose you!"

She had slept and every time she awoke he was still there. Always there.

Priorities. With Channing gone, Faith decided to add another full-time employee; someone trained in food services and preparation who would essentially run the Ganley restaurant. Channing had been working for the museum. The new person would be working for Have Faith. This would free her up; Niki, too. And Trisha Phelan would be starting as a paid apprentice. She wanted to learn the business, but couldn't afford to take courses. Faith knew Trisha was talented and had already picked up a lot. It would be an extra pair of hands.

Tom had been more than pleased with her plans and admitted he'd been reacting to Ben, not Faith. In his frustration he'd flailed out at the nearest—and dearest—target.

She heard the front doorbell and went to greet the Averys—and their pies. Patsy's sweet potato and pecan pies were so good that they'd become the Fairchilds' Thanksgiving favorites instead of pumpkin and mince.

Tom beat her to the door, and as he opened it, Faith saw Patsy and her husband, Will, standing on the stoop beaming. Two children stood between them—a serious-looking little girl who appeared to be about five years old and a cheerful-looking boy about three. The Averys guided them into the hallway and Patsy said, "This is Kianna and her brother Devon."

Will was helping them off with their jackets. "These nice children are our new family members," he announced. "You're going to be seeing a lot of them. They're our little girl and boy now."

On the phone earlier Patsy had told Faith that the adoption would proceed quickly because they had agreed to take two siblings, which were hard to place—hard also since they were older. Weeks ago the

Averys had come to the realization that what was most important to them was raising children together, not reproducing themselves, and started working with an agency.

Love again, Faith thought as she took Devon's hand and put her arm around his sister's shoulder.

"Happy Thanksgiving and welcome to our house," she said.

Kianna smiled.

Author's Note

F ood and Art. Food in Art. The Art of Food. Whatever the formulation, the two words go together
and have throughout history. Friezes in the tombs of
the pharaohs depict food in all forms from cultivation
to preparation to feasting. A wall painting from Hercu-
laneum circa A.D. 50 shows four luscious peaches and
a simple carafe half filled with sparkling clear water.
Nimble Norman needleworkers depicted steaming
cauldrons and early shish kabobs in the Bayeux tapestry. Brueghel invites us to sit down with the revelers
at the *Peasant Wedding* and share the abundant cakes
and free-flowing ale. Seventeenth-century Dutch still
lifes conveyed the quality of the artist's patron's table—
plentiful game, rare fruits, and gleaming plate—in such
exquisite detail that we are tempted to pluck a grape

from the canvas. Chardin's eighteenth-century works such as *Kitchen Still Life* and *Back from the Market* show simpler, but equally appetizing, fare—crusty bread and a *poulet* for the pot.

The Impressionists were interested in painting food—Cézanne's fruit, Manet's asparagus, and both Manet's and Monet's *Déjeuner sur l'Herbe*. Manet's was a pretty skimpy picnic, a few cherries, some other fruit, a roll or two, compared with Monet's generous spread that included roast chickens, bottles of wine, fruits, bread, and a large *pâté en croûte*. Besides immortalizing food in paint, the Impressionists also liked to cook it. One of my favorite books is Claire Joyes's *Monet's Table: The Cooking Journals of Claude Monet*. Beautifully illustrated, it is as much a feast for the eye as its recipes are for the mouth. When Monet moved to Giverny, he painted the dining room a sunny yellow and put blue and white tiles in the kitchen that overlooked the gardens, which included an extensive kitchen garden. The artist entertained his friends and family frequently, recording his recipes and some of theirs—Cézanne's bouillabaisse, Millet's *petits pains*.

I have recently discovered another book, *The Artist's Palate: Cooking with the World's Greatest Artists* by Frank Fedele, which has recipes from Michelangelo (based on three of his existing grocery lists: bread, grapes, anchovies, tortellini, spinach, fennel, "mellow wine"), Matisse (*soupe de poissons,* French fish soup), Mary Cassatt (chocolate caramels), Jackson Pollock and Lee Krasner (bread and cheese hominy puffs), Andy Warhol (a traditional Thanksgiving dinner), Grant Wood (strawberry shortcake), and Red Grooms (confetti egg salad) created by chefs well known for their artistry in the kitchen: Mario Batali, Ming Tsai, André Soltner, David Bouley, and Jean-Georges Vongerichten. Fedele's descriptions of the artists' culinary predilections, based on interviews with friends and family where possible, are fascinating. According to Al Hirschfeld's wife, "Everyone from Charlie Chaplin to Whoopie Goldberg has tasted it!"— Hirschfeld's famous caviar with rice crackers. And Louise Bourgeois eats the same meal every Sunday: linguini with American cheese, served in a frying pan, after which she has coffee ice cream served in the same pan. Both accompanied by a soda. The book is sumptuously illustrated with photographs of the artists and reproductions of their work.

Yet, when it comes to cookbooks paired with art, it's two older ones I love the best. The first is *Picasso and Pie,* a slim volume that you can still find on the Internet. It was published by Lynne Thompson in 1969 and is a collection of recipes that were served at the Blue Hill Buffet in Blue Hill, Maine, part of the Maine Gallery in Blue Hill. Perhaps it's the title that enchants—pairing a great artist with a great dessert—but recipes like Blueberry Ambrosia also stand the test of time. This is a fruit soup with its roots in Scandinavia that is served very cold with whipped cream. The Buffet's Blue Hill Fudge Cake was the 1951 *New York Times* cake of the year and there's also a great fish chowder recipe with instructions to serve it properly with Pilot biscuits.

The other book, *The Art Lover's Cookbook*, was published in 1975 by the Summit Art Center in Summit, New Jersey, as a fund-raiser for the center, which started in 1933 when a small group of artists began meeting in one of their studios to paint and discuss art. After various incarnations, the center moved into its own architecturally striking building in 1973 with plenty of studio and exhibition space. It's still going strong. My mother, who was a painter, was an active member. Each artist provided one or more recipes for the cook-book and each page is a work of art, illustrated and let-tered by the artist. A pen-and-ink sketch of a Greek port accompanies Hella Bailin's tzatziki; my mother's Norwegian fish pudding (it's like a mousse) features a delicate pencil drawing of several fish. Jane Crow enti-tled her offering "Beef in Beer or More Time in the Studio," and pictured herself before her easel, a smile on her face. A note on fund-raising cookbooks: They are addictive. I have them from organizations ranging from churches and libraries to service organizations and historical societies. Besides recording regional recipes that are disappearing all too fast, they provide an intimate glimpse of a group—usually women—and the way food brings people together. My current favorite is *Food to Die For, A Book of Funeral Food, Tips and Tales*. It's the creation of the Southern Memorial Association (www.gravegarden.org/cookbook.htm), which uses the profits to preserve and manage the historic Old City Cemetery in Lynchburg, Virginia.

I can't conclude these thoughts on Food and Art without mention of what I call the "Food Museums," my favorites being the food halls at Harrods in London and Fauchon in Paris. Food is displayed to appeal to the eye first and foremost. The offerings are positively Lucullan and over the top. If it's "location, location, location" in real estate, then it's "presentation, presentation, presentation" in cooking. You have only to watch *Iron Chef* to learn that. (My mother the artist always served food on white plates, so the colors and textures wouldn't fight with a pattern.)

And finally a nod to some additional modern artists. Andy Warhol's Campbell soup cans tapped into a visual iconic symbol of American life, but they also played upon a gustatory one. Few of us do not have strong, positive associations with that "Mmm, Mmm Good" tomato soup or chicken noodle flavor from our childhoods.

Wayne Thiebaud's marvelous paintings of cakes, ice cream, pastries, hot dogs are visually arresting, but make our mouths water, too—like all the other artists starting with the unknown Egyptian sketching baskets of grain and, even earlier, the Lascaux cave paintings of bison and other game. I always think of the old Automat when I look at Thiebaud's rows of slices of cakes each on a plate. They remind me of the walls of delicious offerings behind the little glass doors just waiting for our quarters.

Edward Weston's black-and-white photographs of vegetables, particularly peppers, are sensual delights. Maine photographer David Klopfenstein turns pears into evocative portraits that challenge us to place them in a particular era. The same is true of Isabelle Tokumaru whose shimmering, jewel-like oils of cherries, plums, pears, and satsumas evoked the following words from her writer husband, Joe Coomer: "Here is the perpetual fruit you desire and never tire of eating." This sentence is the perfect description for all the works of art I've mentioned.

Roman mosaics, medieval tapestries, Indian temple sculptures, Japanese prints—I've barely scratched the surface in this short note. The pairing of food and art is natural; the consumption of both, a necessity.

Excerpts From
Have Faith in Your Kitchen

by Faith Sibley Fairchild
(A WORK IN PROGRESS)

Chicken Stroganoff

2 pounds boneless, skinless
    chicken breasts
1 tablespoon unsalted butter
1 tablespoon olive oil
1 medium yellow onion
¾ pound mushrooms
1½ tablespoons unsalted
    butter

1 tablespoon flour
1 cup unsalted chicken
    broth
½ cup sour cream
¼ teaspoon grated nutmeg
½ teaspoon paprika
Salt and pepper to taste
½ cup dry white wine

Cut the chicken into strips, removing any fat. Dice the onion and slice the mushrooms.

Heat 1 tablespoon butter and 1 tablespoon olive oil in a large frying pan or wok and stir-fry the chicken. When done remove to a warm plate.

While the chicken is cooking, melt 1½ tablespoons of butter in a covered flameproof casserole. Add the flour and whisk to make a roux. Slowly add the chicken broth and stir until smooth and thickened. Add the sour cream and seasonings, stirring well.

Sauté the onions and mushrooms in the same pan used for the chicken. You may need to add a bit more butter and olive oil. When the mushrooms are nicely browned, add the mixture to the sauce and fold in. Deglaze the pan with the wine and add to the mixture. Finally fold the cooked chicken in, cover, and simmer. At this point the dish may be served or refrigerated, brought to room temperature, and reheated the next day.

Serve over egg noodles and sprinkle some finely chopped parsley on top of each portion.

Serves 4 to 6.

Replacing the chicken with beef, the chicken broth with beef broth, and nutmeg with dried mustard brings the dish back to its original roots.

As with most recipes, these roots are gnarled. The dish is indisputably Russian and the name comes from Count Pavel Alexandrovich Stroganoff, who lived in St. Petersburg in the late nineteenth century. Some accounts state that the count's chef won a kind of Romanov bake-off with the recipe and named it in honor of his employer. Others ascribe its invention to the time the count spent in Siberia when his chef was forced to cut the frozen beef into thin strips before he could cook it. Still another states that the count had bad teeth and couldn't chew large chunks of beef. Whatever the name, it seems clear that the basic recipe had been in use throughout Russia since the eighteenth century and may possibly have been cribbed from a fifteenth-century Hungarian dish. Whatever its true origin, Beef Stroganoff made its way to the United States and appeared early on in one of Faith's favorite cookbooks, *The Mystery Chef's Own Cookbook,* published in 1934. The author, John MacPherson, whose motto was "Always be an artist at the stove, not just someone who cooks," was the host of a very popular radio show and appeared twice a week on one of television's first cooking shows on NBC in Philadelphia. He was originally from Britain and the term *Mystery Chef* was a nom de plume he assumed out of deference to his mother, who was appalled that he had not kept what she called his "hobby" under "his hat." The name stuck and MacPherson says in his introduction, "Who I am doesn't matter. It is what I have to say that counts." Which could serve as a mantra for many chefs (and mystery fiction writers).

The Russian Tea Room in New York City served the

dish and it was a favorite of James Beard's, who rightly pointed out that the secret was in cooking it quickly.

Serving Beef Stroganoff at a dinner party in suburban northern New Jersey when I was growing up there in the 1950s and 60s meant the hostess was someone with flair—slightly edgy *international* flair. She probably used La Choy chow mein noodles on top of her string bean and mushroom soup casserole instead of Durkee's French fried onions. She may even have added water chestnuts. She might, in fact, have been a relative of Faith's.

Endive Spears with Chèvre

2 heads endive
Fig vinegar (Cuisine Perel
  brand if possible)
5 ounces fresh chèvre at
  room temperature
4 ounces cream cheese at
  room temperature
1 tablespoon half-and-half
  or light cream
Whole shelled walnuts

Look for endive that is fresh and a tight head. If you can, find the slightly purple variety; it's nice to alternate the spears on your serving platter.

Discard the outer leaf and cut a thin slice from the bottom to make it easier to remove the leaves. You may have to do this again. Save the small core of inner leaves for a future salad.

Lightly brush the spears with the vinegar.

Arrange the spears in circular rows or any other way that is attractive on a serving platter or tray.

Combine the two cheeses and half-and-half in a food processor and pulse until creamed together. Fill a pastry bag with the mixture and pipe about a tablespoon on the wide end of the spear. You may also spoon the mixture on the spear. Top with a walnut half. In season you can use pomegranate seeds or a piece of fresh fig. Dried cranberry is also good or a piece of candied ginger for a very different taste.

You can prepare the cheese mixture ahead of time and refrigerate, bringing it to room temperature before assembling.

Serves 6.

Pantry/Fridge Soup

2 tablespoons olive oil

1 large clove of garlic

1 onion

4–5 mushrooms

1 can tomatoes, diced or
　　whole

1 can chickpeas or
　　cannelini beans

4 cups chicken broth

4 chicken sausages,
　　12-ounce package

¼ cup orzo or other small
　　pasta such as ditalini or
　　conchigliette

2 teaspoons dried
　　rosemary

Salt and pepper to taste

Mince the garlic and dice the onion and mushrooms. You may use whatever onion you have in the fridge and any variety of mushrooms, adjusting the amount for size. For this dish, Faith used plain old white mushrooms and a yellow onion.

Heat the oil in a Dutch oven or other covered soup pot and sauté the garlic, onion, and mushrooms for about 5 minutes.

Rinse and add the chickpeas or beans. Add the tomatoes and seasonings. Almost any other herb may be used—thyme, oregano, parsley—and use fresh ones if handy. Add the broth, canned, in a box, or homemade. Bring the soup to a boil and add the sliced sausages. (You do not need to precook the sausages.)

Bring the soup back to the boil—it doesn't take long—and add the pasta. Cover and simmer until the pasta is done. Add grated cheese on top if you have some in your fridge or freezer.

Serves 4.

The above is merely a template. Faith uses the chicken sausages, widely available now in a variety of flavors, because she always has some in her freezer and they make for a heartwise dish. You can substitute beef broth and beef or pork sausages. If you have scallions or shallots, use those instead of the onion. A pepper may be added to or replace the mushrooms. The beauty of this recipe is in its speed and how creative it makes the cook feel. Try the teriyaki ginger chicken sausages with garlic or sesame oil instead of olive oil. In season, add fresh chopped chard or kale a few minutes before serving. Leave out the pasta and serve with a warm crusty baguette or loaf of sourdough.

Parsnip Puree

2 pounds peeled parsnips cut in quarter-inch pieces

6 tablespoons unsalted butter, softened

½ cup heavy cream

½ cup chicken broth

2 tablespoons white horseradish, drained

Salt

Put the parsnips in a large saucepan and cover with water. Bring the water to a boil and simmer for about 10 minutes or until the parsnips are tender. Drain, return the parsnips to the pan, and dry them over moderate heat. Shake the pan to thoroughly dry.

Heat, but do not boil, the cream, butter, and broth.

Puree the parsnips in a food processor with the warm cream, butter, broth mixture. Add the horseradish last. Increase the amount to taste.

Add salt to taste.

Serves 8.

This is a wonderful any-time-of-year dish, but a staple of our family Thanksgivings, and is another of cousin Luis's great recipes.

Red Velvet Cake

2¼ cups sifted cake flour

2 tablespoons unsweetened
    cocoa powder

1 teaspoon baking soda

1 teaspoon baking powder

1 teaspoon salt

1½ cups sugar

½ cup unsalted butter at
    room temperature

2 large eggs

1 cup buttermilk

2 ounces (¼ cup) red food
    coloring (for a very
    deep red)

1 teaspoon vanilla

1 tablespoon white vinegar

Preheat the oven to 350 degrees.

Grease and flour two 9-inch round cake pans.

Sift the flour, cocoa, baking soda, baking powder, and salt together. Set aside.

Cream the sugar and butter. Add the eggs, one at a time, beating well after each addition.

Add the flour mixture to the butter and sugar, alternating with the buttermilk.

Add the food coloring, vanilla, and vinegar. Beat well.

Bake for approximately 30 minutes or until a toothpick or broom straw comes out clean.

Cool on a cake rack.

Frosting:

8 ounces cream cheese at room temperature

½ cup unsalted butter at room temperature

1 box (1 pound) sifted confectioners' sugar

1 teaspoon vanilla

Cream the butter and cheese. Add the sugar, beating until the mixture is fluffy. Add the vanilla and beat some more.

Fill and frost the cake.

You may add chopped pecans or walnuts to the frosting or use them on top of the cake. Some cooks like to sprinkle coconut on top.

Serves 6 to 8.

HARPER LUXE

THE NEW LUXURY IN READING

We hope you enjoyed reading
our new, comfortable print size and found it
an experience you would like to repeat.

Well — you're in luck!

HarperLuxe offers the finest in fiction and
nonfiction books in this same larger print size and
paperback format. Light and easy to read, HarperLuxe
paperbacks are for book lovers who want to see
what they are reading without the strain.

For a full listing of titles and
new releases to come, please visit our website:

www.HarperLuxe.com